EMMA WAS EVERYTHING THAT CIMARRON WANTED IN A WOMAN

When Cimarron was awakened in the night by Emma Dorset's lips, he realized how long he had been without a woman. And when she skillfully stroked his hard flesh, then pressed her naked body against his, he realized he had never had a woman to match this beautiful, wanton mistress of a missionary preacher.

She eagerly matched his savage thrusting. Her hands clutched his buttocks as if she were trying to force him deeper inside her. She moaned beneath him, sweating as he was, clawing his body and biting his neck.

And when he rested for a moment before beginning again, she murmured, gentle as the rain, "We're good together, aren't we, Cimarron?"

Emma was good—too good to be true—the best-laid trap a man ever plunged into. . . .

CIMARRON AND THE HANGING JUDGE

by

LEO P. KELLEY

A SIGNET BOOK
NEW AMERICAN LIBRARY
TIMES MIRROR

PUBLISHER'S NOTE

This novel is a work of fiction. Names, characters, places, and incidents either are the product of the author's imagination or are used fictitiously, and any resemblance to actual events or persons, living or dead, is entirely coincidental.

NAL BOOKS ARE AVAILABLE AT QUANTITY DISCOUNTS WHEN USED TO PROMOTE PRODUCTS OR SERVICES. FOR INFORMATION PLEASE WRITE TO PREMIUM MARKETING DIVISION, THE NEW AMERICAN LIBRARY, INC., 1633 BROADWAY, NEW YORK, NEW YORK 10019.

SIGNET, SIGNET CLASSICS, MENTOR, PLUME, MERIDIAN AND NAL BOOKS are published by The New American Library, Inc., 1633 Broadway, New York, New York 10019

First Printing, February, 1983

1 2 3 4 5 6 7 8 9

PRINTED IN THE UNITED STATES OF AMERICA

CIMARRON . . .

. . . he was a man with a past he wanted to forget, and a future uncertain at best and dangerous at worst. Men feared and secretly admired him. Women desired him. He roamed the Indian Territory with a Winchester .73 in his saddle scabbard, an Army Colt in his hip holster, and a bronc he had broken beneath him. He packed his guns loose, rode his horse hard, and no one dared throw gravel at his boots. Once he had an ordinary name like other men. But a tragic killing forced him to abandon it, and he became known only as Cimarron. *Cimarron,* in Spanish, meant wild and unruly. It suited him. *Cimarron.*

1

Cimarron awoke as the cook let out the first of his usual predawn yells, which sounded like a cross between a Comanche war whoop and the bellow of a bull caught in a canebrake.

The fingers of his right hand were curled about the grips of his single-action Frontier Colt. He stared up at the stars in the sky above him.

Around him on the ground, the lightest sleepers among the trail hands stirred in their blankets and suggans. Other men continued to snore. Somewhere in the thick night a man yawned noisily.

The cook yelled a second time and followed his yell with a loudly shouted threat: "I'll dump this breakfast in the river over there if it ain't eaten in the next two minutes!"

Cimarron sat up, throwing aside his blanket. He clapped his hat on his head, reached for his cartridge belt, and holstered his Colt. After shaking out his boots, he pulled them on and then strapped on his work spurs. He rose, strapped his cartridge belt around his hips, and strode over to the chuck wagon, where he turned the spigot on the water barrel and splashed cool water on his face. After drying himself with the community towel, he went over to the fire trench that the wrangler had dug for the cook the night before.

The cook, cursing enthusiastically as was his early-morning custom, was bent low over a stewpot that rested on the iron rods spanning the trench, vigorously stirring its contents. A Dutch oven also sat on the rods and next to it was a soot-blackened coffeepot. At one end of the trench an uncovered skillet rested on the rods.

Cimarron got a tin plate, cup, and utensils from the wagon and went up to the cook, who slopped grits onto his plate, ladled redeye gravy over them, handed Cimarron a sourdough biscuit, put chunks of boiled beef on his plate, and filled his cup with steaming black coffee.

Cimarron sat down on the ground close to the fire trench, taking care to remain out of the cook's way, in order to benefit from the heat of the cooking fire because the May morning was unusually chilly. He ate in silence as the cattle that were lying down in the distance got lightly to their feet in the single swift and graceful motion characteristic of longhorns.

As he ate, the first pale light that preceded the dawn began to fill the sky that was becoming cloudy.

One of the hands, a man named Jefferson who had seated himself next to Cimarron, belched loudly.

"I'll take that as a compliment," the cook growled at him.

"A truly deluxe meal from first course to last," Jefferson responded cheerfully. Then he leaned over toward Cimarron. "These grits are more water than grain and the beef's about as tough as boot leather. But it surely don't do a man no good to talk mean to a cook. If he does, he might find himself hungering all the way from Texas to Dodge City on account of the short helpings he'll get handed out to him. Most cooks are meaner'n cougars."

"Fact," agreed Cimarron.

"I knew one once," Jefferson said, "we were moving beeves up to Abilene that time—who was so mean I'll be able to recognize him in hell with his hide all burned off."

Cimarron continued eating. "I'll know him," Jefferson went on, "on account of the wonderful way he could curse! He'll be down there cursing out the pitchfork crew and swearing steady at the stokers. That's how I'll know him for sure."

When Cimarron remained silent, Jefferson said, "There was a cook down on the Bar D Ranch when I was working there, who'd swear at the sun for setting and the moon for rising. At any damn thing a'tall, living or dead. Said it kept him in practice."

Jefferson laughed uproariously, spilling some of his

coffee as he did so. He got up and refilled his cup. When he was seated beside Cimarron again, he took a swallow of coffee and said, "Too early to talk, is that it?"

Cimarron glanced at him. "I'm usually not a talkative man."

"Noticed that. You don't let a man get up too close neither. Noticed that too."

Cimarron mopped up gravy with the remains of his biscuit. "Some men, they're like lost calves looking for their mamas. They follow you around. Practically climb into your lap. Tell you all kinds of stories. Ask you all kinds of questions. Other men, now, they're more like mountain lions. They tend to go about their business on their own."

"You saying you're the mountain-lion type?"

"I'm saying I don't run with any pack."

"Well, you sure are the lonest wolf I ever did meet up with and that's the truth."

"It can be a good way to live."

"Lonely, though."

"A man has to pay a price for what he wants."

"That rifle of yours—that seventy-three Winchester repeater you're toting—I'll bet you paid a pretty price for that."

Cimarron ate the last of his beef.

"You figure you'll be needing a rifle on this drive?"

"Might. We're in Indian territory now."

"You're the only one of us has got a rifle. You don't think just your six-gun'll do?"

"Likely it'll do. But a rifle's a comfort to a man like me."

Jefferson started to say something but his attention was diverted by the arrival of the young wrangler who had been out rounding up the remuda and who was now bringing the horses into camp.

As the boy began to set up a makeshift rope corral, Jefferson got to his feet. "Got to go out and help relieve the men on the last guard." He shivered. "Sure is getting cold, ain't it? Feels more like November than May."

Cimarron glanced up at the dull gray sky.

Jefferson said, "I can feel the cold all the way down in my bone marrow. Storm coming, maybe, and I've had me a whole bellyful of rain on this drive so far. I hope we don't get us another drop."

Cimarron sat cross-legged on the ground as Jefferson

walked away, barely aware of the clanging of the Dutch oven in the cook's hands or the lowing of the cattle in the distance as he finished the last of his breakfast and emptied his cup.

He set his plate and cup on the ground in front of him and thrust his utensils into the cup. Then, rising, he took a jackknife from his pocket and began to shave off the thick calluses that covered his hands.

He was a tall, leanly limbed man, an inch over six feet in his socks, taller when wearing boots. He was solidly, if slenderly, built, with thick shoulders and strong arms. The trunk of his body formed a V with its narrowest point at his hips, its broadest at his shoulders. His hands were large and thickly knuckled, but their movements were surprisingly graceful, almost giving the lie to the strength they so obviously possessed.

His stance was an easy one, but there was an odd air about him, a suggestion of wariness, of a readiness to meet and eagerly grapple with whatever he might suddenly or unexpectedly confront.

His bronzed face was as lean as his body and strongly, even strikingly, featured. His jaw was square, his lips a thin, not quite grim line beneath a straight, wide-nostriled nose which was bordered by slightly sunken cheeks below pronounced cheekbones. His forehead was broad and as creased as was the skin at the corners of his eyes and mouth. His was a face that showed unmistakable signs of weathering, a face that had been burned by the sun and blasted by the wind. His face revealed—but to an astute observer only—unsuccessfully hidden signs of suffering which might well be mistaken by a more casual observer for mere signs of a life led ruggedly. His emerald eyes were set deep beneath his brow and they watched the world with a kind of mournful uneasiness. They were often narrowed, sometimes cruel, always alert.

A painter—depending upon how he interpreted the expression on and the features of Cimarron's face—might choose to use it as a model for Francis of Assisi—or for one of the demons under Satan's dominion.

On the left side of his face was a leaden scar that began just below his eye, curved down over his cheekbone, and ended just above the corner of his mouth.

Framing his face was a thick growth of straight black

hair that hid both his ears and the nape of his neck from sight.

Not a few women had found his face handsome. More than a few men had learned to fear it.

Over his collarless brown shirt, he wore a fringed buckskin jacket and around his neck he had tied a tan cotton bandanna. His nankeen trousers were tucked into once-black knee-high boots which were now gray with trail dust from their square toes to their underslung heels. The hilt of a bowie knife protruded from his right boot. On his head was a badly battered and sweat-stained slouch hat with a curled-up brim and indented crown. Every loop of the black leather cartridge belt he had strapped around his hips upon awakening was occupied by a bullet.

Cimarron snapped the jackknife shut and returned it to his pocket.

"You finished with these?" asked the wrangler as he suddenly appeared between Cimarron and the fire trench. He pointed to the empty plate and cup on the ground.

"I am, Willy," Cimarron answered.

"Cook's cleaning up. He told me I'd best get busy. I'm not so sure I was cut out to be a wrangler. Clean up. Wash dishes. Gather brush and buffalo chips for the next fire. Most wrangling's work for a woman."

"Not many women know horses the way you do," Cimarron commented. "You got yourself a good and gentling way with them, I've noticed."

Willy smiled. "It sure does me good to hear somebody say some kind words to me now and then. All I ever get from the cook is curses."

"Wrangling is the lowliest job on a cattle drive, I'll admit. But it's not so lowly that a man"—Cimarron looked directly into Willy's eyes—"can't learn a lot if he looks and listens sharp. You'll be riding point someday not too far from now."

"You think so?"

"I don't say what I don't believe to be true."

The cook gave a shout and shook a fist at Willy.

"See you at dinner," Willy said. He grabbed Cimarron's plate and cup and ran around the fire trench toward the cook.

Later, as Cimarron was gathering his gear, Muncy, the trail boss, respectfully and unfailingly addressed as "Mr. Muncy" by the trail hands, rode up to him.

"'Morning, Mr. Muncy," he said pleasantly as he straightened up.

"'Morning, Cimarron. You about ready?" When Cimarron nodded, Muncy said, "We'll move the herd out onto the trail right away. I don't want to give them time to graze. There's a heavy dew all over the grass, and if they graze it for any length of time, it'll start to soften their hooves."

As Muncy was about to ride off, Cimarron said, "Mr. Muncy, that wrangler of yours—that boy named Willy."

"What about him?"

"He has a mighty strong yearning to turn himself into a full-fledged cowboy. To do that, well, he'll need a chance—and somebody to give it to him. Mr. Muncy, if it suits you, let Willy take my place with the herd this morning. I'll look after his remuda."

Muncy shook his head. "I want you riding point on the left of the herd as usual. You're too good a trail hand to spend your time nursing along the remuda."

"I thank you, Mr. Muncy, but—"

Muncy shook his head a second time. And then, "I'll tell you what I will do for you, Cimarron. I'll let Willy join the drag riders. That boy does seem to have an appetite for dust. He seems bound and determined to corral the remuda too close to the chuck wagon every time we stop for a meal so that we wind up with the dust the horses kick up on our food instead of seasoning. I'll tell the cook Willy's to ride drag this morning and I'll set one of the other boys to looking after the remuda. Like I said, you'll ride point on the left of the herd as usual."

Cimarron nodded and Muncy rode off.

A few minutes later, as Cimarron was heading for the rope corral with his Denver saddle slung over his shoulder and carrying his rifle and gear, Willy ran up to him.

"Cimarron! The cook, he told me that Mr. Muncy wants me to ride drag this morning!"

"Mr. Muncy evidently knows a good man when he sees one." Cimarron dropped his saddle and untied the bandanna from around his neck. He held it out to Willy.

"What's this for?"

"Tie it around your nose and mouth and at the back of your neck, else you'll likely choke to death on the dust the herd'll kick up before you've gone much more than a mile."

"Cimarron—thanks, Cimarron."

Cimarron strode on, after picking up his saddle. He ducked under the rope and entered the corral, shouldering his way through the horses until he reached his dun.

He slipped a curb bit into the horse's mouth and a split-ear headstall over its head and then led the animal out of the corral. He examined its back for saddle sores, and when he found none, he threw his saddle blanket over the horse and proceeded to saddle the animal. When he was finished, he slid his Winchester into its boot.

In the corral behind him, trail hands were selecting their mounts for the morning and heading out toward the herd. Cimarron heard the chuck wagon rumble away from the campsite.

He swung into the saddle, turned the dun, and moved out.

The herd moved northwest along the bank of the winding river, past the whitened skulls of dead buffalo that had been placed at half-mile intervals to mark the cutoff from the main Chisholm Trail that led to Dodge City.

Cimarron rode point on the left of the herd with Jefferson riding point on the right. Behind them came the swing and flank men and just ahead of Cimarron on the left rumbled the chuck wagon.

On both sides of the river the seemingly endless prairie that was covered with lush yellow-green stipa grass rolled and undulated.

Dust billowed up from the wide grassless trail which had been severely eroded by wind and water until it was below the level of the surrounding prairie.

Cimarron was only vaguely aware of the sounds of the cattle's ankle joints cracking as they moved along, of their hooves thudding on the packed ground, of their long horns occasionally clattering against one another.

He looked back over his shoulder. He couldn't see Willy or any of the other men riding drag. He saw only a billowing cloud of dust behind the cripples and orphaned yearlings at the rear of the herd.

Well, he thought, the boy wanted a taste of cowboying. He's got it.

Just before noon, a blustery north wind rose and sent the trail dust swirling over the herd and trail hands. Absently, Cimarron reached for his bandanna and then remembered that he had given it to Willy. He rubbed his eyes as he rode on, keeping his head down.

Getting cold, he thought as the wind whined around him. He dropped the reins and buttoned his jacket. Then he pulled a pair of buckskin gloves from his jacket pocket and put them on.

He looked up at the sky. The sun was nowhere in sight. The sky was the ominous color of slate.

Up ahead of the herd, Muncy veered sharply to the right, rode in a circle, and then halted broadside to the herd.

Cimarron recognized the mute message Muncy had sent the point men and he eased his dun toward the nearest of the cattle while Jefferson, on the far side of the herd, fell away from them. Cimarron yelled over his shoulder to the swing man behind him and pointed off to the right. Gradually the trail hands moved the herd forward to the spot which Muncy had chosen for their nooning.

When the herd was in place, Muncy designated two men to ride loose herd on the cattle while they grazed. As he was about to turn and head for the chuck wagon, Cimarron spoke to him.

"I spotted a cow that's got a bad case of lump jaw," he said. "Maybe the cook has some Fleming's Lump Jaw Cure in his possibles drawer."

Muncy shook his head. "Can't take a chance on the disease spreading while we take time to treat it—if it turns out we have anything to treat it with. Shoot the animal."

Cimarron wheeled his horse and rode over to the herd. His dun, a good cutting horse, soon had the diseased cow racing away from the herd. Riding behind it, he drew his Colt, spurred the dun, and when he was riding alongside the cow, fired. His bullet went into the animal's brain and it fell to the ground. When it convulsed one final time and then lay still, Cimarron rode back toward the chuck wagon.

As he was serving himself bacon, beans, and sourdough biscuits, he heard Muncy call for the hands' attention. He carried his plate and cup of black coffee around the chuck wagon to where the hands were gathered, and sat down on the ground.

"Up ahead," Muncy said, "the cutoff leaves the river. Boys, we got about a hundred miles of dry drive ahead of us from that point on to the Arkansas River and

Dodge City. Normally we'd cover that territory in eight days. I'm proposing that we cover it in four. If we don't, we're likely to lose a whole lot of cattle because of a lack of water. Those that don't die outright are likely to go blind from thirst. If it doesn't rain during those four days, we're going to have our hands full keeping those beeves from turning back to the river for water. I know I can count on you all to do your best. It won't be easy. But it's a job we've just got to try to do."

Cimarron turned his head as Muncy headed for the chuck wagon. Something about the herd, the uneasy bellowings from it, bothered him. He studied the animals and noticed that almost none were grazing. None were drinking at the riverbank. Nearly all of them were moving restlessly about in a mill as the strong north wind whined over the prairie. He looked up at the sky.

Dark as a Denver jail, he thought. Storm coming. The cattle can sense it.

An hour later, the trail hands had changed mounts and the cook had smothered his fire.

Cimarron turned his dun over to Willy, who, as a result of the cook's complaint and Muncy's subsequent order, was once again in charge of the remuda.

"Here's your bandanna back, Cimarron," Willy said, and handed it over.

"How was your ride?"

Willy grinned. "I surely do prefer eating these Pecos strawberries and this overland trout," he said, pointing with his fork to the beans and bacon on his plate, "to eating all that dust a man must when he rides drag."

"It's good experience, though," Cimarron told him. He selected a bay for his remount and proceeded to transfer his saddle and gear from the dun to it. He waved to Willy as he rode away toward the herd.

By early afternoon the river had been left far behind the herd and completely lost to sight. Miles of empty prairie stretched out in every direction. The sky continued to darken and the temperature to drop. The north wind no longer whined. Now it howled.

The first powdery flakes of snow fell in midafternoon. In less than fifteen minutes, thick wet snow was falling and the wind had picked up speed as it swept relentlessly southward.

Up ahead of Cimarron, a steer suddenly bolted from

the herd, swung around, and headed back toward him. He spurred his horse and headed it off, forcing it to come to a skidding halt and then veer to its left and rejoin the herd.

Cimarron rode on at a gallop until he reached Muncy, who was riding ahead of the herd. "Mr. Muncy, this storm's going to get a whole lot worse before it gets any better."

"It's May," Muncy said casually. "It'll end any minute."

"The air's frigid," Cimarron observed. "This snow'll be around for a spell." He paused. "I was in a blizzard on a drive down in Texas last year." He paused again and then added, "In *May* of last year."

Muncy said, "I've been lucky. Never faced a blizzard on the trail. I don't think I'm about to face my first."

"We got through that blizzard," Cimarron persisted. "But we lost a lot of stock in the getting, including twelve of the horses in our remuda. They all froze to death."

Muncy turned in his saddle and stared at Cimarron through the falling snow. "Just what are you trying to get at?"

Before Cimarron could answer, one of the swing men rode up and said, "The storm's thickening fast, Mr. Muncy. Maybe we'd better stop till it blows over."

Cimarron said, "Stopping's a bad idea. The herd should be turned away from the wind and started south."

"We'll lose time," Muncy snapped.

"Better to lose a little time, seems to me," Cimarron said soberly, "than risk losing the herd—or most all of it—if things get really bad."

"We move on," Muncy said firmly, and spurred his horse, leaving Cimarron and the swing man, whose name was Preston, behind.

"I'm with you, Cimarron," Preston said. "It's foolhardy to keep riding into this fierce wind."

"Mr. Muncy's the boss," Cimarron said, and wheeled his horse.

When he and Preston reached the herd, Cimarron asked Preston to spell him for a few minutes. "I want to get myself ready for what I think's coming," he explained.

Preston said he would, and Cimarron promised him he'd do the same for him in a few minutes. As Preston took up his position with the herd, Cimarron reined in his bay and dismounted.

He untied his bedroll and took a dirty pair of socks

from his war bag, which was wrapped in it. He pulled off one boot and pulled a sock over the clean one he was wearing. Putting on his boot, he repeated the process with his other foot and then used his bowie knife to cut a slit in the middle of one of his two blankets. Blinking away the snow that was flying into his face, he cut two more slits on either side of the first one and slipped the makeshift poncho over his head. He thrust his arms through the two side slits and then untied his oilskin slicker and put it on.

He slipped the bowie knife back into his boot and pulled his hat down low on his forehead. Hunkering down then with his back to the wildly wailing wind, he took a waterproof container of matches from his pocket and lit one after another, letting each of them burn down until their flames almost touched his fingers. He used the sooty matches to blacken the skin beneath his eyes in order to avoid going snow-blind once the storm ended and the sun came out.

After putting his bedroll together, he tied it behind the cantle of his saddle and boarded the bay again. He rode to where Preston was doing his best to keep the cattle, which were bawling their fright into the wind, in line. He told Preston he'd take over.

Preston immediately dismounted and struggled into his slicker while the wind seemed to be trying to tear it from his body.

The herd began to race in random patterns through the storm, which was rapidly becoming a blizzard as the velocity of the wind increased and the temperature continued to drop sharply.

Cimarron rode hard and, with the help of Preston and the flank man, managed to get the cows back into line. As the drive proceeded in an orderly but slow manner, Cimarron tied his bandanna around his mouth and nose to keep the sleet that had begun to mix with the snow from his face. He turned up the collar of his jacket, but snow got under it, melted, and ran in a cold stream down his back. He leaned over his horse's neck and brushed the snow from its eyes before it could freeze and blind the animal.

"We've got to turn back, Cimarron," Preston shouted. "We don't, these cattle are goners!"

Cimarron didn't respond. He kept his eyes on the dim shape of Muncy in the white distance, certain that the man would turn back, disbelief stunning him as the minutes passed and Muncy rode steadily northward, leading the herd into the open jaws of the blizzard.

But after he had seen several cows and a yearling drop to the ground and lie there without moving, Cimarron could restrain himself no longer. He yelled to Preston and then across the herd to the muffled figure of Jefferson.

"Turn them south!"

Jefferson stared at him in surprise. Only the man's eyes were visible. His hat covered his eyebrows and he had wrapped a sheepskin-lined cinch around the lower part of his face.

"The cattle are suffocating," Cimarron shouted. "They're breathing sleet into their lungs. It's killing them. *Turn them south!*"

"Do like he says," Preston shouted to Jefferson. "We'll lose them all if we keep up like this!" He galloped around Cimarron to aid Jefferson, who was moving forward to turn the herd.

Cimarron turned his horse and rode back to the flank man, whom he told to ride up to the front of the herd and help get the cattle marching south with their backs to the rushing wind and its burden of wet snow and sleet. He then yelled the same message to the flank man on the right of the herd, telling him to pass it on to the swing man riding ahead of him.

"Once they're heading south," he shouted, "bunch them up. They'll stay warmer that way. *Don't let them drift!*"

"Cimarron!"

Cimarron turned and saw Willy waving wildly to him through the driving snow and sleet. He rode over to the boy.

"Cimarron, look at their legs!"

Cimarron looked down at the legs of the horses in the remuda. The hair and, in some cases, the hides of the horses had been stripped away up to and even above their hocks because of the thick frozen crust that was forming on top of the thick blanket of wet snow.

"They're bleeding bad, Cimarron," Willy yelled as loudly as he could, but the wind whirled his words away.

Cimarron caught only one of them. "Bleeding."

He pointed south.

Willy understood at once. He began to turn the remuda.

Muncy rode up behind Cimarron. "Are you the man that's responsible for this?" he bellowed.

"I told the men to head the herd south, yes," Cimarron roared back. He pointed at the downed cows and the yearling that lay sprawled in the snow not far away. "Dead," he shouted at Muncy. "Suffocated. Sleet in their lungs!"

Preston rode up. "Cimarron did the right thing, Mr. Muncy."

"Turn them north," Muncy shouted at the top of his voice. Preston looked at Cimarron.

Cimarron shook his head.

Muncy rode rapidly north, grabbed the reins of a rider, and shouted something. The man looked back to where Cimarron was sitting his horse in the swirling snow. Cimarron raised his right arm and pointed south. The rider ripped his reins away from Muncy and rode south, close to the hurrying herd.

When cattle strayed from the tightly bunched herd, Cimarron, Preston, and the other men drove them back.

Blood stained the snow as it flowed from the cut legs of both cattle and horses. And then it quickly vanished as the snow continued to fall, only to promptly reappear as the bleeding, like the wind-whipped snow, continued.

Cimarron eased his horse forward. The animal had great difficulty lifting its legs out of the freezing snow. A few minutes later, it halted and dropped its head between its knees, its nose almost touching the crusted snow.

Cimarron sat in the saddle, letting the animal rest and try to catch its breath. Billows of steam shot from the bay's nostrils, to melt some of the snow beneath them.

Cimarron applied light pressure with his knees and the horse reluctantly moved forward, blood flowing down its legs.

Snow melted on the warm bodies of the cattle at the edges of the herd, forming icicles. The icicles swung from side to side, and then, as the slow southward journey continued, they broke loose, tearing away patches of hide from the animals' bodies as they did so and leaving raw red wounds from which blood dripped onto the snow.

An hour passed. And then another one.

The snow and sleet continued to fall. The wind did not diminish.

Some of the nearly exhausted cattle slumped down in the snow.

Cimarron drove them to their feet to keep them from freezing to death. The animals, many of them blinded now by the snow that had frozen shut their eyelids, plodded slowly on as the merciless slivers of sleet continued to pelt their exposed bodies.

Cimarron rode on, mile after weary mile, uncomfortably aware of the unsteady gait of the bay beneath him, wondering if the animal would make it through the blizzard.

Suddenly the sun pierced the clouds in the northern sky. The crystalline snow on the ground glittered brightly in its light.

Cimarron looked up at the still-leaden sky directly above him. He removed his bandanna, pocketed it, and rode on, letting the bay pick its way around the drifts, as the clouds began to break up and the snow lessen and finally stop falling altogether.

An hour later as a cow dropped and died, he yelled to Jefferson, who was riding off to his left. "We'd best spend the night here. The stock's worn out."

Some time later, he heard someone cry out. He turned in the saddle, to see Willy clawing at his face. He rode over to the boy and, as he got closer to him, saw that Willy was not clawing at his face but at his eyes.

"I can't see," the boy cried wildly.

"Willy, it's Cimarron. You've gone snowblind from the reflection of the sun on the snow. Sit tight in your saddle. You'll be out of harm's way up there. Later on, put some salt poultices on your eyes."

"Cimarron, I lost the remuda!" Willy moaned. "When my eyes went, I—"

"You didn't lose them," Cimarron said as he dismounted. "They're all here." He glanced at his dun, which was standing nearby with the other horses, apparently basking in the warm and welcome sunshine.

"Damnation!" Muncy muttered as he rode up to Cimarron. "We're all the way back to the river!"

Muncy's remark was not strictly true. They were more than a mile north of the river, but they could see it in the distance, bright sunlight reflecting from its surface.

Muncy turned his gaze from the river to Cimarron. "I could have gotten them through," he said.

Cimarron, listening to the dying wind, said, "You might have. But I doubt it."

"You're a troublemaker, Cimarron," Muncy muttered. "You made me look like a damn fool back there when you went against my orders and turned the herd south. My guess is that my men won't take any more orders from me now unless they see that you're willing to take them first. And now I know I can't count on you following my orders."

Cimarron said nothing.

"You're fired," Muncy told him. "And the sooner you ride out of here, the better I'll like it." He reached into his pocket, pulled out a wad of folded bills, counted out several, and handed them to Cimarron.

"Get your horse," he barked, "and get going!" He rode away.

Willy said, "I heard what Mr. Muncy told you, Cimarron. I sure am sorry he feels the way he does."

Cimarron looked up at Willy, who sat stiffly aboard his horse, his eyes wide open but blinded.

"You'll be able to see in a little while, Willy. Snow-blindness is only temporary. Now, don't you forget what I told you this morning. You'll be riding point in no time at all. Maybe sooner than I first figured, since Mr. Muncy's short a man at the moment."

"Where you headed, Cimarron?"

Cimarron tilted his hat back on his head. "Well, I can't answer that on account of I just don't know."

"What'll you do?"

"Don't know the answer to that one neither. I'll find something. Or it'll find me."

"So long, Cimarron. It was real good knowing you."

"I wish you the best, boy." Cimarron, leading the bay, strode in the direction of his horse, which was pawing the snow in a vain effort to reach the grass beneath it.

2

When Cimarron reached his horse, he gently stroked its neck and then stooped and carefully examined each of its legs.

They were, he found, badly cut by the frozen crust of snow. In places, the blood had dried. But some still trickled in thin red lines down the dun's legs.

He transferred his saddle and bridle from the bay to the dun, and then, leaving the animal to continue pawing the snow in search of graze, stripped off his slicker and makeshift poncho and tied them behind his saddle. Then he turned and walked north.

When he reached the dead cow that had been his destination, he pulled his bowie knife from his boot, knelt down in the snow, and deftly skinned one of the cow's haunches. He cut off the haunch, wiped his knife clean in the snow, and returned it to his boot. Carrying the bloody haunch of beef, he retraced his steps and filled his canteen from the chuck wagon's water barrel. Then he headed for his horse, gripped its reins in his free hand, and walked the animal south.

Gradually the sounds the trail hands were making and the sound of the bawling cattle faded behind him. The only sound he heard now was the crunching of his boots and the dun's hooves on the snow's thick crust.

When he reached the river, he dropped the bloody haunch he was carrying in a deep snowdrift and led his horse down to the river to drink. He maneuvered it so that all four of its legs were, at one time or another, standing more than hock-deep in the water.

He pocketed the buckskin gloves he had been wearing and pulled his bandanna from his pocket. He soaked it in the river and then led the dun onto the bank, where he bent down and, using the wet bandanna, gently cleaned the wounds on the horse's legs. When he was satisfied with what he had done, he washed his bandanna in the river and, noticing his face reflected in the water, also washed away the soot from the charred matches that he had rubbed on his skin. He got up, and after spreading his bandanna across his saddle to dry, he hunkered down and used his bowie knife to cut thin strips of meat from the dead cow's haunch, which he then hung on the branches of a nearby chokeberry bush to dry.

As the sun disappeared below the western horizon, he built a small fire that sputtered and threatened to go out because of the wetness of the chokeberry branches he had used to make it. But by blowing on it often and by drying some branches in its heat before adding them to the fire, he was able to keep it burning.

He cut off several slices of beef from the haunch and spitted them. As he held them over the fire, the burning blood sputtered and hissed. When the meat was brown and sizzling, he withdrew it from the fire. The outside of the meat was crusty, almost charred, but the inside was rare, and Cimarron ate with an appetite that bordered on the ravenous. He wiped grease from his lips with the back of his hand as he watched the green-necked buzzards circling in the north above the carcasses of the dead stock.

Later, as twilight deepened into night, he cleared snow from a space between the river and his fire. He deliberately let the fire burn low until it was little more than embers, and then he placed his slicker, oilskin side down, on the wet ground and covered it with the ground sheet he took from his bedroll. He placed the blanket that had served him as a poncho on top of the ground sheet, spread his second blanket on top of the first, and placed his war bag on the bed he had made.

He unsaddled the dun and took a picket pin from his war bag and pounded it into the ground with one booted foot; then he tethered the animal to it.

He looked upriver and downriver with his back to the fire to maintain sharp night vision. Then he looked north.

In the distance, he could see the remains of the cook's fire, which, like his own, was nearly dead. He kicked out his fire and then got between his blankets, placing his Colt beside him on the bottom blanket.

He lay there a few minutes staring up at the half-moon and the stars, and then turned over and was almost instantly asleep.

He awoke as abruptly when he caught the sound of crunching snow.

His fingers closed around the butt of his Colt, but the rest of his body remained motionless as he listened. Slowly he swiveled his head. Nothing in sight.

He listened warily to the sound of a rider coming toward him. As he listened, the rider moved west. The sound of crunching snow faded. Then it grew louder as the rider turned back.

Cimarron was up on his feet in one swift fluid motion, shaking off his blanket, calling out into the night, "I've got you spotted! Don't move!"

The figures of the horse and rider blotted out some of the stars on the northern horizon. Were it not for that fact, they would have been invisible. But Cimarron had long ago learned to see what other men might miss simply by taking note of any change, major or minor, in the normal appearance of the world around him. Hidden stars were one such aberration.

The mounted figure in the near distance was a deeper blur on the dark night. Cimarron could not make out the rider's face in the thin light of the half-moon.

"Cimarron? That you?" The male voice was low, tentative. "Cimarron, it's me . . . Willy. I still can't see so good from close up. Things is fuzzy around the edges. Cimarron?"

Cimarron's hand that held his Frontier Colt lowered. He returned the gun to its holster leather. "Boy, you might have got yourself killed sneaking up on a man in the night like that."

Willy's horse moved forward, the snow crust cracking beneath its hooves. When it was within a few yards of Cimarron, Willy got out of the saddle. In his hand he had a gunnysack which he held out to Cimarron.

"What's that?" Cimarron asked.

"Some things I brought you. I saw your fire before you put it out. I figured I'd bring you these." He took a step toward Cimarron, still holding the gunnysack out in front of him.

Cimarron took the sack and reached inside it. He felt, but could not see, what he quickly identified by touch as potatoes, raisins, dried fruit, and cornbread. "A man can get mighty hungry alone out on the prairie," he said in a low voice. "I do thank you, boy. But I wonder why you did it."

"The cook told me," Willy said.

"He told you to bring me these edibles?"

Willy shook his head. "No, he told me that the only reason he let me loose to ride drag this morning was because Mr. Muncy made him do it. He said Mr. Muncy told him that you wanted to switch places with me so I could get a chance to ride herd."

"So you decided to give back as good as you got, that it?"

"I owed you something, Cimarron. But it wasn't just that. It was . . ." Willy looked down at the snow, which glistened in the moonlight. "It was—well, I kind of think of you as my friend."

"I am that."

"Maybe we could build a fire, Cimarron. We could sit and talk some."

"No fire. Never can tell who might be prowling around out here. A big old lobo wolf—or a stray wrangler."

Willy smiled. "Cimarron . . ."

Cimarron waited.

"I've been thinking maybe I'm not cut out to be a trail hand. I've been thinking maybe I'd ride on back to Texas."

"I ride alone, boy."

"I wouldn't cause you any kind of trouble, Cimarron."

"Listen up, boy. The cook curses at you. The trail hands, some of them maybe, let on that they're better than you. Probably they are. They know more about cattle, horses, and weather than you do at the moment.

"But you bear this in mind. A cook's curses don't amount to more'n a mess of gnats aiming themselves at a buffalo. And those cowhands had to learn what they now know just like you've got to. Takes time. If you quit now, you'll never learn, and it'll get to rankling deep down inside you and festering too so that pretty soon you won't like yourself for a real good reason. Because you quit and didn't give yourself a fair chance to learn cowboying."

"That Mr. Muncy sure is a bullheaded man."

"You'll meet a lot of Mr. Muncys before you lay yourself down to die. Can't be helped. But you can learn to handle them."

Willy looked to the north. "Well, maybe I'd best be getting on back."

"You do that, boy. And when you get to Dodge, you pay a visit to the Long Branch and a lady you're likely to find there name of Jessica. Tell her I told you to look her up. Tell her I said she'll find you little more than a colt—but a colt that's got bottom."

"Jessica," Willy repeated softly. "Nice name."

"Nice lady," Cimarron said, and held out his right hand.

Willy shook it and then quickly got into the saddle and rode noisily north through the frozen snow.

Cimarron awoke just before dawn. His body was stiff from the chill of the surrounding snow. He spent a few minutes working the kinks out of his muscles and a few more eating some of the dried fruit and cornbread that Willy had given him.

By the time the sun rose, he knew that it was going to be a hot day. Already the snow was melting beneath his boots and running in rivulets along the almost bare ground that sloped down toward the river.

The sight of the melting snow disturbed him. Melting snow, in time, meant muddy ground underfoot. It meant slow traveling. But it wasn't the prospect of slow traveling that bothered him. Cimarron was worried about his horse. The mud could easily cause an infection in the animal's wounds. And infection, if severe enough, could mean the loss of the horse, and the loss of a man's horse in Indian territory could mean serious trouble.

No use worrying about trouble, he told himself, glancing at the raw legs of the dun. Not till you meet up with it on the trail.

He went over to the chokeberry bush and turned the strips of beef to facilitate their drying. Then he kicked the picket pin loose, picked it up, and led his horse away from the river to where a patch of clover poked through the melting snow. The horse bent its head and began to nibble the clover.

Cimarron went over to the remains of the haunch he had left in what had been a snowdrift the night before but now was little more than a wet white dust covering the ground. He bent down, pulled his knife from his boot, and sliced several gobbets of fat from it; he placed them on a flat stone. He picked up one of the pieces of fat and went over to his saddle, where he proceeded to rub the fat into the leather. He worked slowly, feeling the warmth of the sun on his back, and when he was finished nearly an hour later, his saddle, straps, latigo, fenders, and stirrup leathers gleamed in the sunlight.

He got up and went over to the chokeberry bush, selected several pieces of jerky from the many he had draped over the branches of the bush, and carried them to the flat stone on which he had placed the pieces of fat he had cut from the cow's haunch. Using another smaller stone, he began to pound the jerky and fat, mixing them well, until he had made what he considered to be a sufficient quantity of pemmican. He balled it and placed it in the gunnysack Willy had given him.

A sudden buzzing sounded in his ears and he turned quickly, an eager expression on his face. The buzzing continued as bees swarmed down toward the river.

Elated, he studied the course of their seemingly wayward flight. He knew he could find their hive by simply backtrailing along their line of flight. He walked away from the river and five minutes later found a lightning-blasted stump of a dead redbud tree. The bees were streaming out of the shattered stump. Flapping his hat to ward them off, he successfully raided the hive. Scooping both hands full of honey, he ran back the way he had come, and when he reached his horse, he knelt down on the ground and began to smear the honey over the horse's wounded legs.

"That'll fix you up just fine," he said to the dun as he wiped his hands clean in the grass. "It'll bind up the edges of your torn flesh. It's a good antiseptic too. You'll heal in no time."

He decided to spend another night where he was in order to give the honey time to do its work.

Nobody's waiting for me anywhere, he reminded himself. I've got no place in particular to go and all the time in the world to get there.

Next morning, after breakfasting on potatoes he had taken from the gunnysack and roasted in the ashes of the fire he had built, Cimarron washed the honey from his horse's legs and then headed back to the hive he had found the day before.

He made another raid on it, but this time two bees left their stingers in his neck.

He carried the honey he had gathered back to his camp and applied it to the horse's wounds.

After saddling up, tying his bedroll and slicker in place, and smothering his fire, he swung onto the saddle and began to ride southeast along the Chisholm's cutoff. The river, on his right, glistened in the bright sunshine, drowning in it.

He rode slowly, the reins held loosely in his right hand, guiding the dun by knee pressure alone. The horse's gait was slow but, Cimarron noted with relief, steady.

The sun was riding high in the sky when he reached the point where the cutoff joined the main branch of the Chisholm Trail. He turned south and followed the hard-packed trail.

The snow left by the blizzard had almost completely vanished from the face of the land, a victim of the sun, which had blazed in the sky for the past two days.

Cimarron had gone no more than a mile down the trail when he spotted a herd of about fifty cows coming toward him. It was moving slowly and he knew why. There were two calves among the herd. No steers or bulls. An easy herd to move, he thought, were it not for the calves.

Only two men were driving the small herd.

Cimarron halted his horse and moved it to the right. When the herd reached him, he nodded to the two men driving it.

Both of them, he noted, were young. Not much older than Willy, he guessed. They looked tired as they leaned on their saddle horns, watching him.

"Nice day," he said.

"Better than day before yesterday," one of the two men said.

"Bad blizzard, that one," Cimarron said. "You lose any stock?"

"Five head. Three died. Two run off."

The companion of the man who had spoken said, "We'll

likely be losing our two calves too. Their mothers won't let them near to nurse."

Cimarron considered advising the men to shoot the calves. They'd make better time without them. He said nothing. It was none of his business.

"Don't know what's wrong with those cows," the man who had just spoken added. "It ain't natural for cows not to let their own calves nurse."

Cimarron dismounted. "Which ones are the cows that calved?"

When the two cows had been pointed out to him, he got down on one knee and examined each of them, running his fingers lightly over their udders. Both of the cows bawled and pulled away. He straightened and said, "Their udders are sunburned on account of the sun that was reflecting off the snow. That's why they won't nurse their calves. Their udders are too sore."

"Dade," said the man nearest to Cimarron. "Look there!"

Cimarron saw the Indians riding up, saw Dade pull a revolver from his waistband.

"Get your iron, Pete," Dade said grimly.

As Pete went for his six-shooter, Cimarron said, "No need for guns."

Both men looked at him in surprise.

"Put them away," he said, pointing to their guns. "These Indians are Shawnees. It's not likely they mean trouble."

The Indians rode up and halted their horses, their eyes on the cows. Then one member of the party turned and pointed first to his mouth, then to his stomach, then to the cows.

"You'll move north a lot faster without these calves," Cimarron said in a low tone to Dade and Pete. "They'll most likely die on you anyway, since they can't nurse. Turn them over to these hungry Indians."

Dade started to protest, but Pete overruled him and pointed to the calves and then to the Indians.

Instantly the Indians were off their horses and on the ground, knives in their hands. They slit the throats of the two calves, but before they could begin skinning them, Cimarron let out a yell.

When the Indians looked up at him, he held up one hand. Then, to Dade and Pete, he said, "You'd best cut the mothers of those calves out of your herd. Take them over to their calves and let them smell them so's they'll know they're dead. You don't, you'll have trouble with them running back along the trail to look for their calves once their udders are healed."

Dade and Pete did as Cimarron had suggested, and when they had the two cows, bawling over their dead calves, back in the herd, Cimarron pointed to the Indians and then to the calves.

The Indians dropped to their knees and began to skin the dead calves. When the job was completed, they sliced pieces of meat from the carcasses and began to eat them, blood running down their chins, broad smiles on their faces.

Pete grimaced and looked away.

Later, their meal completed, the Indians packed the remaining meat in the bloody calf hides and rode away with it without a word.

"My partner and me," Dade said to Cimarron, "we've never been in Indian territory before. I thought those Indians were bent on killing us. I've heard awful stories about them."

"Thanks for your advice," Pete said to Cimarron. "We appreciate it."

"Good luck to you," Cimarron said, and swung into the saddle. He rode around the small herd and continued journeying south.

Several hours later, he saw a meadowlark fly up from the ground off to his left. It was quickly followed by a second one. He wheeled his horse and rode over to where the birds had taken wing. As he had suspected, there was a small creek winding through the low buffalo grass. He watered his horse and filled his nearly empty canteen before heading back to the trail.

He dismounted when the sun had passed its meridian but did not stop to eat despite the hunger he felt. The gunnysack of edibles, he knew, would be empty soon enough. The thing to do now was to make them last as long as possible.

By midafternoon as the sun's rays slanted down from the sky, Cimarron stopped walking and sat down on the ground in the shade cast by the body of his horse. As the dun began to graze, he took off his hat and wiped the sweat from his forehead and face. He was in the act of putting his hat back on when he heard the sound of riders heading down the trail. He quickly got to his feet, clapped his hat on his head, and shielding his eyes with his hand, looked north.

There were two riders coming toward him.

His horse looked up at them and then dropped its head again.

As the riders came closer to him, Cimarron was surprised to find that one of them was a woman. She was wearing trousers, a shirt, a vest, and a stetson. Her long hair was yellow, almost golden, and she had tied it at the nape of her neck with a narrow scarlet ribbon. Her eyes, bright blue, were on Cimarron, and on her far-from-plain but not-quite-beautiful face was a smile.

The man also wore a stetson. His coat and pants were brown, his shirt white, and his boots black.

He sat taller in the saddle on the quarter horse he was riding than did the woman on her roan. His face was weathered and heavily lined, making him look older than Cimarron guessed he really was. His eyes, as black as his hair, were set deep beneath his bristling brows. His cheeks and chin were covered with a light black stubble and his lips were compressed in a long thin line.

The pair pulled up short in front of Cimarron.

He looked from the woman to the man and then back again.

"Good afternoon," said the man with a nod to Cimarron. "You're alone on the trail?"

"I am." Cimarron's right hand moved almost imperceptibly closer to his holster.

The woman, still smiling, said, "This is a terribly lonely land even when you have company to travel with. My name is Emma Dorset and this gentleman beside me is Reverend Philip Griffin."

"Glad to know you both," Cimarron said, his fingertips less than an inch from the butt of his gun.

"We mean you no harm, sir," said Griffin. "You won't need your gun."

Cimarron was surprised. He hadn't thought a preacher would be the kind of man to notice another man making ready to unholster his six-shooter should it prove necessary to do so.

"You know our names," Emma said. "May we know yours?"

"Cimarron."

"That's all?" Emma asked, her eyebrows lifting. "Just Cimarron?"

"That's all."

"I see," she said, and glanced at Griffin.

"Which way are you headed, Mr.—Cimarron?" Griffin asked.

"South."

"So are we—until we reach the North Canadian River. Would you mind if we rode along with you?"

Cimarron shot a glance at Emma, a coolly appraising glance.

"I suppose we could all ride along together, if you've a mind to," he said.

"Fine," Emma said, her eyes on Cimarron's face.

"Splendid," Griffin said. " 'For a friend of mine is come to me in my journey . . .' Luke, chapter eleven, verse six."

Cimarron swung into the saddle and the three of them rode south.

"We're missionaries," Emma volunteered as they rode side by side.

Cimarron said nothing. He was thinking that Griffin's quarter horse was an especially fine specimen to belong to a preacher. It was sleek, looked strong, and strained against its bit as if it were yearning to run. The man's clothes, although a bit grimy with trail dust, were a cut above what the average townsman wore.

"We are going to work among the Cherokees," Emma said, glancing at Cimarron, whose eyes were on the trail ahead.

Boots, Cimarron thought. Never met a preacher yet who wore boots.

Griffin intoned, " 'For my brethren and companions' sakes, I will now say, Peace be within thee.' One hundred and twenty second psalm, verse eight. That is the message Miss Dorset and I are bringing to our red brethren."

He doesn't wear a gun rig in Indian Territory, Cimarron thought. He must be a very trusting—or foolhardy man.

"You're not a very talkative man, are you, Cimarron?" Emma asked.

"I can be when I have something worth saying."

"But you don't have anything worth saying?" she prodded.

"Not at the moment, I don't."

" 'In the multitude of words,' Emma," Griffin said, " 'there wanteth not sin: but he that refraineth his lips is wise.' Psalms, chapter—"

"Good place up ahead to make camp, looks like," Cimarron interrupted. He pointed to the edge of the eastern woodlands that could be seen in the distance. "There's good shelter. Wood for a fire."

"Shelter," Emma repeated, and glanced back over her shoulder.

When they reached the mixed stand of locust and elm trees, Cimarron rode in among them and then halted his horse. To his surprise, Emma rode deeper into the trees whose branches interlocked overhead.

"We won't feel a bit of wind in here," she declared, looking around. "How very nice and snug it is."

"We'd invite you to share our food, Cimarron," Griffin said, his expression morose. "But the fact of the matter is that neither of us had the foresight to pack sufficient provisions for our journey. We've already eaten what we had with us."

"Be right back," Cimarron said, and slid his Winchester from its scabbard.

He walked out from under the trees and scouted along the edge of the woodlands. It took him almost half an hour to find what he had been looking for—game. It came to him in the form of a flock of prairie chickens. He brought his rifle up to his shoulder and sighted through the rear and along the front sight. He squeezed off a shot and one of the birds dropped. His second shot downed one of the other birds in the flock.

He went over and picked up the two quivering bodies and retraced his steps.

"Wonderful," Emma exclaimed when she saw him coming through the trees with his kill. "But what do we do with them?"

Cimarron eyed her for a moment and then, without answering her question, plucked and gutted the birds. He lopped off their heads and feet, set the ends of two notched branches he broke from an elm in the ground, spitted one of the fowls, and laid the spit across the notched branches.

Griffin hurried up to him carrying some branches he had broken from a locust tree.

"Green wood," Cimarron said. "Won't burn easy and

it'll make too much smoke when and if it does catch." He got up and went over to a deadfall and returned carrying some wood he had taken from it. He cut away the outer wood, which was still damp from the snow, and placed the dry inner wood beneath the spit.

When he had a fire going, he said, "The smoke'll get lost up there in the tree branches. We're pretty well hidden in here. It's not likely anybody'll spot our fire."

As he turned the spit, Emma peered out through the trees at the prairie beyond them and asked, "Who do you think might see our fire?"

"We're pretty far east for any Comanches to come upon us," Cimarron answered. "But you never can tell. Some braves just might be ranging this far from home hunting buffalo."

Emma shuddered and moved closer to Griffin.

Later, as she and Griffin ate the portions of the prairie chicken Cimarron had cut off and given to them, he spitted the second bird and proceeded to roast it.

"You two ever lived with the Cherokees before?" he asked as he slowly turned the spit.

Emma shook her head. "But our people have a mission at Tahlequah and a small staff to operate it. I'm told the Cherokees are quite civilized."

"They're tame enough," Cimarron said. "They're one of what some call the Five Civilized Tribes."

"But," said Griffin eagerly, "they cannot be called truly civilized until they have all begun to reap the benefits of the Christian religion."

"You may have yourself a point there," Cimarron said as he continued to turn the spit. "But an arguable one."

"I'm not sure I understand," Griffin said tentatively.

"I've known some churchgoing men in my time," Cimarron said. "Seemed to me they forgot to practice what they'd heard preached even before they'd ducked past the preacher on the way out after services."

" 'For the wages of sin is death; but—' "

"Want some seconds, Miss Dorset?" Cimarron asked to silence Griffin.

"No, thank you, I've had quite enough. It was delicious."

"Reverend?"

Griffin shook his head.

Cimarron removed the spit and, holding it in both

hands, began to consume the second bird. When he had finished, he smothered the fire and said, "I'll see to my horse and then it'll be about time to turn in. Sun's down. It'll be dark before long."

He rose and led his horse to one side where he unsaddled it. He took some raisins from the gunnysack and fed them to the animal. He offered the dun a dried peach but the horse refused it. He ate it himself.

He shook out the animal's saddle blanket and hung it over a low tree branch and then pulled a handful of grass and began to rub the horse down. It nickered softly and tossed its head. He checked its legs and found that they were healing nicely.

"What's his name?"

Cimarron turned to find Emma standing just behind him. "Him? He hasn't got one."

"I thought all cowboys named their horses."

Cimarron leaned back against a tree and folded his arms. "You take me for a cowboy?"

"Aren't you?"

"You start slapping labels on a man before you know anything about him, you might be setting yourself up for a surprise or two."

"I imagine that you can be a surprising man, Cimarron."

Cimarron said nothing as Emma stepped closer to him, her features almost invisible in the gathering darkness that was trapped among the trees.

"If you're not a cowboy, Cimarron, what exactly are you?"

"I didn't say I wasn't a cowboy."

"I know one label that I'm sure fits you," Emma said, almost whispering.

"What might that be?"

"You're a man."

"That's plain to see."

"You're right," Emma said. "It certainly is." She quickly turned and hurried back to where Griffin was standing and watching her.

3

Cimarron awoke and was instantly alert, his index fingers tight on the trigger of his Colt. The sound that had awakened him came again. A rustling. Someone or something was moving through the underbrush toward him.

He cocked his Colt, peering into the darkness.

And then a slender hand, white, appeared out of the darkness and reached out to touch his face.

"I'm afraid of guns," Emma Dorset whispered. "Put it away."

"You could have got yourself shot," Cimarron snapped in exasperation. "Creeping up on a man like that in the middle of the night!"

Emma placed the tips of her fingers against his lips. "*Sshhh,*" she whispered. "Do you want Reverend Griffin to hear you?"

Cimarron tried to speak but Emma's fingers prevented him from doing so. As he reached up, intending to remove them from his lips, she removed them herself, and kneeling down beside him, she leaned over and pressed her lips against his.

Cimarron surprised himself by having the presence of mind under the exciting and decidedly unexpected circumstances to ease the hammer of his .45 back into place.

Emma's kiss was a brief one, but it had been passionate enough to inflame Cimarron. She withdrew her lips from his and stretched out on the blanket beside him.

"You won't need your gun," she said softly, "I won't

hurt you, so hadn't you better put it away? It might go off."

As Cimarron hesitated, Emma took the gun from his hand and, reaching across his body, placed it a safe distance away. "Now, isn't that better?"

Cimarron could make out her face in the moonlight filtering down through the trees. She was smiling. Her eyes caught the moonlight and gleamed as she ran her fingers over his lips and then down his chin and neck. They slipped inside his shirt.

"Miss Dorset, you—"

"I wanted you from the minute I first saw you," she said, running her fingers lightly over his chest. "From the very first instant, as a matter of fact." She began to unbutton his shirt. "And you wanted me. Oh, I could tell. You had that hungry look in your eyes."

"Hell, honey, you're not blaming me for that, are you now?"

"Sit up."

When Cimarron did, Emma slipped his jacket and shirt off. "I'll be ready in a minute." She stood up and hurriedly began to remove her clothes as Cimarron, on his feet now and pushing aside the questions that tumbled about in his mind, hurriedly removed his boots and trousers.

"You don't waste any time," Emma murmured.

"I don't want to give you a chance to change your mind," he said, taking her soft body in his arms.

Her hand slid lightly along the length of his hardened flesh and she murmured, "I just knew you were built big."

Cimarron placed his lips against hers and eased his tongue between her teeth.

She sucked on it, holding him tightly as she did so. Then she pulled his arms from around her body and lay down on the ground, reaching up wordlessly.

Cimarron knelt down between her spread and bent legs, his hands cupping both of her breasts.

"Is this what you're going to teach the men of the Five Tribes?" he asked her, grinning.

"If a man has to be taught, I'm not interested," she responded.

"How'd you know you might not have to teach me?"

She laughed lightly. "I know a real man when I see one. And when I saw you, I knew at once that you wouldn't need any teaching. Or coaxing."

Cimarron dropped down upon her and, despite his intention to use restraint, thrust himself all the way into her. The suddenness of her appearance beside him in the night and the abruptness of her seduction had washed away any inhibitions he might have had as well as any capacity to indulge in any gentle foreplay.

She eagerly matched the almost savage thrusting of his body. Her hands clutched his buttocks as if she were trying to force him deeper inside her. She moaned beneath him, sweating as he was, clawing his back and buttocks and biting his neck.

Fiery minutes later during which the only world Cimarron knew was the woman he felt and heard beneath him, he erupted within her. When his shuddering body stilled, he remained inside her.

Her knees were bent and her feet were anchored against the insides of his thighs. She sighed and he raised his head so he could look into her eyes.

"Am I good?" she asked him, smiling up at him.

"The best."

"You're even better than that." She paused and smiled mischievously. "I feel like I've just been had by a wild horse."

"Honey, I'm sorry—"

She pressed her fingers against his lips. "I meant that as a compliment."

Although still stiff, he started to withdraw from her.

"Don't" she muttered almost angrily. *"Don't!"*

He eased all the way back into her again and, after lying still for a moment, began to move his hips in a gently rocking motion. He swiveled them, rocked, swiveled again.

Emma's breath gushed from between her lips along with a low, drawn-out moan.

This time, aware of her need and desire, Cimarron maintained a slow, deliberately tantalizing rhythm, and when he felt her body lurch beneath him as she achieved orgasm, he increased the rapidity of his thrusting and, a moment later, exploded inside her a second time. Before she could speak, he withdrew from her and dropped down on the ground, hands clasped behind his head as he lay on his back staring up into the trees above him.

Emma reached out to fondle him.

"You'll wear it out on me," he said, grinning. "Give it a rest."

But she continued to fondle him as she said, "You and I, we're very good together."

"I can't remember when or if I ever had it so good." He paused and then, raising himself on one elbow to look down on her, asked, "Only I wonder why you came stalking me."

"I do like modesty in a man," she said with a sly smile, and squeezed him.

He let out a cry that was a blend of pleasure and pain.

"Sshhh!"

"If the good reverend were to find out—"

"He won't." Emma sat up, pushed Cimarron down, and took him into her warm wet mouth.

It was Cimarron's turn to sigh as again the world slipped away from him and the nervous nickering of a horse in the distance might have been a sound made on the moon.

Their lovemaking went on for nearly another hour until at last Emma declared herself tired. And more than satisfied.

"Think about it," she whispered.

"About what?"

"Tomorrow night," she answered.

And then she was on her feet and getting into her clothes.

When she had gone and he had dressed, Cimarron, slipping down into a deep sleep, thought with lusty anticipation of Emma and the night to come.

He awoke at first light and automatically reached for his Colt. It lay not far from him where Emma had placed it. His war bag, gunnysack and rifle lay on his opposite side.

As was his habit upon awakening, he surveyed his surroundings before getting up. He looked first to where he had picketed his horse before climbing into his blankets. He sat up quickly.

His horse was gone! So were his saddle, bridle, and saddlebags which he had not removed from the dun the night before.

Near where he had picketed it stood Griffin's horse.

He got up fast, and after holstering his Colt, he walked over to the animal. Griffin hadn't unsaddled it the night before. He looked around. Emma's horse, also still saddled and trailing its reins, had wandered to the edge of the woodland, where it stood idly grazing.

Emma herself, wrapped in a suggan, was still sleeping not far from where Cimarron stood.

He strode to the edge of the woodland and peered out across the prairie. Where, he wondered, had Griffin gone? And why? A morning constitutional on top of a horse? The man was nowhere in sight.

Cimarron started back beneath the trees, wondering if his dun had pulled its picket pin and wandered off. But even if that had happened, he reasoned, it wouldn't explain Griffin's absence.

Why, he asked himself, hadn't he heard the horse—or Griffin—moving through the underbrush when both, either separately or together, had obviously done so? The answer to his question was not hard to find. Emma. Emma had occupied his full and undivided attention for more than an hour during the night.

Had Griffin heard or seen them? Was that why he had left the camp? But, if so, why had he not taken his own horse?

Emma awoke at that moment, and when she saw Cimarron, she smiled and said, "Good morning."

"Did the two of you make plans to part before the night ended?"

"Part?"

"You and the reverend."

"Why, no, of course not. Why do you ask?"

"He's gone."

Emma looked around. "But his horse is here."

"Mine isn't."

Emma looked up at Cimarron. "You think Reverend Griffin took your horse?"

"That's what I think."

"But why would he do that?" Emma frowned. "Do you suppose something might have happened to him? You mentioned Comanches last night."

Cimarron shook his head. "You two didn't plan on him riding on ahead to your mission, then?"

Emma shook her head. "I've no idea where he could have gone—or why. But he'll come back, won't he?"

"I don't intend to wait to find out," Cimarron said. "Get up and get ready to move out of here. We'll trail him."

"But—"

"On your feet! I don't know how much of a head start he has on us. There's no time to waste."

Emma scrambled to her feet and began to fold her suggan.

Cimarron was in the saddle of Griffin's horse and waiting for her by the time she was ready to leave. "I've found sign," he told her. "We came into the woodland up there. There's trampled grass over that way. He's headed northwest. You hungry?"

"Yes, I am, a little."

Cimarron took out his gunnysack, which he had placed in Griffin's saddlebag, and handed it to her.

She reached into it and came up with the balled pemmican. "What is this?"

Cimarron told her.

She made a face.

"Try tasting it before you turn it down."

She did and said, "It's—why, it's quite good."

"There's also some raisins and dried fruit in there."

"Aren't you having any?"

"Not hungry. Hurry it up and let's move out."

A moment later, after Cimarron had returned the gunnysack to the saddlebag, they rode out of the woodland.

Cimarron kept his eyes on the ground and the grass. He spotted a trace of blood on a clump of curled buffalo grass. Some time later, he spotted horse droppings lying in the bent grass. He got out of the saddle and examined them. They were, he found, still moist.

"He's not far ahead of us," he told Emma. He got back into the saddle and touched the flanks of his mount with his spurs to move it forward into a trot and then into a gallop. He almost forgot about Emma as he rode, scanning the ground ahead of him. Her cry, which came from far behind him, caused him to turn and then rein in the quarter horse to wait for her to catch up to him.

"I can't travel this fast," she declared breathlessly when she was beside him again. "I simply cannot."

"You'll have to."

Emma's eyes flashed. "I will not!"

"Suit yourself. I like to let people do what they have a mind to do. Now if you want to turn back and head for that mission of yours, you're welcome to do so. But I intend to get my horse, rifle, and gear back from your friend Reverend Griffin."

The fire in Emma's eyes flickered and then died. "You know I wouldn't be able to find my way to the mission by myself."

"Then you'd best try awful hard to keep up with me." Cimarron spurred his mount and galloped across the prairie, following the trace of bent grass.

Emma rode not far behind him.

Thoughts raced through his mind. The horse under him was superior to his dun even if the dun's legs had been uninjured. It had good wind and seemed to prefer galloping to trotting or walking. Now why, Cimarron asked himself, would a man steal a horse that was inferior to his own?

The Texas saddle beneath Cimarron was as good as his own Denver saddle. Some men, he knew, preferred one; some the other. Some men found the forty-pound Denver saddle too heavy because its weight tended to cause saddle sores. But Cimarron found it more comfortable than the Texas saddle and he avoided saddle sores by keeping his saddle blanket clean and his horse in good condition.

The saddle, then, he concluded, was not the reason for the theft. And the dun itself couldn't be the reason because Griffin's quarter horse was the superior animal. Cimarron found that he could discover no reasonable motive for what Griffin had done.

A short time later, as the Chisholm Trail came into view in the distance, Cimarron slowed his horse and stood up in the stirrups.

Two riders were moving down the trail.

Griffin and a companion?

He yelled to Emma and waved her up to him. He thought she hesitated for a moment, but he wasn't sure.

The two of them rode toward the approaching riders.

As the distance between them lessened, Cimarron was disappointed to see that neither of the two men was Griffin. He looked down at the ground and swore. He had lost Griffin's trail. The man must have cut to the right or left and Cimarron had missed the cutoff at some point after having spotted the approaching riders.

He tightened his grip on the reins and brought his horse to a stop. Emma rode up beside him, breathing hard. One of the two riders pointed at them.

"Do you know those men?" Emma asked.

Cimarron shook his head. "But they seem mighty interested in us. And they're both wearing badges."

The two men rode up, reined in their mounts, and glanced from Emma to Cimarron.

"That's it, Tracy," one of the pair said, swiftly unholstering his Dance revolver and aiming it at Cimarron.

Tracy ripped his Winchester from its scabbard and aimed it at Cimarron. "Don't move, mister!"

"You're fixing to throw down on me," Cimarron said in a calm voice. "Might I know the reason why?"

"Where'd you get that horse?" Tracy asked, pointing to the quarter horse.

"A man stole my horse last night and left me his—this one." Cimarron reached out to pat the animal's neck.

"Hold it," the man with the Dance yelled at him. "Don't make any fast moves!" The Dance rose until it pointed at Cimarron's head.

Cimarron raised his hands above his head. "What is it about this horse under me that interests you two?"

"It belonged to a friend of ours," Tracy said, his expression grim and his eyes cold as they studied Cimarron. "A man named Brent. He was a deputy marshal same as us."

"Until you killed him," snapped the second man. "Marshal Brent was trailing a man who'd robbed some banks over in Arkansas and then come over into the Nations and we came across Brent—dying he was. But before he died he told us you shot him in the back because you wanted his horse."

Tracy said, "He told us you were traveling with a woman and another man who was driving a spring wagon. Well, we got *you* anyway," he concluded, his eyes riveted on Cimarron.

"I don't know anything about a man driving a spring wagon," Cimarron said. "I do know I didn't kill Brent."

"You not only killed him," Tracy snarled, "but you went and robbed him first. Took his money and the ring he was wearing."

"I didn't kill Brent," Cimarron repeated. "Maybe the man who—"

Emma interrupted him. "He did, Marshal," she cried to Tracy. "I was with him and I saw him do it!"

Cimarron, without taking his eyes from the guns in the marshals' hands, said quietly, "She's lying."

"Who are you, ma'am?" Tracy asked.

"My name is Emma Dorset. This man . . ." She pointed at Cimarron. "I was with my father's cattle drive. This man worked for my father. Just before we reached the Kansas border, he and another hand abducted me. They made me ride out with them in the middle of the night."

"Where's the other jasper?" Tracy asked.

"He left," Emma answered. "Yesterday."

"We got him for murder, Wickers," Tracy said to his companion. "Now we can add kidnapping to that."

Emma began to sob. "You'll find the money he stole from the marshal in his saddlebag. I saw him put it there."

"Get his guns, Tracy," Wickers said.

"Keep me covered." Tracy slowly rode up on Cimarron's right.

He was reaching for Cimarron's revolver when Cimarron suddenly grabbed the barrel of his rifle and jerked it out of his hand.

As Tracy let out an oath, Cimarron savagely spurred his horse.

It leaped forward, colliding with Wickers' mount. Cimarron spurred the horse again, sending it thudding against Wickers' horse a second time. He swung the Winchester by its barrel. The stock struck Wickers on the shoulder and he started to slide out of his saddle. Before he could regain his balance, Cimarron swung the rifle again and knocked Wickers from the saddle. Before the man hit the ground, Cimarron turned his horse and swung the rifle again in a wide arc, this time knocking the six-shooter, which Tracy had halfway out of its holster, to the ground.

He spurred his horse and galloped back the way he had come, Tracy's rifle clutched in his right hand.

Behind him, a shot sounded. It was quickly followed by another one. Cimarron urged his horse on, thankful that it was not his dun beneath him. He was almost grateful to Griffin now for having stolen the dun and for leaving the quarter horse in its place.

He looked back over his shoulder. They were coming after him and firing at him. But they had only their six-shooters now and he was out of range of their guns.

He rode on, and when the western fringe of the woodland came into sight, he spurred his horse again.

When the trees loomed directly in front of him, he rode

in among them, slowed his horse, and finally brought it to a halt.

He leaped from the saddle, tossed Tracy's rifle into some underbrush, and sprinted for cover. He found it where he had known he would: at the site of the previous night's camp. He leaped over the deadfall from which he had taken wood for the fire he had made only hours earlier and flattened himself on the ground behind it.

When he heard them coming after him, he drew his Colt. Tensing, he waited behind the deadfall that served him as a breastwork.

One of his pursuers gave a shout.

Cimarron didn't catch the man's words. But he thought he knew what to expect. They would dismount and come after him on foot. Astride their horses, they would make easy targets but on foot the trees would provide them with cover.

Did they intend to take him alive? he wondered. Of only one thing was he certain: they intended to take him.

He heard them moving cautiously through the trees. He could see neither man. But the sounds they were making told him their location. They were within range of his Colt now, but he didn't intend to fire unless he had to because a shot would give away his location. Silence wouldn't betray his position.

Cimarron had been careful to keep out of any of the shafts of sunlight that were streaming through the trees. He lay in deep shade, a spot he had deliberately chosen, with the sun at his back and the marshals walking into its rays that fell through the branches of the trees. He took off his hat and placed it on the ground beside him.

Wickers suddenly ran out from behind a tree to take cover behind another one closer to where Cimarron lay prone on the ground.

Cimarron, out of the corner of his eyes, saw the quarter horse amble into sight among the trees.

"He's around here somewhere," Wickers shouted from behind the tree. "There's Brent's horse!"

"You spot him yet?" Tracy yelled from somewhere behind Wickers.

"Not yet!"

The quarter horse, searching for grass and finding little on the forest floor, turned and headed toward the deadfall.

It had almost reached it when it stopped and blew nervously through its nostrils.

Cimarron knew the animal had scented him.

The horse swung its head up and then stepped almost daintily forward. When it reached the deadfall, it bent its head and nuzzled the back of Cimarron's neck.

Cimarron endured the animal's attentions without moving a muscle.

A shot rang out.

Wickers had fired it from behind the tree that still shielded him. The bullet slammed into the deadfall and sent splinters of wood flying into the air, several of which struck Cimarron's face and neck.

The quarter horse spun away and galloped off to the left.

"Found him," Wickers yelled, and to Cimarron's surprise, sprinted back the way he had come, dodging from tree to tree.

Cimarron looked around for the quarter horse. It was nowhere to be seen. But, if he could find it, he thought, he might be able to get to it, get aboard it, and get out of the woodland and away. First, however, there was a more important move he had to make. Because he'd been spotted, he had to change positions.

He clapped his hat on his head and wriggled backward along the ground away from the deadfall and deeper into the trees. Then he sprang to his feet and ran to the left on a course paralleling the one the quarter horse had taken. He stopped and dropped down on one knee behind the trunk of an old elm.

He considered his position, focusing on the fact that Wickers, instead of continuing to fire at him when he was down behind the deadfall, had instead run back toward the edge of the woodland. He asked himself why Wickers had done that and came up with an answer: Wickers probably wanted to confer with Tracy and plot their strategy.

A thought occurred to him. Maybe one of them would try to circle around and come in behind him. He shifted his position until he was facing the spot where the deadfall lay on the ground. Minutes later, he saw Wickers moving through the underbrush and coming up on the deadfall from the rear.

Cimarron's finger tightened on the trigger of his Colt. He cocked its hammer.

He kept Wickers in sight as the man moved, crouching, closer to the deadfall. Then he eased around the trees and said to the man, "Drop it!"

Wickers turned quickly, saw Cimarron, and dropped his revolver.

Cimarron moved toward him from tree to tree and called out to him in a deliberately loud voice, "If your partner's got me in his sights, he'd do well not to fire. I'll take you same time as he takes me."

Cimarron moved closer to Wickers and then around behind him. "We're getting out of these woods," he told the man. "Let's go!"

Wickers obediently began to move through the trees in the direction Cimarron had indicated. Cimarron, his Colt held firmly in his hand, moved cautiously along behind him.

They had almost reached the point where the woodland ended and the prairie began when Wickers suddenly dropped down and flattened himself on the ground.

A shot sounded and Cimarron's body lurched as a bullet struck his right thigh.

"Let go of your gun!"

Cimarron obeyed Tracy's shouted order, which had come from somewhere behind and above him. He handed his Colt to Wickers, who was getting to his feet.

Wickers took it from him and, grinning, aimed it at Cimarron's chest. "I got him," he yelled. "You can come on down now, Tracy!"

Behind him, Cimarron heard Tracy climbing down from a tree. Now he understood why Wickers had dropped to the ground. The man must have known exactly where his partner had treed himself. He had dropped to the ground to give Tracy a chance to get off a safe shot. It had been a risky move on Wickers' part, but it had worked. Cimarron found himself unable not to admire the man, however grudgingly.

He looked down at the spot where Tracy's bullet had ripped through his thigh. His pants were torn, revealing the bloody flesh beneath them. He hadn't felt the pain when the bullet had struck. But he felt it now and it was sharp and searing.

Tracy came up behind him and Cimarron felt the man's

gun barrel come to rest in the small of his back, urging him forward. He stepped out, and as he did so, Wickers took up a position on his right.

It took them only minutes to reach the edge of the woodland. When they did, Tracy spoke to Wickers.

"See if you can round up that horse of Brent's. If you can't, this man's going to have a long walk ahead of him."

"Got to get my gun he made me drop back in there too."

Wickers returned to the woodland again and Tracy stood guard over Cimarron who was staring off into the distance to the point on the prairie where he could see Emma Dorset still sitting astride her horse.

She began to trot toward where he and Tracy were standing in total silence. When she reached them, she dismounted and said to Tracy, while her eyes remained on Cimarron's face, "I'm so glad you caught him, Marshal. I've been so frightened."

Ignoring her, Cimarron said, "Tracy, you going to give me a chance to bind up my leg wound?"

Tracy didn't answer immediately. But then he said, "Go ahead. But first hand over your gun belt." When Cimarron had done so, Tracy said, "Any moves you make, you make them nice and slow." He backed away, well out of Cimarron's reach. "Ma'am," he said to Emma, "this one's a tricky fellow. Better stand clear of him."

Emma took a step backward as Cimarron examined his wound. The bullet, he saw with relief, had gone through the flesh of his thigh. Bending over, he bound his bandanna loosely around his thigh. Better to let the blood flow a bit, he silently told himself, the way the Indians do to keep a wound clean.

He knew that Tracy's eyes were on him, but he felt he had to take the chance—the only chance that remained to him to regain his freedom. Still bent over and ostensibly still examining his wound, he swiftly pulled his bowie knife from his boot, but before he could throw it, Emma screamed, and a bullet tore into the ground at his feet. He let the knife fall to the ground and stared silently out over the plain.

"Step away from that knife," Tracy shouted.

Cimarron obeyed the order.

Tracy cautiously approached, picked up the knife, and

then backed farther away from Cimarron than he had the first time.

"You and Griffin planned the little party you invited me to last night, didn't you?" he asked Emma. "Did he send you to me or was it your idea to keep me from hearing him make his getaway?"

Emma stared at the ground in silence.

"Griffin—he's no preacher, is he? Preachers, as a rule, don't go around shooting deputy marshals in the back and stealing all they have. You two weren't heading for any Cherokee mission, were you? You—both of you—were on the run after murdering and robbing that marshal."

Emma looked up as Wickers, carrying Tracy's rifle and his own six-gun, came out of the woodland leading the quarter horse. "Take a look in this mount's saddlebag, Tracy," he said. "See if Brent's money is there like the lady said it was."

Tracy opened the saddlebag and then spun around to face Cimarron, his fist holding the paper money he had removed from the saddlebag. "Less than ten dollars," he bellowed at Cimarron. "You killed Brent for less than ten damned dollars, his ring, and his horse!" He removed Cimarron's Winchester from its scabbard and cradled it in his left arm. "What did you do with his ring? You aren't wearing it."

Before Cimarron could answer, Emma said, "He gave it to the other man he was riding with. He kept the money and the horse."

"This horse," Wickers said, "has scratched himself up some. But he's fit enough for the ride we got ahead of us."

"Where do you plan on taking me?" Cimarron asked him.

"To Fort Smith on the Arkansas border," Wickers replied.

"To Judge Isaac Charles Parker," Tracy added. "You ever hear tell of Judge Parker?"

"I have," Cimarron replied. "Folks have taken to calling him the Hanging Judge."

"He deserves the name," Tracy said. "Ever since he became the federal judge at Fort Smith, he's hanged scores of men. Well, that's not strictly true. George Maledon did the hanging. Judge Parker positively dotes on handing down death sentences and that old boy, George, he goes and does his job with real gusto."

"Gather our mounts," Wickers said to Tracy. "It's time we were riding out of here."

When Tracy had gone, no one spoke. Cimarron's eyes were on Emma. She had turned her back to him and was staring out across the prairie. Wickers stood motionless, his Dance aimed at Cimarron.

When Tracy returned with the horses, he began to uncoil a rope that had been hanging from his saddle horn. "Come over here with me, Wickers," he said. "Stand behind him," he said, gesturing at Cimarron, "while I tie his hands."

Emma turned and looked at Cimarron. He met her gaze but said nothing.

"Hold 'em out, mister," Tracy said as Wickers' Dance jammed into Cimarron's back.

Cimarron held out his hands.

Tracy tied them together at the wrists. "Now climb up into the saddle."

Cimarron got into the saddle of the quarter horse and Wickers stood guard over him as Tracy cut the rope he was using, bent down, and tied one end of the remaining length of rope around Cimarron's right ankle. He ran the rope under the horse and tied its other end to Cimarron's left ankle.

"Better not fall off that horse," he said when he was finished. "You do, you'll likely be dragged to death."

"Might be a better way to go," Wickers suggested. "I've seen how Maledon weaves and oils that hemp rope of his. It's guaranteed to break the neck of any man whose neck it drops around."

"You ready to go, ma'am?" Tracy asked Emma.

"Yes," she answered.

"The court'll find you accommodations in Fort Smith," Tracy told her, "till it's time for you to give your testimony against—" He glanced at Cimarron. "What's your name, mister?"

"Cimarron."

"Cimarron, huh?" Tracy burst into laughter. When his laughter had subsided, he said, "Wickers, won't it be real interesting to watch this here Cimarron swing at the end of old George's rope?"

"It will be that," Wickers said with evident enthusiasm. "Let's ride."

Emma mounted her horse and moved out behind the men.

Cimarron kept his eyes straight ahead as they rode into the eastern woodland and his blood continued to soak the bandanna he had tied around his right leg.

4

An hour later, as they were riding along the flood plain of the North Canadian River, the widely scattered homes of some of the inhabitants of the Seminole nation visible on the southern bank of the river, Tracy suddenly let out a lustily shouted greeting.

Cimarron had spotted the wagon that Tracy had just hailed a moment before Tracy did. It was heading northeast, angling away from the Seminole nation. Its bed was piled high with boxes and burlap bags among which sat three men and a woman. It was being drawn by a team of two horses which looked to Cimarron to be not much better than crow bait. The driver was angrily urging them on with a ragged buggy whip. Riding beside the wagon were six men. Three armed men rode horses. Three unarmed men rode mules. Accompanying the odd caravan were extra horses and mules.

"It's Jim Regan and a posse," Tracy yelled happily, and let out another wild greeting.

"Move out real smart," Wickers barked, and prodded Cimarron's horse with the barrel of his rifle.

Cimarron rode out, gripping the saddle horn tightly with both bound hands, and when they reached the caravan, Tracy got out of the saddle and shook hands with one of the three armed men who were mounted on horses.

Cimarron stared curiously at the three unarmed men aboard their mules, one of whom was an Indian. All three stared just as curiously at him.

"Where you been, Regan?" Tracy asked the man he had shaken hands with.

Regan, a gaunt man, shifted the wad of tobacco he was chewing, spat, and answered, "All over hell's half-acre, seems like. At the last—in the Shawnee Hills. Picked up that jasper with the beard and greasy grin there where he'd gone to ground. He raped two Choctaw women down in Caddo, killed one of 'em after, and then holed up in the Hills. But we flushed him out."

"You're wrong, Marshal," declared the burly bearded man Regan had pointed out to Tracy. "I didn't rape those squaws. They *see*-duced me and the one you claim I killed, why, she had such a down-and-out good time all during that she just wore herself out and gave up the ghost once we had completed our little business."

Regan ignored the outburst. "That one," he said to Tracy, "the one without so much as a pinfeather on his face—he was peddling the ardent to the Chickasaws out of the bottom of a buckboard. And that Cherokee over there robbed his partner while they were collecting tolls from the drovers moving their herds through Cherokee Nation. The ones we got in the wagon are witnesses in other cases Fagan sent us to serve summonses on."

"You're a liar!" the white man Regan had indicated roared indignantly. "You *planted* that whiskey in my wagon!"

Regan clucked his tongue in mock sorrow and Cimarron caught the wink he gave Tracy before he leaned over and slammed a fist into the prisoner's jaw, sending him hurtling to the ground.

"Get up," Regan said to the man he had downed. "And learn to talk respectful of the law."

"You had yourself quite a haul, Regan," Tracy commented, and then added, "We didn't do so bad ourselves."

Regan glanced in Cimarron's direction. "What'd he do?"

It was Wickers who answered the question. "Brent's dead. This man killed and robbed him. That's Brent's horse he's sitting."

"Well, I'll be damned," Regan exclaimed. "I'm real sorry to hear that. Brent was a helluva good man." He paused and winked again at Tracy. " 'Course he cheated something awful at poker."

"You figuring on reaching Fort Smith by tonight?" Tracy asked Regan.

Regan shook his head. "We're going to make us a camp for the night somewheres up ahead. It's too far to make it to town before midnight at best and we don't want to have to rouse everybody in the whole jail to see to these prisoners of ours in the middle of the night."

"We'll join you," Tracy declared.

The caravan moved out, the three prisoners riding behind the wagon, flanked by Regan and the other two deputies. Behind them came Cimarron, who was flanked by Tracy and Wickers.

Cimarron could not see Emma Dorset. He supposed she was riding somewhere behind him. He discovered with no surprise that he had no desire to see her.

As dusk settled on the land, the setting sun first reddened the ragged clouds streaking the sky and then purpled them. They rode past the point where the Canadian joined the North Canadian and on into the fertile valley of the meandering Arkansas River. They made camp under some Gambel oaks beneath which grew snowberry bushes and a profusion of dandelions in full yellow bloom.

Cimarron remained in the saddle until Wickers finally got around to untying his ankles. Then he threw his left leg over his saddle horn and slid down to the ground.

"Get yourself over there by the wagon where I can keep an eye on you," Wickers ordered him.

Cimarron went over to the wagon and, obeying Wickers' peremptory gesture, sat down on the ground. Wickers sat down some distance away from him, Tracy's rifle resting on his crossed legs, warily watching as Cimarron picked some dandelion leaves and began to chew them, undaunted by their bitter taste.

The other three prisoners, like Cimarron, took up positions on the ground around the wagon and two deputies stood guard over them as Wickers was guarding Cimarron.

Cimarron turned his head and saw that a fire had been started. Tracy was helping Regan prepare supper. Cimarron's belly rumbled and he realized that he was very hungry. He saw Emma Dorset approach the fire, a coffeepot in her hand. She didn't look in his direction.

The meal, when it was served to Cimarron and the other prisoners, consisted of beans and rice. As Tracy held out a tin plate to Cimarron, Cimarron looked up at him and held up his still-bound hands.

Tracy shook his head. "You can hang on to that plate tied up as you are and still make do. I'm not taking a chance on you without that rope in place."

Cimarron took the plate from Tracy and, holding it in both hands, bent his head and began to lap up the rice and beans which rested on it. He looked up as Tracy dropped a slab of hardtack on the ground beside him.

"Now that was real thoughtful of you," he said soberly. "I just hope the ants don't get to that morsel before I have a chance to."

Tracy turned abruptly and went around to the rear of the chuck wagon.

As Cimarron managed to devour the last of the beans on his plate, the prisoner Regan had accused of rape and murder, who was seated near him, said "Move over some, mister. You don't give a man much elbowroom."

Cimarron moved away from the man and toward the prisoner on his right. He put down his plate, picked up the piece of hardtack Tracy had tossed on the ground, wiped it on his shirt, and began to eat it.

The bearded man put out a boot and shoved it against Cimarron's hip.

Cimarron stopped eating and stared at the man.

"I need more elbowroom," the man told him.

"You must have mighty big elbows," Cimarron said quietly.

"Move!"

Cimarron swiftly swung his bound hands, which had become fists. They caught the man on the side of his face and he toppled backward.

As the prisoner struggled to his feet, Cimarron was up and ready for him.

Wickers leaped up and stepped between them. "Sit down! Both of you. *Now!*"

Cimarron waited until the bearded prisoner, muttering obscenities, had once again seated himself on the ground before he did the same. As Wickers moved away, he finished eating the last of the hardtack.

"He's a real mean one."

Cimarron turned to face the prisoner on his left, who was sitting with his back braced against the wagon's rear wheel. "Most skunks are," he said, making sure he spoke loudly enough for the bearded prisoner to hear his words.

"Why, you big bastard, you," the man roared, and started to get to his feet.

Wickers intervened and started to march the man around to the other side of the wagon. Calling back over his shoulder to the other deputies, he said, "Keep your eyes on that one Tracy and me are bringing in. Tricky devil, he is."

"His name's McIntosh," the prisoner on Cimarron's left volunteered, referring to the man Wickers was marching away. "Best to stay clear of him."

Cimarron was staring at the witnesses—and Emma Dorset—who were seated around the fire, talking quietly as they ate.

"You'll hang, you know."

Cimarron turned to face the prisoner beside him. "I don't plan on letting myself be hanged."

"What do you plan on doing?"

"Staying alive."

"You got yourself a name you go by?"

"Cimarron."

"Well, I wish you good luck, Cimarron. But that's going to be mighty hard thing for you to be doing—staying alive, I mean—once you get yourself hauled up before Bloody Parker, as some correctly calls him. He's hanged men by the bunches."

"So I've heard tell."

"These two deputies have got the goods on you, have they?"

"I didn't kill that deputy."

"That won't lighten the dark days that lie ahead for you," the prisoner said mournfully. "By the way, my name's Jack Boyd. I'm innocent too. Like I said before, those deputies planted that whiskey in my buckboard. But a man can claim he's innocent until the cows come home and it won't do him much good in Parker's court. And if Parker gets a jury to convict you, you're a goner. There's no appealing Judge Parker's decisions."

The Indian appeared and bent down to pick up Cimarron's empty plate.

"Trusty," Boyd muttered to Cimarron with a nod in the direction of the man who was now picking up Boyd's plate from the ground. "But I wouldn't trust that Cherokee as far as I could throw him."

"How does a man get to be a trusty?" Cimarron asked, an idea forming in his mind.

"By licking deputies' boots," Boyd muttered contemptuously. "You thinking of trying to become one—a trusty?"

"Was. But boot licking's just not my style."

"Figured it wasn't."

"Tracy," Cimarron called out.

When Tracy left the fire and came over to him, Cimarron said, "My leg wound could stand some washing. I figure you could march me down there to the river, untie my hands, and let me see to myself."

Tracy hesitated a moment and then said, "Go ahead." He raised the rifle he was carrying as Cimarron got to his feet and started down toward the river.

Tracy called the trusty, and when the Cherokee had joined them on the riverbank, Wickers ordered him to untie Cimarron's hands, which the Cherokee promptly did.

Cimarron removed the bloody bandanna he had tied around his thigh and rinsed it in the river. Balling it in his hand, he swabbed the crusted blood from his thigh and again rinsed his bandanna.

"You happen to have any whiskey I could pour on this?" he asked Tracy, pointing to the torn flesh of his leg.

"Get a bottle of that stuff we confiscated from Boyd," Tracy ordered the Cherokee.

While he waited for the Indian to return with the whiskey, Cimarron knelt on the riverbank and drank deeply. He splashed water on his face and rubbed his eyes with the backs of his hands. He was standing up when the Cherokee reappeared with a whiskey bottle in his hand, which he held out to Cimarron.

Cimarron took the bottle, opened it, and poured some of its contents onto his raw flesh, wincing from the sting of the spirits as he did so. He handed the bottle back to the Indian and proceeded to retie his bandanna around his wound.

"Back to the wagon," Tracy said to him, waving his rifle.

Cimarron started back toward the wagon. On the way, he said, "I'd like to see to my horse if you've no objection."

"*Your* horse," Tracy said, and grinned. "I thought you said *your* horse was stolen and the one you were riding left in its place."

"Just a manner of speaking, Marshal."

"Don't worry none about that horse."

"A man does well to take care of his horse, Tracy. You must know that. That quarter horse should be rubbed down and fed some grain—or at least some grass."

They had reached the wagon and Tracy pointed to the ground. As Cimarron sat down on it, Tracy barked an order to the Cherokee, who bent down beside Cimarron and quickly tied his hands to a spoke of the wagon's rear wheel.

"If you're planning to run off during the night," Tracy said with a sly grin, "you'll just have to take the wagon with you."

Cimarron merely stared up at him.

When Tracy and the Cherokee had left him, Cimarron shifted position, trying to make himself as comfortable as possible under the circumstances. His efforts were only partially successful. The rope bit into his wrists and the hub of the wagon wheel jutted into the small of his back.

The fire, he noticed, was almost out. The witnesses were spreading blankets on the ground. He heard Regan give orders to his men concerning the night watch. Two-hour shifts were assigned. One man was to stand guard on each shift.

Cimarron looked up at the sky, which was spangled with stars but in which no moon rode.

He watched Emma Dorset, who was seated near the fire, as she stared into it, seemingly unaware of him or of her surroundings. The firelight flickered on her features, revealing them in its orange light, then allowing them to plunge into momentary shadow. She didn't, Cimarron thought, look like an accomplice to murder. A thought crossed his mind. Maybe she wasn't an accomplice. Maybe she was the one who had shot and killed Deputy Brent.

The lone guard began to patrol the camp, passing and repassing Cimarron.

The horses on the picket rope stirred. One snorted.

An owl hooted and Cimarron heard a *whoosshh* of air as it swooped out of an oak and across the top of the wagon.

He closed his eyes. But the hub of the wagon pressing into the small of his back held sleep at bay. Finally he did slip into sleep only to awaken minutes later. He slept again. He dreamed of a long rope. And awoke gasping for air until he realized he had been merely dreaming.

Cimarron was awake before first light, and as dawn came, he stared up at the thick white clouds that were scattering before a breeze. He kept his eyes on a cloud that looked a little bit like a bird of no identifiable species as the camp began to stir and a deputy who had been whistling "Garryowen" called the Cherokee trusty over to untie Cimarron and Boyd, who had also been tied to the front wheel of the wagon.

"Tie their hands in front of them," the deputy ordered, and the Indian mutely obeyed.

Cimarron stood up and stretched, pretending to ignore the deputy's rifle, which rose ominously as he did. He stretched his arms above his head and stood on the tips of his toes. Then he hunkered down and rubbed his back against the wagon wheel, the hub of which seemed to him to have gouged a hole in the small of his back during the night.

Breakfast consisted of rice and hardtack.

After it, the four prisoners were marched down to the river, accompanied by the witnesses and several deputies, where they all drank before returning to their mounts. The wagon was already moving out, weaving among the thick trunks of the Gambel oaks until it left the grove and moved out onto the open plain.

Cimarron, his hands bound and his ankles again tied beneath the belly of the quarter horse he was riding, listened to the joking of the deputies, the snarl of anger from McIntosh, who had been refused a cigarette by Regan, and the deputy, who was again whistling "Garryowen."

All in all, he thought, we make a fairly merry procession. All we need to really liven things up is a big brass band.

They rode along at a steady pace through the valley of the Arkansas, the peaks of the San Bois Mountains rising behind them.

They forded the Canadian and rode along the southern bank of the Arkansas for nearly an hour before Regan called a halt and began to make arrangements to ferry the caravan across the muddy river to Fort Smith.

The deputies ordered the prisoners to dismount, and after Cimarron's legs had been freed by the Cherokee trusty, he slid out of the saddle and went aboard the ferry with the other prisoners, the witnesses and Emma Dorset bringing up the rear as if they had deferred to the prisoners, allowing them the honor of being the first to go on board the boat. Once the wagon had rumbled onto the ferry and the horses and mules had been led aboard it, the ferrymen freed the stern lines and then manned the sweeps. The boat pulled away from the limestone-and-sand embankment and moved out into the Arkansas' current.

Cimarron, aware of the pungent smell of the river, stood at the railing on deck, aware too of Tracy's rifle aimed at him, as he watched the black children seated on the sandbars on the opposite bank, fishing poles held hopefully in their small hands.

He noted the large crowd that was gathering at the ferry slips that jutted out into the river just in front of the Arkansas Valley Railroad yards. As the ferry eased into an empty slip a few minutes later, Cimarron was surprised to hear a cheer erupt from the throng on the embankment.

He let himself be herded from the ferry by the deputies, and when he was ashore again, he looked around him. South of him were the docks and beyond them in the distance was the confluence of the Arkansas and Poteau rivers. The railyards extended some distance to the north. East of the docks and yards he saw what he considered to be a decidedly second-class frontier town. It was divided into neat blocks, but the streets were dirt and now, as the wind occasionally rose and halfheartedly gusted through the town, dust billowed up, obscuring many of the town's frame and brick buildings from sight.

Wickers ordered Cimarron to remount and this time, when Cimarron did, Wickers did not bother to tie his ankles together beneath the belly of the quarter horse. He rode south with the caravan through the crowd that lined the river front, with Boyd riding beside him.

"Marshal," a woman cried, and pointing to Cimarron, asked, "What, may I ask, did that good-looking Lothario do?"

"Killed a deputy, ma'am," Tracy called back cordially, touching the brim of his hat to the woman.

"Then he's sure as shootin' goin' to meet up with the government suspender," a man shouted gleefully.

"Government suspender?" Cimarron said to Boyd, who

shook his head and said, "That's what they call George Maledon's gallows."

A little boy running on the fringe of the crowd scooped up a small stone and threw it.

The stone struck Cimarron's jaw, but he did not turn his head.

As they rode past the docks, men emerged from the waterfront saloons. Cowboys and steamboat and railroad men gaped at the prisoners. The crowd thickened and continued to follow the procession, hooting and jeering. Someone in the crowd was playing a Jew's harp.

"Town's crowded," Cimarron commented idly.

"Must be a hanging day," Boyd remarked woefully. "A hanging'll bring people out in droves from miles around. Nothing seems to pleasure so many people so much as a hanging."

"Hard to understand," Cimarron commented.

"Not so hard," Boyd countered. "Most people have a mean streak in them somewhere. That's why they flock to see a hanging. But, being good, God-fearing folk, they tell themselves it's to see justice done."

Regan, in front of the caravan, raised an arm and gave a signal, and the procession, with the crowd still following, turned left onto Rogers Avenue. Within minutes, they were turning in at the gate of the old fort that was no longer used by the army.

It extended for the whole of a city block and was surrounded by six-foot stone walls on which cannon bastions were mounted. As Cimarron passed through the gate into the fort, the first thing he saw was the gallows. Thirteen steps rose to its platform, above which three nooses hung suspended. It was a strong structure built of heavy timbers. The four traps that extended the length of the deep platform rested innocuously beneath a twelve-by-twelve I beam that was supported by other heavy timbers. A roof slanted above the platform and at its far end was a back wall.

"Not a very pretty sight," Boyd commented.

Cimarron turned his head toward the two-story brick building, a former army barracks, that was the federal courthouse. Not far from it was a small stone building that had once been the fort's commissary.

Children were perched on the stone walls that surrounded the compound and the place was packed with people.

Friends called out gaily to one another and a worried woman ordered one of the children on the walls to cimb down from his stone perch.

"We'll stop here for a spell," Regan announced, and spat a stream of brown tobacco juice. "It'll be edifying for our prisoners to see the spectacle about to take place."

"It's almost nine-thirty," Tracy said, after glancing at a watch he took from his vest pocket. "Old George is usually punctual. The festivities'll be beginning most any minute now."

As if his words had been a signal, a door in the basement of the courthouse swung open and two clergymen carrying bibles emerged from the jail. They were followed by three prisoners—a white man and two blacks. Flanking the prisoners were two guards armed with revolvers. They all moved slowly toward the gallows. As the prisoners approached it, a man appeared from behind the gallows. He was of average height, gray-bearded, and thin to the point of gauntness. He wore black trousers and a matching coat, high-top black felt and leather shoes, a white shirt and black tie. The hair on the top of his head was thinning and his eyes were dark and cold. Around his waist he wore a shiny leather belt which supported two holsters, both of which were filled with revolvers, their butts pointing forward.

"Maledon?" Cimarron asked Boyd.

"That's him."

The two clergymen climbed the thirteen steps, their lips moving in prayer. Behind them climbed the three prisoners followed by their two guards.

Maledon slowly climbed the steps, head bowed, as if counting each one and, when he reached the platform, wordlessly pointed to the rough plank bench that sat against the gallows' rear wall. When the men were seated, another man, who wore a badge on his vest, mounted the platform and proceeded to read aloud the death warrants of each of the condemned men.

Silence settled on the assembled throng as the lawman read on in an emotionless monotone. The silence was broken briefly by the muffled sobbing of one of the blacks.

When the warrants had all been read, the lawman pocketed them and told each man he could now say any last words he might choose to deliver.

One of the black men, the one who had sobbed, got

shakily to his feet and moved toward the front of the platform, stopping just before his feet touched the deadly trap set in the platform floor.

"I never had myself even half a chance," he said, flinging the words at the eagerly gaping crowd as if they were an accusation or an indictment. "I was born a Cherokee slave, and when I was freed after the war, I had me no place at all to be. I wandered and I wandered with no friend to take my hand or the least little light to steer my bark by. White mens sold me whiskey. White mens kept me down in the dirt. I tried to get up and in the getting I killed myself my first man. The next one was easier and it kept on getting easier. But the good Lord, He understands. He knows how hard it is not to be free and then to be all of a sudden free and not know how to be it in any goodly way. That's all."

The next man, the other black, strode to the front of the platform and, glaring out at the crowd, let loose a string of obscenities, concluding with "And I be seeing you each and every one in the hell-fire and howling. You all no better than me. Not one of you is!"

The white man rose, made a plaintive gesture, looked from side to side, clasped his hands in front of him, and said in a low voice, "It ain't right to kill. And I killed. So I got to die. Only I wonder. My dying—you all hanging me—don't that make Mr. Maledon over there a murderer and you out there his accomplices?"

A chill seized and shook Cimarron as he sat his horse, watching and listening.

The lawman left the platform, and when he was gone, Maledon positioned the men on the trap so that each was standing just below one of the waiting nooses. He bound their arms behind their backs.

"Keeps 'em from clawing at the rope while they're doing their dance in the air," Cimarron heard a man in the crowd mutter to his companion.

When the condemned men were securely bound, Maledon dropped black hoods over their heads, and then, working with the ease that comes of long practice, he placed one of the well-oiled, handwoven Kentucky hemp nooses around each man's neck, adjusting it in each case below the men's left ears in order to ensure that, when they dropped, their necks would be broken and they would not die of slow strangulation.

The two clergymen took turns reciting prayers and then led the crowd in a rousing hymn.

Cimarron caught the words "savior" and "shepherd," the phrases "stamping out sin" and "merciful master." But his mind was not on the hymn. It was trying to focus on a way—any way—to avoid sharing the fate that was about to descend on the three men standing on the deadly platform.

Maledon stepped back. From in front of the platform, the lawman who had read the death warrants gave a signal. A deputy swiftly shot a greased bolt.

One of the prisoners screamed, "Jesus, save—" His words were cut off as he and the other two men dropped, the trap thundering out from beneath their feet.

A hushed and subdued *ooohhh* went up from a cluster of women in the crowd. From the stone wall came the nervous tittering of a child.

The three bodies hung in midair, turning slowly. They quivered. One jerked spasmodically.

"Wickers," Tracy said from beside Cimarron, "you take Cimarron's guns up to the clerk's office and check them in. I'll search him when I get him in the jail, and if he's got anything of value on him, tell Wheeler I'll send it up later. Then come back down here and take Brent's horse over to the livery stable." To Cimarron, he said, "Step down."

Cimarron got out of the saddle and Tracy pointed to the entrance to the basement of the courthouse toward which Regan was herding his three prisoners. Cimarron headed for it as the crowd, laughing and talking animatedly, began to leave the fort's compound.

As he approached the door, he was able to make out the strained faces, most of them very pale, of men at the small barred basement windows. He followed the other prisoners through the door and found himself in a small vestibule that was approximately eight by ten feet square.

Regan unlocked a door at the far end of the vestibule, and McIntosh, Boyd, and the Cherokee trusty went through it. Cimarron, hesitating, felt the barrel of Tracy's rifle come to rest in the small of his back. He moved forward, went through the door, and entered a room filled with prisoners. The rank odor of urine and feces struck him like a fist. The dampness of the huge room settled on him like an invisible fog. The ceiling was no more than eight feet above the floor. The tiny windows were the only source of light and ventilation. The floor was made of flagstones neatly fitted together. The size of the jail measured twenty-nine by fifty-five feet.

Cimarron recalled a zoo he had once visited in Saint Louis. It was a paradise compared to the jail he now found himself in.

The prisoners were of all ages, sizes, and colors. Blacks and whites, Indians and half-bloods. Some were middle-aged or old men with seamed faces and ugly eyes; others were little more than boys on whose faces flickered bravado, despair, or simple fear.

"Empty out your pockets," Tracy ordered him.

Cimarron handed over the money he had received as his pay before leaving the trail drive. His jackknife. A few odd coins.

"That all?" Tracy asked him.

"That's everything I own," Cimarron replied.

Tracy used the jackknife to cut the rope that bound Cimarron's hands. Then he and Regan left the jail. The door slammed behind them. A key turned in its lock.

The light in the room was dim, and as Cimarron turned around to take a closer look at his surroundings, he noted that the walls had once been whitewashed. He became aware of a smell that was not that of human excrement—a sharp odor. He recognized it—lime. Some had been sprinkled on the floor, where traces of it still remained. But the awful stench of urine and feces easily overpowered it.

Cimarron strode over to one of the windows and looked out into the compound. Maledon was out there cutting down the no-longer-quivering bodies that had so short a time ago been men. All, Cimarron noted, had soiled themselves when their sphincter muscles had involuntarily loosened at the moment of their violent deaths. The crowd was gone. The stone walls were bare.

"What does a man have to do," Cimarron asked a prisoner crouching against the wall, "to get to use the privy?"

"Why, nothing more than to just step right up to it," the prisoner declared, looking up in surprise at Cimarron.

"Beg pardon?"

"Right over there," the man said, and pointed to a bucket that sat in one of the basement's old chimneys. "There's a slop pail set in each one of the chimneys," the prisoner added. "Only difficulty you'll encounter is finding one that's not full. They don't empty 'em out all that often. You can tell that, though, by the stink in here."

"I can."

As Cimarron started toward one of the buckets, the prisoner he had spoken to called after him, "If you've a mind to take a bath, why, you can use that barrel in the corner." He pointed to a kerosene barrel that had been cut in half.

But before Cimarron could reach the chimney and the bucket sitting in it, a blow landed on the side of his neck, causing his knees to buckle. As he straightened, but before he could turn around to face his assailant, another blow struck him on the side of the head, briefly blurring his vision.

Someone kicked him viciously.

He fell.

5

Cimarron hit the flagstones, his knees cracking against them, and rolled over. He sprang to his feet and spun around to face whoever it was who had attacked him.

He found himself staring into McIntosh's face. The man's eyes were narrowed and his lips were parted as he stood crouching, waiting for Cimarron to make his move.

The other prisoners in the room stood silent, watching the two men as they faced each other, McIntosh glaring, Cimarron evaluating his opponent.

"You think you can hit me like you did back there on the trail and get away with it?" McIntosh muttered, his hands clenching and unclenching as he continued to glare at Cimarron. "Well, mister, you can't. I'm going to do for you."

"You're welcome to try." Cimarron estimated that McIntosh, a big man, outweighed him by maybe as many as twenty pounds. He knew McIntosh would try any trick at all to win the fight that was about to begin between them. McIntosh had proved that, not only by attacking without warning and from behind but also by the vicious kick he had given Cimarron. Well, he thought, a fight's a fight, fair or foul. What counted most was, if not exactly winning, at least not losing.

Cimarron, thrusting hard with his legs, took a sudden dive and hit McIntosh just below the knees.

McIntosh went down, his breath hissing out from between his still-parted lips. He tore at Cimarron with both hands and managed to break Cimarron's grip on his legs.

He pulled them free and drew back his right boot, ready to smash it into Cimarron's face.

But Cimarron grabbed the boot, twisted it, and McIntosh let out a grunt as he was forced to roll over. Cimarron released him, stood up quickly, and hauled McIntosh to his feet. He drew back his right arm and then brought it smashing forward, striking McIntosh's jaw a savage blow. He heard his opponent's teeth click as his fist connected. He let go of McIntosh, whom he'd been holding with his left hand, and was about to connect with a right uppercut when McIntosh raised his left arm and warded off the blow. McIntosh said, "So you're a fighter, are you?"

"When I have to be," Cimarron replied as he ducked McIntosh's wildly thrown punch and came up with a quick right and an equally quick left that caught McIntosh in the ribs and on the left shoulder.

McIntosh threw a left jab that hit Cimarron squarely on the nose. Blood began to flow from his nostrils. And then McIntosh, head down and arms outstretched, was coming at him and Cimarron stepped back, grabbed the man by the ears, and pulled as hard as he could, momentarily unbalancing him. He brought a fisted hand down on the back of McIntosh's neck. The blow sent the man to his knees.

Cimarron became aware of the shouting in the jail. The other prisoners, most of them, were urging him on. Some were yelling for McIntosh to get up. One prisoner, looking dazed and oddly haunted, sat in a corner, his arms on his knees, staring dully at the floor beneath him, seemingly oblivious to the fight taking place in the room.

Cimarron reached down for McIntosh, but McIntosh evaded his grasp by rolling to one side and then leaping to his feet. He smashed a blow into Cimarron's face with his right fist and Cimarron landed one just under McIntosh's heart. As Cimarron was about to follow up with a left uppercut, McIntosh kicked out viciously and Cimarron moved fast, turning his body, so that McIntosh's kick caught him in the hip instead of the groin, which had obviously been McIntosh's intended target. He turned, feinted with a left, and swung hard with his right fist, which caught McIntosh on the left ear.

As McIntosh staggered backward a few steps, Cimarron reached up and hurriedly wiped the blood from the stubble on his upper lip and then wiped his slick fingers on his trousers. He waited, and when McIntosh, growling deep in his throat, went for him, Cimarron ducked and came in under the blow and hit him with a hard right to the gut. His fist seemed to sink into the man's thick flesh. He pulled back, and as McIntosh charged again, he thrust out his right foot and caught McIntosh behind his left ankle, toppling him and sending him down hard on his backside.

McIntosh swore, scrambled up, and leaped forward. His right foot came down hard on Cimarron's left instep. The pain snapped something in Cimarron.

Fury rose within him. Until now, he had fought coolly, watching for any advantage, making one where none existed. But now he was enraged and his rage mingled with the pain in his foot and the aches McIntosh's blows had aroused in his face and body, and he grabbed McIntosh in both hands, hauled him up, and then sent him crashing down to the floor again.

McIntosh, stunned, was kneeling on the flagstones shaking his head. Cimarron booted him in the backside, sending him tumbling forward to crash headfirst into the wall.

"Kill him," someone in the room shouted. "Stomp the bastard!"

Cimarron didn't know whether the man who had shouted was shouting to him or to McIntosh, nor did he care. He stood over McIntosh, panting, his chest heaving, the blood that was flowing from his nose trickling between his lips, where it blended with his saliva to produce a brassy, bitter taste.

McIntosh got to his feet slowly. He rubbed his head and turned toward Cimarron, who stood crouching, waiting. He began to circle Cimarron, who moved warily out of his way, also circling, certain that the man wasn't finished, not yet. Cimarron spat a mixture of blood and saliva and blinked the salty sweat from his eyes. He had lost his hat and his hands hurt, as did his body, but he was determined not to let McIntosh best him. The man had a weight advantage, but Cimarron had discovered that his opponent fought with little grace or agility and less intelligence. He simply struck out, almost blindly, certainly wildly. It was not, in Cimarron's opinion, a good way to hand-to-hand it. A man needed a brain working behind his blows. McIntosh was a powerhouse of brute strength, but Cimarron conducted himself in a fistfight like a general out to win a war, battle by bloody battle.

McIntosh suddenly lunged, battering Cimarron brutally with both fists, first one, then the other. Cimarron let himself be driven back a few steps and then he feinted, warded off a blow with his left forearm, and landed a well-aimed right uppercut on McIntosh's jaw. The blow didn't seem to affect McIntosh, who kept rushing, coming in, dancing bearishly backward, and then coming in again.

Cimarron went down under a sudden rough onslaught delivered by McIntosh that turned the room red before his eyes and seemed to silence the loud shouting of the other prisoners. He saw McIntosh throw himself forward and down, and he failed to move out of the way fast enough.

McIntosh landed on top of him, his fingers circling and cruelly tightening on Cimarron's throat. The room turned from red to bright orange and Cimarron's breath struggled to get out of his lungs and through the open but blocked aperture of his throat.

Cimarron tried to break the iron grip of McIntosh's fingers, but he couldn't. As his vision blurred, he brought his knees up, lifting his opponent's heavy body; then, with a mighty upward thrust of his knees, Cimarron sent McIntosh flying over his head, to crash down on the floor behind him. He fought his way to his feet, breathing hard, cold green eyes on the man he had thrown.

McIntosh, grimacing wildly, got up and lunged at Cimarron, head down, butting him back into a group of prisoners who scattered as Cimarron brought his right knee up fast and his kneecap struck McIntosh's chin, jerking the man's head upright. Cimarron swung ferociously and his right fist glanced off McIntosh's cheekbone. He swung again, his left fist this time, and deliberately landed a blow on McIntosh's windpipe.

McIntosh seized his throat in both hands and gagged.

Cimarron backed up and then sprang swiftly forward, both fists flying, both of them relentlessly striking bone and flesh over and over again.

Badly battered, McIntosh sank to his knees.

Cimarron brought both of his bruised fists down on the back of the man's neck, sending him sprawling facedown on the flagstone floor. He stood over McIntosh, gasping for breath, unmindful now of the blood that still ran from his nose, watching the downed man, resisting the urge to kick him, and kick him hard.

McIntosh rolled over, moaned, and spit out part of a broken tooth, which hit the flagstones with a faint *tink* in the suddenly quiet room.

McIntosh's eyes were closed. His chest heaved. His fingers clawed at the smooth flagstones.

Cimarron said, "You finished?"

McIntosh didn't answer him. Instead, he opened his eyes, threw himself to one side, and when he was on his feet, he had the cut-down kerosene barrel in his hands. He raised it above his head and threw it at Cimarron.

Cimarron turned sideways and the flung barrel glanced off the side of his body. The blow unbalanced him, and as the barrel fell to the floor, McIntosh sprang forward, seized it, raised it high above his head, and brought it down on Cimarron, who had dodged, but not fast enough.

Cimarron bent double as the barrel struck his shoulders and shattered.

McIntosh grabbed Cimarron, locked his arms behind him, and then thrust him hard against the brick wall. Cimarron almost lost consciousness, but he fought to remain on his feet, struggling like a berserk animal to free his limbs. When he found that he couldn't, he threw himself backward and McIntosh hit the floor again, Cimarron landing on top of him.

The fall broke McIntosh's grip and Cimarron turned swiftly and straddled his opponent, hooking the toes of his boots on the insides of McIntosh's thighs to keep the man from getting to his feet or using his legs to throw him. Keeping his knees tight against both sides of McIntosh's rib cage, Cimarron unmercifully landed blow after blow against his downed man's jaw, cheeks, nose, and ears. For Cimarron at that moment, the man he had pinned beneath him was someone to be destroyed, however long it took.

It didn't take long. On the sixth blow, McIntosh went limp beneath Cimarron, and Cimarron, feeling weak and dazed, let his fists fall to his sides and slowly unclench. He stared down at the unconscious McIntosh a moment and then slowly disengaged his boots and rose to his feet. Hands hanging limp at his sides, he stood there looking down at McIntosh for a moment, and then stepped backward, turned, found his hat and put it on, and walked over to the bucket in the basement chimney toward which he'd been headed when McIntosh attacked him.

By the time he had finished using the primitive privy, his nose had stopped bleeding and McIntosh had regained consciousness and had crawled into an empty corner of the jail, where he sat silently, his wary eyes on Cimarron.

Cimarron doubted that the man would try another sneak attack upon him. But if he did, he was sure he'd be able to give him another lesson in discouragement. He kept his distance from McIntosh, aware all the time of every move the man made.

He went over to one of the windows and looked out into the compound. Maledon was still out there, and now, stacked neatly in front of the gallows were three pine boxes. Cimarron watched a weeping woman accept a piece of paper from Maledon along with a pencil. The woman wrote on the paper and handed it back to Maledon, who folded it and stuffed it into his coat pocket, from which it protruded. A wagon drawn by a team of horses pulled up; the man driving it got down and, with Maledon's help, loaded the obviously heavy coffin in the back of the wagon. The driver climbed back onto the wagon and the woman climbed up beside him. As the wagon drove out through the gate of the compound, Maledon tucked the protruding piece of paper, which was obviously a receipt signed by the woman who had claimed the body of one of the hanged men, deeper into his coat pocket.

The door of the jail swung open and a man stuck his head into the room and yelled, "Sick call!"

There was a stirring among the prisoners and a line began to form at the open door. Cimarron watched McIntosh join the line and stand in it, impatiently shifting his weight from foot to foot.

Boyd came up to Cimarron and said, "If I'd've had any cash, I'd have bet it on you in that brawl. You sure were hell on the border and then some!"

"I do my best."

"Aren't you going to get in line?" Boyd asked. "You're pretty bruised up. Anything busted?"

"Don't think so. Unless maybe my nose. Only I think it's just bent a little, not broken."

"What happened to your leg?" Boyd inquired, glancing down at Cimarron's torn trousers and the bandanna wrapped around his thigh.

"When I met up with Tracy and Wickers on the trail in the Nations, Tracy managed to put a bullet through me."

"Oughtn't you to see the doctor about that wound?"

Cimarron considered the question. "Might not be a bad idea. If I don't, it might get infected and before you know it my leg'll be liable to fall off and I don't think even Judge Parker'd have the heart to hang a one-legged man." Cimarron grinned and Boyd's serious expression gave way to a smile.

He strode across the room and got into the line of men waiting to see the doctor, who apparently practiced in the small vestibule beyond the door. When his turn came, Cimarron wordlessly displayed his leg to the doctor, who as wordlessly took a bottle of alcohol from his black bag and proceeded to swab the wound, after which he applied a clean dressing.

Then, looking up at Cimarron, he said, "Try to keep it as clean as you can, which will not be an easy task, considering the condition of that pigsty in there that the law sees fit to keep you men penned in."

"Much obliged, Doctor."

As Cimarron was about to return to the jail, the doctor called out to the jailer. "Charley Burns, I've told you and I've told Parker too. That jail is a disgrace. Worse, it is an abomination in the sight of both God and man. Don't you, for Christ's sake, have any disinfectant you can use in there?"

"Judge Parker," Burns said with a trace of indignation in his voice, "applied to Congress for funds to upgrade conditions in there. Congress didn't see fit to appropriate any money. Yell at our congressmen if you must, Doc, not at me!"

Cimarron turned and went back into the jail.

Minutes later, when the last prisoner had been treated, the door was slammed shut and locked.

That night, as Cimarron sat with his back braced against the stone wall in the damp, dark jail and men were sprawled everywhere on the flagstone floor as they tried to sleep, he let his thoughts roam back over the years and the trails he had ridden, all of which had, he thought grimly, finally converged and landed him here where he now was.

It was hard, he thought, to say exactly what had been the cause—or causes—of his being here in this filthy jail on this dark and lonely night with no man to call friend and no woman to wonder where he was or when he would return to her. He had no place to return to, he thought. Neither did he have a place to go to. But it had not always been this way. There was a time, he remembered, when he had had a name like other men and was not known only as Cimarron. There had been a time when he belonged in a special place in central Texas among people who cared about him.

He recalled her now, his ma, a woman made partly of the rich earth and partly of iron. She was a fighter, his ma, a fighter for her home and family and for what she spoke of sometimes as "a body's rights." She had walked behind a horse, her hands gripping the wooden plow handles, down uncountable furrows. She had weeded and anxiously watched the sky for signs of rain as she had seemed to coax the corn to grow. And grow it did—tall, green, rustling, and sweet on the tongue after having been smeared with freshly churned butter and a touch of salt.

Her hands were rough, but oddly, when they caressed the boy that Cimarron had once been, they seemed to him to be as tender and as soft as early spring breezes.

"Don't fret so," she would say to him. "You've got a ways to go before you're through with being a boy. A man's road is long and troublesome, and you'll set foot on it and learn to walk it soon enough, and that's a fact."

"He won't let me do nothing, Ma. And I'm near to fourteen."

"Your pa knows what's best. Didn't he teach you how to shoot straight? Didn't he show you how to trap and skin? Don't he say you're near as good a horseman as he is himself?"

He hung his head. But he nodded. And then, stormily, "But Pa's always so strict with me. Thrashed me again yesterday, he did, just on account of I said a bad word. Either me or that belt of his is going to wear out first and *I* ain't aiming to be the first to go."

Ma sighed and ran her fingers lightly through his unruly black hair. "It's true that your pa is a righteous man and that he fears the Lord. He has strong notions of what's right and what's wrong and he aims to teach you those notions so's you'll learn to walk the straight and narrow path in this life and then go on to glory in the next."

"I don't want to go to glory! I want to get all I can right here on earth while I've got time for the getting!"

"Hush, here he comes. Don't you dare let him hear you talk that kind of blasphemy or that belt of his'll be out of its loops before you can say, 'God made little green apples.' "

And so the days passed on the home place. There was always work to do and he had done it. He went, at times, to the school in town, where he learned to read, write, and figure. All the time he dreamed—yearned—for the world beyond the home place. The world that was the only real one to him—the world of cities and steamboats and trains that was chock full of dreams a boy could drown in happily.

When Pa caught him in the loft of the barn with Rae Ellen Smith the following Fourth of July while the older folks were picnicking in the pasture, his usually stern visage grew even sterner as he ordered Rae Ellen to pull up her drawers and ordered his son to remain as naked as he was.

As Rae Ellen climbed shamefacedly down the ladder and ran from the barn, Pa's belt swished through the air and his leather met his son's flesh. His son gritted his teeth and did not so much as whimper as the belt rose and fell, rose and fell with a kind of bitter inevitability.

That night, taking only the clothes on his back and the worn work boots on his feet, he left the home place and by morning he was miles away and on his way to pay a visit to the real world.

The years that tumbled their debris down upon him after that came and went quickly.

He learned to gamble on Mississippi riverboats, to consort with the painted women on the Barbary Coast. He killed a man in Denver who had challenged his three-card monte game, and he did time in the federal penitentiary for the killing. When he got out, he rode with other hard cases and relieved stagecoaches and banks from Missouri to Texas of their money.

Until the day in the Texas panhandle when the bank robbery he was participating in was interrupted by a gaunt and bitter-eyed man wearing a sheriff's badge.

He had been emptying the safe behind the tellers' barred cages when one of his confederates had shouted something about the law. He didn't take time to think; he acted instinctively. He was up on his feet and his Colt was blazing and then he and the others were running for the door, past the dead sheriff lying sprawled faceup on the floor.

He had already passed him, having only briefly glanced down at the dead man in passing, and then he suddenly froze.

His confederates yelled for him to come on, to ride, and to ride hard.

But he was paralyzed.

Slowly he turned around and looked down again.

The dead sheriff was his pa. And he had killed him.

He stood there, his Colt in his hand, smoke still drifting out of its barrel, the terrified customers and bank clerks staring at him in terror as he barked questions at them.

The dead man, they answered him, had come to the town from central Texas a year ago. After his wife died, he had taken the job as sheriff when the townspeople recognized him for the fearless and righteous man he was.

He grimaced at the sound of the word "righteous."

It was enough. It was too much. Too much by far.

He turned and, holstering his Colt, ran for his horse, leaped into the saddle, and rode away from the town, never to return. He did not try to rejoin the men he had been riding with. Something had broken within him that day, and he knew the men who had been his companions for more than two years would not, not a single one of them, know how to repair that suddenly and sadly broken part of himself. He rode off, and he rode by himself. In the years that followed, he always rode alone, letting no one come too close to him, drifting, rootless and solitary. He hired out as a hand on ranches, drove Texas herds north to Kansas railheads, caught, broke, and sold wild mustangs. His lonesome and free ways earned him the name "Cimarron," a name that stuck, one he neither liked nor disliked. One he learned to hide behind.

He let no one know that he was a broken man—a man always riding on in search of something, he always told himself and almost always believed his lie. But deep down, down in that dark and grieving place where he was broken and in pain, he knew the truth. He was not searching for something. He was riding on, hurrying on, his eyes often on his back trail, afraid that he might see the father he had murdered riding relentlessly after him, an awful question on his dead lips, the single word thundering in the air, eclipsing the sun, drowning the world in a blood-red tide.

"Why?" his father would call out to him, and the word would reverberate in his mind, which would begin to bleed, and he would not be able to stop himself from screaming in an effort to drown out that voice and the terrible question that had no understandable answer.

Cimarron opened his eyes, which he had not realized he had closed, and remembering where he was and why, he gritted his teeth and listened to the men around him scratch at the vermin that infested them, listened to them shift and turn, turn and shift, all the while trying to see far enough ahead on the trail he was traveling in the hope of making out whom he might meet who would be able to mend his brokenness with a secret word that only the wisest and the best knew and that would be as soothing and ultimately as healing for him as balm of Gilead.

In the morning, after the prisoners had been fed, Cimarron watched the head jailer, Charley Burns, supervise the deputies who were placing handcuffs and leg irons on one of the several men scheduled to appear in Judge Parker's courtroom promptly at eight o'clock in the morning. The others were left unfettered.

As the prisoners scheduled for trial left the jail and the door closed behind them, Cimarron went over to one of the windows and stared out into the empty compound. The gallows stood silent and empty, no nooses suspended above its trap. Cimarron gazed at the stone walls surrounding the compound and imagined himself running across the bare ground, vaulting up to the top of the wall and then leaping down from it. There would be a horse waiting. He would be in its saddle and riding hard, riding away from the old fort toward freedom, away from . . .

He was in the bank in the Texas panhandle again and there was a dead man at his feet and something else that was dead—the freedom which had died for him at the moment he had killed the man who had been his father.

He silently swore, knowing that there was no horse waiting for him beyond the stone wall bordering the compound. He would not vault to freedom over that wall. Would he hang?

The thought left him untouched, as if it were merely a rhetorical question, one that had to do with some other man, not him. He could not imagine his own death. He could more readily imagine the end of the world cindered by fire, foundering in flood.

He did not hear the door behind him open. At first, he did not hear his name called as he stood staring out the window and wondering why a man like George Maledon had chosen to earn his living in the deadly way that he had.

"Cimarron!"

The second summons registered in his brain and he turned from the window to find Charley Burns standing in the doorway. When their eyes met, Burns beckoned, and Cimarron, curious, strode across the room to stand before the jailer.

"Man outside to see you. Counselor-at-law. You can talk to him in the vestibule."

Cimarron followed Burns into the vestibule and found not one but two men in the small enclosure. One was wearing a badge. So the other one, Cimarron thought as he turned his attention to the little man wearing a store-bought suit and a woebegone expression on his face, must be the lawyer.

"I'm Francis Owens," the little man said, squinting up at Cimarron.

Cimarron held out his hand and then let it drop when the lawyer ignored it. "Name's Cimarron."

"For the purposes of the court, I'll have to know your real name," the lawyer said, looking as if he were about to weep. "A procedural matter."

"You can use Cimarron. The name's done for me till now. It'll go on doing, I figure."

The lawyer shook his head in resignation.

"I didn't hire you," Cimarron said, faintly belligerent, feeling himself slipping down into the morass of the legal system of which he wanted no part but which was, he felt, beginning to crowd him, and crowd him hard.

"The court appoints lawyers in the cases of indigent prisoners. They turned your money over to me—"

Cimarron swore.

"And the court will pay the rest."

"They gave you the money they found in the saddlebag of the horse I was riding?" Cimarron asked.

Owens shook his head. "That's evidence against you and

is needed for your trial. And speaking of evidence, how much do they have on you?"

Cimarron told Owens what had happened, what Emma Dorset had accused him of, about her and Griffin, all of it.

When he finished, Owens rubbed his sweating hands on his suit coat and looked down at the floor. Then, with a glance at the armed deputy standing guard in the vestibule, he took Cimarron by the arm and led him as far away from the lawman as he could. In a whisper, he asked, "Is what you've told me the truth?"

"It is."

"The money," Owens said, "is just circumstantial evidence. Miss Dorset—now, she is quite another matter. As a self-proclaimed eyewitness to the crime, she can be very damaging to your case."

"I'll testify that she lied about me."

"Your word. Her word. One can never tell who the jury will believe. And to make matters worse, you're accused of killing a lawman. That will not sit well with most jurymen. They've heard—and some of them have seen—the horrors perpetrated in the territory. They are fed up with violence."

"I didn't perpetrate anything."

"Where are you from, Cimarron?"

"Nowhere in particular."

"Do you have friends I can call as character witnesses?"

Cimarron shook his head.

"Is there any way you can prove that this Mr. Griffin was with you and Miss Dorset?"

Cimarron shook his head again. "But he was there. I didn't imagine him. My guess is he's the one who killed Brent and then set me up to stand in for him as the man's killer."

"Possible," Owens mused. "But proving it is another matter altogether." He paused and then added, "With the exception of Miss Dorset's testimony, which is likely to be severely damaging to your case, the remainder of the evidence against you—the money found in the saddlebag, the fact that you were riding Marshal Brent's horse—is purely circumstantial. Now, in order for a jury to convict on circumstantial evidence alone, the evidence presented must clearly exclude all other possible explanations of your situation.

"You could have found the horse abandoned on the

plains. The money could have been planted by Griffin and/or Dorset in the saddlebag on Brent's horse."

"It *was* planted, had to be. I didn't put it there. I never saw it until Tracy took it out of that saddlebag."

"Yes, yes, I understand. Now, let me think a moment. We have a chance. Yes, decidedly. About Miss Dorset. Is there any way that you can think of by which you might discredit the testimony she is intending to give against you?"

Cimarron told Owens what had happened between him and Emma Dorset during the night the trio had camped in the woodland, concluding with "The way I figure it now, she wanted to make sure I had other things on my mind when her friend Griffin snuck off with my horse and gear during the night. Matter of fact, as I recall it now, I did hear a horse nicker while we were having at it, Emma and me. That horse might have been unsettled by Griffin making off, but I didn't pay the animal any attention at the time, though normally a horse in a nervous state claims my attention fast."

"Manslaughter," Owens said thoughtfully, glancing up at Cimarron.

"What're you getting at?"

"If you were drunk at the time you killed Brent, it would not be murder but manslaughter. Manslaughter is not a hanging offense."

Cimarron's eyes narrowed. "Let's get one thing straight between you and me, Counselor. I didn't kill Brent. And I don't much like the way your mind's tracking."

"If you would be willing to plead to a lesser charge—a charge like manslaughter—a few years in the federal penitentiary at Fort Leavenworth would be all—"

Cimarron held up a hand and the gesture, faintly ominous, caused Owens to sputter and then back away from him, glancing over his shoulder as he did so to where the deputy was still standing.

"I didn't kill Brent," Cimarron repeated in a low tone. "Now, it's your job to prove I didn't. I'll give you all the help I can. But you'd best stop entertaining any notions that I might have done what Emma Dorset is bound and determined to say I done."

Owen sighed. "I told you that jurymen in this court are sometimes all too willing to convict in a case like yours. They are interested in seeing law and order come to the territory. I can't blame them. The Nations have long been a terrible, terrible place. It is no wonder that people have taken to saying that there is no Sunday west of Saint Louis and no God west of Fort Smith."

"I hope there's justice *in* Fort Smith," Cimarron said.

Owens shrugged.

6

On Cimarron's third morning in the Fort Smith jail, after he and the other prisoners had been fed, Charley Burns appeared in the doorway leading to the vestibule. He was accompanied by two deputy marshals, one of them carrying handcuffs and leg irons.

"Cimarron," Burns yelled, and beckoned to him.

Cimarron walked over to Burns and stood in front of the man without speaking, his eyes on Burns' stern face.

"Your case will be heard this morning," Burns told him, and motioned to the deputy at his side.

The deputy handed Burns his revolver and Burns stepped back, the gun leveled at Cimarron, as the deputy dropped to one knee and snapped a leg iron around Cimarron's left boot just above the ankle.

"What are these irons for?" Cimarron asked angrily. "I'm not armed and you've got a gun on me."

"Just a precaution," Burns replied as the deputy snapped the other leg iron in place, the heavy chain connecting them resting on the floor between Cimarron's ankles. "We use them on prisoners we believe to be dangerous."

Cimarron recalled the man he had seen shackled earlier before being led away for trial among the other unfettered prisoners.

The deputy snapped the handcuffs on Cimarron's wrists and then retrieved his revolver from Burns, who motioned to Cimarron.

Cimarron stepped around the deputy and headed for the

door at the far end of the vestibule, the deputy directly behind him with his gun in his hand and Burns bringing up the rear.

When they reached the far door, Burns stepped forward and unlocked it.

As Cimarron stepped out into the compound and the bright sunshine flooding it, he blinked in the yellow glare, so unfamiliar after the nearly always dark jail from which he had come.

Burns led the way around to the front of the federal building and went up the steps.

Cimarron, his leg irons clanking, made his slow way up the steps behind Burns and past a small group of spectators gathered on the landing at the top of the steps. They made way for him, stepping back quickly as if they were afraid he might reach out and touch them, contaminate them in some mysterious and possibly fatal way.

A woman, as Cimarron passed her, fanned herself vigorously with a paper fan, more out of nervousness than because it was hot.

It was not. The morning was cool but the day held the promise of becoming hot before it ended.

Burns led the way down the main hall past the judge's chambers and the jury room and on past the spectators waiting to enter the courtroom who were being assiduously searched for weapons by two deputy marshals.

Cimarron shuffled along, unable to walk normally, his leg irons an unwelcome weight he dragged along, his hands cuffed in front of him, his eyes staring straight ahead.

"Take off your hat," Burns said, and when Cimarron had done so, the trio entered the courtroom, which was already almost filled with men and women calling out to one another, jumping up from their seats and hurrying across the room to exchange embraces and greetings with friends, eating sandwiches taken from the paper sacks they held on their laps.

When Cimarron appeared in the courtroom, a hush fell upon the crowd. Heads turned to stare at him. Women whispered among themselves. Men looked him up and down, nodded to themselves. One chewed his lips. Others stroked their beards.

Cimarron looked around the room. The spectators were seated to his right on oak pews that hinted oddly of a secular church. Behind the rows of pews were high windows looking out on the compound. In the middle of the room was a wooden railing beyond which, on a raised platform, was a cherry-wood desk covered with green felt. Just inside the railing were tables for the defense and prosecuting attorneys and in front of the tables was the court clerk's desk. The jury box with its oak swivel chairs was against the far wall and in front of it was a small table used by the court reporter.

"Take a seat," Burns ordered Cimarron, who moved forward, dragging his leg irons, to where Owens was seated at one of the tables just beyond the wooden railing. He went through the swinging gate and sat down next to Owens.

"Wasn't figuring on being tried so quick," he muttered.

"Judge Parker shunted aside some minor cases to take yours," Owens commented. "Might as well get it over with."

"Might as well," Cimarron agreed, listening to the crowd behind him, which had become noisy again. As the jurymen began to file into the box, he studied their faces.

Undistinguished, all of them. None of them noticeable even in a small crowd, he thought. They wore jeans and shirts or roughly tailored suits over their collarless shirts. Some of the men were bearded; most were not. None wore hats. None looked at Cimarron.

Not at first. But, once seated, having shifted their weight in their swivel chairs, one by one they shot either bold or surreptitious glances at Cimarron, who met their stares and was amused when most of the men quickly, somewhat nervously, looked away from him.

A door opened in the wall opposite the jury box. A man wearing a black robe came through it and, without a glance at the spectators or at Cimarron, made for the cherry-wood desk. He mounted the platform and sat down behind the desk, folding his hands in front of him on it.

Through the glasses he wore, he gazed down at Cimarron.

Cimarron stared up at Judge Parker, meeting the man's steady gaze.

Parker, a tall man, was an imposing figure, Cimarron decided. He would be, he thought, even when he was not wearing his black judicial robe. Cimarron guessed the man must weigh close to two hundred pounds. His cheeks were clean-shaven, but he wore a tawny mustache and goatee, both neatly clipped. His forehead was broad, his nose straight, and his eyes a bright icy blue.

The bailiff, a man wearing the badge of a deputy marshal, rose and intoned, "Oyez! Oyez! The Honorable Court of the United States for the Western District of Arkansas, having criminal jurisdiction of the Indian territory, is now in session, the Honorable Isaac C. Parker presiding. God bless the United States and the Honorable Court!"

Judge Parker looked away from Cimarron, took off his spectacles, and with the thumb and index finger of his right hand rubbed the spot on his nose where the spectacles rested. Then, opening his eyes, he looked down at the spectators, from whom was coming a low murmuring, and said one word: "Silence!"

The crowd went immediately mute.

"I see counsel for the defense," he said. "But where is Mr. Clayton? I trust he has not had any misgivings about prosecuting this case for the United States?"

The door at the rear of the courtroom burst open as if in response to Parker's question and a man bustled down to the railing and through it.

"Sorry, Judge," he said as he plopped a briefcase on the prosecuting attorney's table and sat down with a sigh. "I'm afraid I overslept."

Parker said, "Let the grand-jury indictment be read."

It was read by the bailiff and Cimarron heard himself indicted for the murder and robbery of Deputy Marshal James Brent and the kidnapping and rape of Emma Dorset.

As the bailiff sat down, the court reporter scurried into the room and took his place at his desk, spreading notebook and sharpened pencils out before him.

"Punctuality is a virtue," Parker declared without looking at his reporter, who flushed and busied himself with his pencils. His eyes on Cimarron, Parker asked, "How does the prisoner plead?"

Cimarron rose, his leg irons clanking as he did so, and said, "I'm not guilty. Not of murder or robbery either."

Parker nodded to Clayton.

Clayton leafed through papers he had taken from his briefcase and then rose and strode over to stand in front of the jury box. "The United States," he began, "will prove that the defendant, the man who calls himself Cimarron, did intend and did commit murder upon the person of Deputy Marshal James Brent, after which he robbed said Brent."

As Clayton continued with his opening statement, Parker took off his spectacles and gazed solemnly at Cimarron, who sat with his hands folded in his lap, his legs thrust out beneath the table.

"The government is pleased," Clayton continued, "to have an eyewitness to the murder of which the defendant is charged. Gentlemen of the jury, you will hear Miss Emma Dorset relate in horrifying detail how this dastardly crime was committed and how, following it, she herself—who had earlier been cruelly abducted by the defendant—was then savagely molested by the defendant."

"What the hell . . ." Cimarron muttered, and turned to Owens. "I told you what happened that night. If anybody was molested that night, it was me!"

"*Sshhh!*" Owens hissed, giving Parker a weak grin.

Clayton finished his opening statement and sat down.

"Mr. Owens," Parker prompted.

Owens rose and went to stand in front of the jury box. "The defense will show, gentlemen, and show clearly, that my client is innocent of the crimes of which he has been wrongly accused. The defense will show that only circumstantial evidence exists, which the eminent prosecutor will use to try to convince you beyond the shadow of a doubt that he did indeed kill and rob Marshal Brent. But we will show, gentlemen, and show to your full satisfaction, that Cimarron is the victim of a malicious woman who will give false testimony against him, for which, I might add, she may later be tried for perjury."

There was more, and Cimarron listened to it with a sinking feeling that Owens was mere bluster and bravado. He watched the little man pace back and forth in front of the jury box and almost winced as Owens shook a skinny index finger at the jurymen at one point as if he were a schoolmaster chastising reluctant scholars.

When Owens had finished what Cimarron considered to be something only a little short of a harangue, he sat down and Parker leaned back in his chair and said, "Call your first witness, Mr. Clayton."

"I call Emma Dorset to the stand."

Cimarron straightened in his chair as she came through the door that led to the jury room.

She was no longer wearing the clothes she had been

wearing on the trail. Now she wore a street dress of bright-blue silk with just the hint of a bustle. On her head was a pert white hat trimmed with violets. Her hands were demurely covered with black lace gloves. As she stood beside the witness chair waiting to be sworn, the patent-leather toes of her pumps peeked out from beneath her dress. She did not look in Cimarron's direction.

After having been sworn by the court clerk, Emma sat down in the witness chair and arranged her hands in her lap, her eyes downcast, as if she were about to perform a sad but necessary duty.

"Please state your name," Clayton said to her.

"Emma Dorset."

"Where do you reside, Miss Dorset?"

"Father sold our homestead before setting out on the cattle drive from which I was abducted. Father and I had hoped to settle in Abilene when the drive was completed."

"You know the defendant?" Clayton asked with a wave of his arm in Cimarron's direction.

Emma shot Cimarron a quick glance and then immediately lowered her eyes again. She nodded.

"You must state your answer aloud for the benefit of the court," Judge Parker advised her.

"I know the defendant," Emma said softly.

Clayton asked her how she knew him.

"He and another man abducted me."

Clayton asked Emma to describe her abduction and Cimarron listened in disbelief as she told her lies with an earnestness that had the men in the jury box leaning toward her in sympathy. Cimarron would not have been surprised had one or more of them clucked his tongue in sorrow.

"And after the defendant and his accomplice had abducted you," Clayton continued, "you both met Marshal Brent on the plain. Is that correct?"

Emma nodded and then, apparently remembering Parker's injunction about stating her answers aloud, said, "That is quite correct."

"Tell the court what happened then, Miss Dorset."

Emma described the mythical meeting, and Cimarron, listening to her, silently swore, damning her and the words she was uttering with such easily feigned sincerity.

"And then," she continued, her gaze straying to the

jurymen, "Cimarron—the defendant—shot the marshal. He shot him in the back."

"And robbed him?" Clayton asked.

"Objection, your Honor," Owens said sharply, half-rising from his chair. "My eminent colleague is leading the witness."

"Objection sustained. Rephrase your question, Mr. Clayton."

"Very well, your Honor," Clayton said meekly. "Tell us, Miss Dorset, what happened after the defendant shot Marshal Brent."

"He robbed him of his ring and his horse and all the money he had."

"Objection," Owens declared. "It has not been established that the witness knew exactly how much money the marshal was carrying."

"Overruled." Parker took off his glasses and tapped them on the green felt of his desk.

Cimarron stared steadily at Emma, who was gazing at the jurymen with liquid eyes.

"You saw the defendant remove money from the marshal's person?" Clayton asked.

"I did."

Clayton thrust his hands into his pockets and in a low voice said, "I must ask you the next question, although I know it will be difficult for you to answer, Miss Dorset. Did the defendant molest you while you were with him?"

Emma lowered her head. Her chin quivered. "He— It was the night after he had killed the marshal— Oh, I just *can't!*"

The women in the spectator section began fanning themselves vigorously, many of them leaning forward in their seats.

"Please, Miss Dorset," Clayton said. "Please answer my question."

"He ravished me," Emma said in a voice that was barely audible.

"The defendant?" Clayton prompted. When Emma nodded, Clayton said, "Let the record show that the witness accuses the defendant of rape."

"Aren't you going to object?" Cimarron muttered to Owens.

"I'll have my chance during cross-examination."

"Your witness, Mr. Owens," Clayton said, and sat down.

Owens got up and stood to one side of the witness chair. "I understand you were traveling with a man when you both met my client on the plain, is that correct?"

"No, it isn't," Emma replied.

"Oh, yes, you were abducted from your father's cattle drive—that is what you claimed earlier, isn't it?"

"Objection, your Honor," Clayton said. "The witness did not 'claim' she was abducted. She stated a fact. Counsel is using innuendo to attempt to discredit the witness."

"Sustained," Parker said.

Owens sighed audibly. "Miss Dorset, you *say* you were abducted—"

"Objection!" Clayton roared.

Before Parker could rule, Owens said, "You were abducted from your father's cattle drive by two men. One, you say, was the defendant. What happened to the other man?"

"Cimarron gave him the marshal's ring and he left us."

"Miss Dorset, did your father—with or without the aid of some of his trail hands—come looking for you?"

"I don't know."

"It wouldn't have been hard to find you on an empty prairie if he had, would it?"

"Objection, your Honor," Clayton cried. "The question asks for a conclusion on the part of the witness, one which, I submit, she is not qualified to make."

Parker nodded. "Sustained."

"I'll withdraw the question," Owens said, having made his point.

As he continued to question Emma, she stuck to her story. Owens asked one last question. "Only the person who stole Marshal Brent's money would have known how much the man was carrying, don't you agree, Miss Dorset?"

"I—well, I guess so."

"You did say, did you not, Miss Dorset, that the defendant took *all* of Marshal Brent's money?"

"Yes, but—"

"How could you know that?" Owens shot at her, and before Emma could answer said, "I have no further questions, your Honor." He resumed his seat.

Clayton called Tracy to the stand, who testified that he

had found less than ten dollars in the saddlebag of Brent's quarter horse. When asked by Clayton exactly how much money had been in the saddlebag, Tracy replied that there had been nine dollars and fifty cents.

During cross-examination of Tracy, Owens asked, "Is it not customary for United States marshals to be reimbursed for travel expenses?"

"It is," Tracy replied.

"And do men in your position use some of that money to finance their subsequent trips into Indian territory?"

"A man's got to eat. Buy grain for his horse. Sure."

"And is it not customary for men in your position to level fines on citizens when they see minor criminal acts being committed in the territory?"

"It is."

"But you found only nine dollars and fifty cents in Brent's saddlebag. An unusually small sum under the circumstances."

"Well, he—the defendant could have spent some of it."

"On the plain? Where exactly, Marshal?"

"He might have stashed it away somewhere before we caught up with him."

"But you cannot testify under oath that the defendant did such a thing, can you? Or that he spent any of the money he allegedly stole?"

Tracy's face went red. "No," he said. "I can't do that."

"Thank you, Marshal. That will be all."

Clayton called Wickers to testify and Wickers supported Tracy's testimony.

Owens, under cross-examination, elicited the fact that neither Wickers nor Tracy had actually seen Cimarron take Brent's quarter horse.

Clayton recalled Emma, who testified to the fact that she had seen Cimarron take the animal after he had murdered the marshal. Owens declined to question her.

"He's a bulldog," he whispered to Cimarron, nodding in Clayton's direction. "He served in the 124th Pennsylvania Infantry under Colonel Hawley. He fought at South Mountain, Antietam, and Hooker's Battle of the Wilderness, among other places. He's a fighter, that man is."

Cimarron said nothing. As he shifted position in his chair, his leg irons clanked and all eyes turned in his direction.

Judge Parker recessed the court for dinner.

Cimarron was returned to the jail, after having had his leg irons and handcuffs removed in the jail's vestibule by a deputy under the watchful eyes of an armed Burns.

When court reconvened at two o'clock, Cimarron, shackled and cuffed again, looked around for Emma, but she was nowhere to be seen.

"Clayton will sum up now, no doubt," Owens told Cimarron.

"If it please the court," Clayton said, "I have but one more witness to call before resting."

Owens stiffened.

"I call Ralph McIntosh to the stand," Clayton intoned theatrically.

"Who is he?" Owens asked, the uneasy question directed to himself.

But Cimarron answered it by identifying McIntosh for Owens.

McIntosh was led, unshackled, into the courtroom by a deputy and was sworn.

"Now, then, Mr. McIntosh," Clayton said amiably, "I believe you are acquainted with the defendant, are you not?"

"I know the bastard," McIntosh replied, and a gasp went up from the spectator section.

"You'll use no profanity in this court," Parker exclaimed, pointing a rigid index finger at McIntosh.

McIntosh shrugged and settled into the witness chair.

Clayton turned to Parker. "May the court understand that this prisoner, who is confined in the jail here, asked to see me, conveying his request through Mr. Burns, the head jailer."

"Yes, yes, Mr. Clayton," Parker said. "The court does not concern itself with who delivered messages to whom, only with direct testimony. I suggest you get on with it."

"Thank you, your Honor," Clayton said, and turned back to McIntosh.

"The defendant spoke to you about a personal matter, did he not?"

"He told me how he killed that marshal."

Someone in the spectator section let out a shrill whistle.

"Silence!" Parker thundered, banging his gavel down.

"He admitted having done the killing?"

McIntosh grinned. "He sure did."

"He's a liar," Cimarron said to Owens, gripping the

man's arm with both cuffed hands. He quickly told Owens about the incident on the trail that had occurred between him and McIntosh and how McIntosh had subsequently jumped him in the jail and about the fight that had followed.

"He admitted shooting Marshal Brent?" Clayton asked, his voice sharp.

"I already said so," McIntosh barked back.

"Your witness, Mr. Owens," Clayton said with a slight bow.

Owens rose slowly and as slowly walked to the witness chair, where he stood with his chin cupped in one hand, staring at the floor. Then, without looking at McIntosh, he asked, "Why do you suppose my client told you what you claim he told you?"

"We were friends, sort of."

Owens looked directly into McIntosh's eyes. "But you brutally attacked him in the jail three days ago. Isn't that true?"

"Objection," Clayton shouted. "Not relevant testimony."

Parker, without hesitation, said, "Mr. Owens, will you establish the relevance of this testimony?"

"I will, your Honor."

"Objection overruled, Mr. Clayton," Parker said quietly.

"You were beaten by my client in that fight, weren't you, Mr. McIntosh?" Owens inquired.

"Well, I guess you could say he whupped me."

"And now you are trying to get even for that . . . whupping, as you call it, by giving false and injurious testimony against my client."

"You can't prove he didn't confess to me that he murdered that marshal!"

"Where did my client say he shot the marshal?" Owens angrily asked McIntosh, who just as angrily replied, "Out on the plain somewheres! I don't know where exactly."

"Mr. McIntosh, I'm afraid you have misunderstood me. I mean where in the body did my client say he shot Marshal Brent?"

McIntosh fidgeted in his chair, glared at Cimarron, licked his lips, and answered, "He didn't happen to say."

"But he *did* say that he killed the marshal?"

"How many times have I got to tell you that? Yes, he said it, damn his eyes!"

"That will be all, Mr. McIntosh."

When McIntosh had been escorted from the courtroom by the deputy, Owens turned to Judge Parker and said, "I call my client to the stand."

When Cimarron had been sworn and had seated himself in the witness chair, Owens asked him, "Did you kill Marshal Brent?"

"I never saw the man."

"Just answer my question please."

"I didn't kill him."

"Did you steal Marshal Brent's horse?"

"Griffin—that phony preacher who was riding with Emma Dorset—he's the one who stole it if anybody did."

"Your answer to my question?" Owens asked Cimarron, clearly exasperated.

"I didn't steal his horse or any other horse—ever."

"Did you rape Emma Dorset?"

"It was more the other way around."

A titter ran through the crowd of spectators and Parker promptly gaveled for order.

"I repeat," Owens said, "did you or did you not rape Emma Dorset?"

"I did not."

"Thank you. That will be all. Your witness, Mr. Clayton."

Clayton rose as Owens returned to his seat and stood in front of Cimarron, arms folded, eyes cold. "What is your name?"

"Cimarron."

"I didn't ask you what you were called. I asked you what your name is."

Cimarron met Clayton's cold stare.

"I see. You do not choose to acquaint this court with your real name. Perhaps it is a name you are not proud of."

"Objection!" Owens shouted. "My client's name is not at issue here. His conduct is."

"Sustained. Go on, Mr. Clayton."

"Have you ever been imprisoned before, Cimarron?"

Cimarron started to speak, but Owens objected again and Parker summoned both lawyers to a conference in front of his desk. When it was over, Clayton resumed his questioning of Cimarron. Cimarron, in responding to the prosecutor's questions, denied the charges against him as he had denied them when Owens questioned him.

Clayton at last sat down and Cimarron left the stand.

"Mr. Clayton, Mr. Owens," Parker said. When he had their attention, he asked, "Will you both be able to complete your summations in a reasonable amount of time or shall I recess this court until tomorrow morning?"

Both lawyers said that they could deliver their summations without undue delay.

"Then we will proceed," Parker announced. "Mr. Clayton, if you're ready."

Clayton rose and proceeded to sum up his case.

"You men on the jury have heard Miss Dorset's eyewitness account of how the defendant, brutally and in cold blood, did fatally shoot a United States deputy marshal in the back. You have heard her recount the fact that this defendant—a man with no honor and less human feeling—did abduct her from the care and protection of her father so that he could bend her to his will—to his primitive animal lusts.

"The defendant, may I remind you, gentlemen, is being tried on three charges. Kidnapping. Rape. Murder. All of them, gentlemen, are capital offenses. All of them point a finger at the savagery of the defendant, yea, I might say his soullessness.

"You have heard the evidence against him. You have heard that he was discovered by Marshals Tracy and Wickers riding Marshal Brent's horse. You have been told that he had secreted the money he stole from the man he so viciously murdered in the saddlebag of the horse that had belonged to the man he killed.

"You have heard Miss Dorset testify that this man"—Clayton jabbed a finger in Cimarron's direction—"if such a monstrous person can be called a man—or even human—you have heard this poor woman testify to the fact that he"—again Clayton's finger jabbed toward Cimarron—"did carnally know her despite her vain attempts to fend him off.

"You have heard Otis McIntosh testify that the defendant did willingly and even boastfully admit to the said McIntosh that he had murdered Marshal Brent.

"There thus can be no shadow of doubt in your minds, gentlemen, that this man is as guilty as sin. He stands before you convicted not only by the testimony of Miss Dorset, who was both the victim of and the witness to his crimes. He stands convicted before you by his own words as recounted by Otis McIntosh.

"I therefore ask you, gentlemen, to find him guilty—as indeed he is in the sight of God and man—of all three charges that have been brought against him. In good conscience, you can do no less than to find him guilty as charged. And by so doing, you will have rid this world of an aberration, a monstrosity who, if allowed to go free, at any time in the future will, I can assure you in all sincerity, make the world an unsafe place for all of us as well as for our wives and children. I thank you, gentlemen, for your kind attention."

When Clayton had seated himself, Owens rose and strode, his hands thrust deep into his pockets, over to stand in front of the jury box.

"Monstrosity," he boomed, and grimaced. "Aberration," he shouted. "My esteemed colleague, Mr. Clayton, should not, I submit to you, allow himself such flights of literary fancy. The man you see seated there"—Owens nodded in Cimarron's direction—"is, I submit, no monstrosity and he is no aberration. The man you see seated there, gentlemen of the jury, is a wronged man. An innocent man.

"Emma Dorset testified most eloquently against him, I grant you. She gave damaging testimony, I'll admit that. *But*—and this is important, gentlemen, very important, and I want you to pay close attention to what I am about to say—is there anyone who can corroborate Miss Dorset's testimony?

"*No*," Owens thundered. "There is no one. So what does it all come down to then in the final analysis? Just this: it is Emma Dorset's word against that of my client.

"What's that? You ask about the testimony that Otis McIntosh gave against my client? Was not the man's testimony devastating, you ask—proof positive, in fact, that my client is guilty? *No*!" Owens thundered even more loudly. "What possible weight can you give to testimony taken from a man who is himself accused of rape and murder? Surely, gentlemen, such testimony is tainted.

"Especially when you consider that McIntosh had a grudge against my client for—as he put it—*whupping* him."

Owens paused as several of the men in the jury box smiled, and then he continued, "But what, you ask, about the statements made under solemn oath by Deputies Tracy and Wickers? Those men merely drew conclusions from what they saw. They saw my client riding the quarter horse that had once belonged to Brent. They therefore concluded that my client had stolen that horse. There are other explanations for why my client was riding that horse. He might have found it wandering on the plain after the murder of its owner. He might have bought it from Brent before the man was killed.

"And then consider this. The deputies found nine dollars and fifty cents in the saddlebag of that horse. The deputies therefore concluded that, first, the money had belonged to Brent and had been stolen from him, and that, second, my client stole it from Brent.

"Conclusions, gentlemen, are not sufficient grounds on which to convict. Neither is uncorroborated testimony.

"My client is clearly innocent of all charges leveled against him. I know you will find him so. The defense rests and thanks you."

Parker, after leafing through one of the statute books on his desk, took off his glasses and began to charge the jury.

"Gentlemen of the jury," he began, "you have heard all that has been said here by witnesses under oath concerning the charges brought against this defendant. It is up to each one of you to decide the merits of what you have heard and the credibility of the witnesses. You must carefully weigh all that you have heard and then reach a decision as to the guilt or innocence of the defendant on all three counts contained in the indictment."

As Judge Parker continued with his charge, he stressed more than once that the burden of proof rested with the government. He pointed out that the jurymen must be convinced that the government had proved beyond a reasonable doubt that the defendant was guilty as charged.

"If you believe that the government has failed to so prove," he continued, "then you must find the defendant innocent on one or more of the charges brought against him.

"The defense, I must point out to you, has not argued that the defendant was insane at the time the crime was committed. A murder committed while the perpetrator is insane is punishable by a term of imprisonment to be determined by the court. Such is not the issue in this case. The defendant here is accused of killing a man without just cause and with premeditation.

"Such a crime is punishable by death. Rape, of which the defendant also stands accused, is also punishable by death. Kidnapping too is a capital offense.

"Now, gentlemen, you may go and begin your deliberations. Please bear in mind that a man's life lies in your hands. I beg you to weigh most carefully all that you have heard. I urge you to give serious thought to it all so that you may reach a fair and just verdict in this case."

Cimarron watched the jurymen file out of the courtroom. He looked down at the irons fastened to his ankles and then at the handcuffs binding his wrists. Near his head, a fly buzzed in the afternoon air, which had become hot and humid.

He leaned back in his chair and closed his eyes. He did not know how much time had passed—perhaps he had dozed—when he felt Owens nudging him in the ribs.

"They're coming back," Owens whispered.

Cimarron watched the jurymen file across the front of the room and take their places in the jury box. He stared at the piece of white paper that the jury foreman was holding in his hand. Parker returned to the courtroom and seated himself behind his desk.

"Gentlemen of the jury, have you reached a verdict?" Parker asked, his voice sounding tired.

"Yes, sir, your Honor."

"The defendant will rise," Parker said without looking at Cimarron.

Cimarron's leg irons clanked as he got to his feet. Owens also rose and stood at his side.

"Bailiff," said Parker.

The bailiff crossed the room and took the piece of paper the jury foreman was holding out to him. The bailiff reached up and handed the paper to Parker, who glanced at it and then, peering through his glasses at the foreman, asked, "Is this your verdict?"

"Yes, your Honor. That's it."

"The jury finds the defendant guilty on all three counts. I will pass sentence. The jury may be excused."

There was silence in the courtroom as the members of the jury hurriedly left the room. When they had gone, Parker glanced once more at the piece of paper that the bailiff had handed him and then looked at Cimarron.

"Your crimes have been vicious ones," he remarked almost tonelessly. "A man is dead because of you—a man who was sworn to uphold the law. A man who was dedicated to bringing justice to those who would do evil in Indian territory. A man sorely needed by society if civilization is to reign and the lawless are to be ground down into the dust.

"Because of you a woman has been dishonored. And throughout these proceedings I have detected not the slightest sign of remorse in you. Indeed, your testimony was tinged with a repulsive air of arrogance.

"I feel it is my duty now to implore you to ask forgiveness of your Maker. This court cannot grant you such forgiveness. It can only pass sentence upon you as provided for in the statutes of the State of Arkansas. But first, you are entitled to say whatever might be on your mind."

When Cimarron remained silent, Parker asked wearily, "Have you nothing to say then?"

"I have this to say," Cimarron said. "I'm not guilty of any of the charges. You hang me, you'll be hanging an innocent man."

Parker seemed to suppress a sigh. "Promptly at nine-thirty tomorrow morning, you will be delivered into the hands of the hangman and you will be hanged by the neck until you are dead. May God have mercy on your immortal soul."

Parker banged the gavel down on his desk and quickly left the courtroom.

Two deputies took Cimarron by the arms. He shook them off and strode out of the courtroom, his shackles shattering the silence.

He was aware as he walked of the spectators staring at him, some with looks of intense, almost sensual satisfaction on their faces, others with expressions that might possibly have been pitying.

He walked down the long hall and then went down the steps, Owens hurrying along at his side, insisting that he was sorry, proclaiming that he had done his very best.

"You did what you could," Cimarron told him. "Don't worry about me."

Owens faded away and Cimarron was marched around the courthouse by the deputies who rapped on the door leading to the jail's vestibule. It was quickly opened by Burns, who dismissed one of the deputies, and the ritual of unchaining Cimarron began.

Burns held the deputy's revolver on Cimarron as he had

done before. The deputy knelt and removed Cimarron's leg irons. He rose and inserted his key to unlock the handcuffs binding Cimarron's wrists.

As the deputy removed the cuffs, Cimarron suddenly seized them and, at the same instant, swiftly raised a leg and booted the deputy backward. He spun around toward the startled Burns and swung the cuffs, his fingers tightly gripping one of their steel loops.

7

The free cuff slashed through the air and slammed down hard upon Burns' wrist. Burns let out a howl of pain and the revolver fell from his hand.

Cimarron shifted the handcuffs to his left hand, bent down and retrieved the revolver with his right hand, and covered the cowering deputy and the still-howling Burns with it.

"Shut up, Burns," he snapped.

"You hurt my wrist," Burns bellowed. "It feels like it's broken clear through!"

"*Shut up,*" Cimarron repeated. "I don't want any noise!"

Burns, holding his injured wrist, began to whimper.

"Cuff him," Cimarron ordered, and when Burns looked up at him, he pointed at the deputy. "Hands behind his back."

"I can't," Burns protested. "My wrist—"

"You can, and you will," Cimarron declared, taking a step toward Burns and raising the revolver slightly so that it pointed at Burns' heart.

Burns bent down and picked up the handcuffs Cimarron had dropped. Cimarron watched silently as Burns clumsily handcuffed the deputy's hands behind his back.

"Gag him," Cimarron ordered.

Burns pulled a cotton handkerchief from his back pocket with his left hand and looked at it, then at the deputy, then at Cimarron.

"Do it," Cimarron snapped.

Burns stuffed the handkerchief into the deputy's mouth. The man gagged.

"Get it all in," Cimarron ordered.

"He'll choke," Burns protested.

"Maybe so," Cimarron said, and gestured. When Burns had stuffed all of the handkerchief into the deputy's mouth, he said, "Now you're going up to the clerk's office. You're going to get my rifle, six-gun and cartridge belt and you're going to bring them back here. Now I reckon you might already have got yourself the idea of coming back with a deputy or two by your side. Or maybe you figure on alerting whoever's about so they can shoot me down like a dog once I move out of here.

"Those ideas, I can tell you, won't do you much good. You come back alone or else this deputy dies. Sure, you can probably kill me, but it'll cost you at least one deputy to try. And if you set up an ambush out there, *you'll* die. Because you're walking out of this fort with me. Now get going, Burns!"

Burns backed down the vestibule, felt behind him for the doorknob, found it, turned around, and went out into the compound, closing the door behind him.

The deputy gagged again, his face growing scarlet.

Cimarron didn't give the man a glance. He kept his eyes on the closed door as the minutes passed, too slowly to suit him. But he forced himself to be patient. This way that he had worked out of obtaining his freedom, he was convinced, was the only halfway reliable way of achieving it. If he had made a run for it, Burns and the deputy would have raised a ruckus and he probably wouldn't have made it to the fort's gate alive. But this way—this way, he told himself, I've got a better than good chance to get away with my hide unpunctured.

More minutes passed.

Finally the door opened and Burns entered the vestibule, carrying Cimarron's gun and gun belt.

Burns held them out to him. "Take them and get out!"

Cimarron shook his head. "We're going out together. You're going to carry my gun and gun belt. I'll be right behind you. So will this be." He raised the gun in his hand.

"They'll see us," Burns protested. "Somebody will."

"Maybe they will. What they'll see is me and my gun ready to throw down on you, Burns. If anybody starts anything, you'd better tell them to back off if you've no hankering to die. Now let's go, Burns."

Burns opened the door and went through it, followed by Cimarron, who looked warily around. There was no one in sight.

"Lock the door," Cimarron told Burns, who did so. "Now move out real brisk and head for the gate."

The two men were halfway across the compound when a boy's head appeared above its stone wall. As the boy clambered up onto the top of the wall, he looked down and let out a yell.

Cimarron stiffened. "Keep moving, Burns. Don't look right or left. Just keep right on walking toward that gate."

"Hey, Marshal," the boy yelled from the top of the fence, standing up on it now and pointing down at Burns, "where you taking him?"

The tension that had been building up in Cimarron eased and he almost laughed out loud as he realized that the boy had mistaken him for a deputy engaged in escorting a prisoner.

Cimarron gave the boy a jaunty left-handed wave and marched on, Burns quickening his pace in front of him.

When they reached the gate, the tension had built to a flash point within Cimarron, but he said nothing, nor did he quicken his pace as Burns opened the gate and stepped outside the fort.

Cimarron quickly followed him and kicked the gate shut behind him. "Which way's the livery stable?" he asked Burns, shoving the revolver into his waistband so that only a portion of its butt was visible.

Burns pointed.

"Head for the livery," Cimarron told him. "I'll be right behind you. Let's go!"

They walked along Rogers Avenue toward the river, passing men and women, some of whom greeted Burns, who returned their greetings with a stiff nod.

When they reached the livery stable, Cimarron said, "Inside."

The farrier, wearing a leather apron, looked up as they entered the dim interior of the stable.

"I'm a friend of yours," Cimarron whispered to Burns, hoping the farrier had not attended his trial.

"Afternoon, Mr. Burns," the farrier said cheerfully,

wiping his blackened hands on his apron. "What can I do for you this fine day?"

"This man is a—a friend of mine," Burns stammered, and glanced at Cimarron, who had stepped up to stand beside him.

"Name's Bartlett," Cimarron said quickly. "Deputy Marshal Bartlett. We've come for a quarter horse that desperado we brought in the other day was riding and which we sent over here to be housed."

"Fine animal," the farrier said, glancing back into the stable where the stalls were. "You want him saddled up?"

"Be obliged," Cimarron said.

The farrier nodded and turned, heading for the stalls.

"You won't get far," Burns muttered to Cimarron. "They'll send marshals out after you. They'll track you and—"

"Shut up," Cimarron said, a broad smile on his face for the benefit of the farrier, who had glanced back at them as Burns spoke.

When the farrier led the quarter horse, saddled and bridled, up to Cimarron, he said, "The bill's six dollars and two bits." He looked from Cimarron to Burns, his hands on the horse's reins.

"The court will give you a voucher," Cimarron said, still smiling pleasantly. "Now I've got a question for you."

"What might it be?" the farrier asked, also smiling.

"We had a witness at the trial this morning—Miss Dorset. She—"

"Are they going to hang that man who murdered Marshal Brent?" the farrier interrupted.

"You bet your boots they are," Cimarron answered. "Right, Charley?"

Burns nodded dumbly.

"Is Miss Dorset's horse here in your stable?" Cimarron asked.

The farrier shook his head. "She rode out on it early this afternoon."

Cimarron forced the smile to remain on his face. "Did she now? Did she happen to say where she was heading?"

"Nope." The farrier frowned. "Well, she didn't *exactly* say, is what I mean. What I mean is, she asked me if it was very far to Bent's Fort. 'Far?' I said to her. 'It most surely is,' I said to her. She said something about far being just her sort of luck, and then she left."

"I'll take my gun belt now, Charley," Cimarron said, and held out his hand. When Burns handed the gun belt to him, he quickly strapped it around his hips and holstered his Colt. Then Cimarron stepped into the saddle and the farrier released his grip on the quarter horse's reins. "Well, Charley, it sure has been a pleasure doing business with you."

As Cimarron spurred the quarter horse, Burns let out a yell.

Cimarron galloped out of the door of the livery stable, turned his horse to the right, and rode up Rogers Avenue toward the river. As he neared it, he turned the horse to the right again, and after passing Garrison Avenue, he rode toward the docks. Once past them and the ferry slips that were to the north of them, he rode on past the railyard. He didn't look back.

When the railyard was behind him, he headed northwest, riding along the lush flood plain of the Arkansas River, which was on his left. He entered the Indian territory's eastern woodland, glad of the fact that he didn't have to ride out in the open, certain as he was that he would be pursued. The trees not only hid him from sight but also offered him protection from the sun, which, although low in the sky now, was still hot.

Off to his right, the tracks of the Arkansas Valley Railroad cut through the woodland, and as he rode on, he saw a train heading down the tracks toward Fort Smith. Once the sun had set, he changed direction and headed due north across the railroad tracks and up into the Cookson hills, just south of the Boston Mountains, intending to search for a better place to spend the night than in the woodland.

He rode through a wide gully flanked by two sloping hills that were dotted with the yellow spikes of prince's plume growing beneath the branches of young willow trees. He rode slowly, letting his horse pick its way among the rocks of various sizes that had been eroded from the sides of the hill and that had tumbled down into the gully.

The gully wound its way through the hills, and as Cimarron rode on, the only sound in the stillness that surrounded him was that of the creaking of his saddle leather.

He rode on until he came to a place where the hill on his right jutted out in an overhang from which a thin wall of water spilled down from a stream higher up on the hill which he couldn't see.

The water was a welcome sight.

He dismounted and led his horse over to the pool that had formed beneath the overhang and let the animal drink. Aware that he had not had a bath in a long time, Cimarron, after drinking from the pool as his horse was doing, stripped and removed the dressing the Fort Smith doctor had applied to his leg wound. He examined the puckered flesh, scabbed now, that covered it. He walked out into the pool and then under the water that was spilling down from the overhang. It was cool, almost cold, and he threw back his head and let the water cascade down upon his sweaty face and body. He pulled some grass that was growing at the edge of the pool and used it to rub the dirt and grime from his body. Then, kneeling naked beside the pool, he washed his clothes in it and spread them out on some nearby rocks to dry.

He retrieved his cartridge belt as dusk began to settle in among the hills and then removed the bedroll that was tied behind the quarter horse's saddle. He wrapped himself in the blanket and sat down by the pool, idly watching his horse munch the grass growing at the edge of the water.

He was hungry, he realized.

But there was no sign that any animal had come down to the pool to drink. And it was getting too dark to think of hunting for his dinner. He stared at the surface of the pool, in which the light of the polestar was being refracted—splintering into bright fragments, coalescing, and then splintering again.

Something caught his eye. A movement. He leaned over the pool, looking down into it. Something moved in the shallow depths of the pool. And then Cimarron saw what had caught his eye.

Tadpoles. Some of them, he noticed, had almost grown into young frogs. He made a grab for one, missed it, tried again, and this time caught one of the smaller tadpoles, which he promptly threw back into the pool. As he continued to try to seize some of the larger ones, they continued to evade him by darting beneath the edges of the rocks littering the bottom of the pool.

Cimarron rose, broke off the branch of a nearby willow, and after rubbing it against a rock to sharpen one of its ends, he used the makeshift implement to spear several large tadpoles.

As he took out his matches and built a small fire under the overhang, using willow wood and some dead leaves he found beneath the trees, a night bird called in the distance.

He speared and roasted the tadpoles and ate them, remembering with wry amusement the time he had dined in a French restaurant in New Orleans and had, because of a lady's taunting dare, with some slight trepidation ordered frog's legs for the first time in his life.

He had liked them, relished them so much, in fact, that he had ordered a second helping, to the dismay of the lady he was dining with; her name, at the moment, escaped him. But the memory of the night that had followed that dinner in the French restaurant—the night he had shared the bed of the woman who was now nameless in his memory—had not been forgotten. She had been French. He had seldom found a woman more satisfying.

As a tadpole crackled in the fire at the end of his branch, Cimarron licked his lips. The little creatures tasted, he decided later as he ate them, more like chicken than prairie chickens. Juicier too.

Later, after kicking out his fire and picking up his gun belt, he went to his horse and led it around the thin curtain of water that was trickling down from the overhang and hobbled it far back beneath the rocky ledge. He stripped the gear from it and gently rubbed it down with grass. He left the dim cavern and retrieved his clothes, which he brought back under the overhang and spread on the ground. Unholstering his Colt and placing it on the ground, he gathered the blanket around him and lay down not far from his horse. Lulled by the sound of the trickling water and the occasional haunting cry of the invisible night bird, he was soon asleep.

When he awoke just after dawn the next morning, he automatically reached for his gun. As his fingers closed around its butt, he lay without moving, listening, his eyes roving.

He heard water trickling, splashing down into the pool. He heard his horse moving about behind him in the rocky recess. He saw no movement of animal or man beyond the miniature waterfall.

He rose and dressed, strapped on his gun belt, holstered

his Colt, and then left the rocky shelter and climbed up the hill, crouching there, his hat in his hand, peering out over the thickly massed mounds that were the Cookson hills. He moved only his head for long minutes as he crouched below the crest of the hill, surveying the terrain all around him.

No riders. No sounds made by men.

But he knew that he could not see into every gully, every small valley. He knew, too, that he might not hear a man moving stealthily toward him, hidden in the gray shadows of the looming hills. So he would remain wary. He eased back down the hill and around to the overhang, stopping to kneel and drink from the pool, cupping water in his hands that was as cool and refreshing as the equally cool and refreshing early-morning air.

He stood up and studied the ground beneath his boots. Most of it was rocky, but there were a few patches of sand mixed with mud. In one of those patches he saw the tracks and the drag marks the animal that had made them left as it approached and then left the pool where it had come to drink during the night.

A heavy whitetail buck, judging by the tracks and drag marks, he thought to himself with faint annoyance. He hadn't heard it during the night. He should have heard it, he told himself. He should have heard its hooves striking the rocks around the pool. If the whitetail had been a man . . .

But he had been tired. No excuse, he told himself angrily. Better to lose a little sleep than your freedom. Or your life.

He went in under the overhang and led the horse out to the pool. He left it there to drink and graze and went back and got his gear. He dropped it on the ground and waited until his horse had satisfied itself with water and grass. Only then did he saddle and bridle the animal, which tossed its head and pawed the ground with one front hoof as if it were as eager as he was to be on its way.

He stepped into the saddle and moved out, following the gully that wound its way westward, as the sun began to ascend the sky. He found himself wondering as he rode on through Cherokee Nation why Emma Dorset had asked the farrier about Bent's Fort. The place, he knew, no longer existed. He had heard that, when the cholera epidemic that had been borne westward by gold seekers in 1849 decimated the Cheyennes who had been the mainstay of the Bents' trade, William Bent, after his brother's death, had dynamited the fort rather than let it be overrun by drifters. Now only ruins remained.

But Emma Dorset had asked if it was far to the fort. Clearly that's where she was headed. There could be only one reason, Cimarron decided. She must have arranged to meet Griffin there.

The more Cimarron considered the matter, the more a prearranged rendezvous made sense to him. A woman alone—one not overly familiar with the land—could reach the fort with relative ease simply by following the course of the Arkansas River until it met the Santa Fe Trail, and then traveling west along the Santa Fe. If he was right, Cimarron thought, he could, if he was able to get to the fort before Emma, settle his score not only with her but also with Griffin. Kill two birds with one stone? He grinned.

He rode on through the hills, avoiding their crests, keeping to the valleys, occasionally dismounting to climb one of the hills and scan his back trail. He saw no sign of pursuers, and as the miles fell away, he began to relax.

When the hills were behind him, he made his nooning, such as it was, on the bank of the Arkansas in a thick grove of white pines. He tore moss that was growing on the trunks of the trees loose and washed it in the river before eating it.

He was kneeling to drink at the riverbank when he heard his horse snort. He quickly turned and as quickly leaped to his feet as he saw a woman, completely naked, running out of the pines toward his horse, which had obviously been startled by her sudden appearance.

As the woman leaped into his saddle, Cimarron began running toward the horse. The woman seized the reins and was trying to turn the alarmed animal. Cimarron, as the horse danced under the woman, ran to the left, and as the horse started north, he increased his speed.

The woman was using hard hands on the reins and the quarter horse, the bit tearing at the soft flesh of its mouth, reared in protest.

Cimarron, at the same instant, skidded to an abrupt halt beside the animal, tore the reins from the woman's hand, and with one shove sent her toppling out of the saddle.

He paid her no attention as he worked to gentle the horse, talking softly to it, touching it lightly on the neck, stroking it, his hands loose on the dangling reins. Only when the horse had all four feet on the ground again and was no longer tossing its head, did he turn to look at the woman. She was up and running back toward the pines.

Cimarron leaped into the saddle and set out after her.

He caught up to her in less than a minute and, reaching down with his left hand, seized her by her long black hair. He hauled her up and laid her across his horse's neck just in front of his saddle horn. He halted the horse, dismounted, and then dragged the woman down beside him, his left hand still gripping her hair.

She pummeled him with her fists, clawed at his face, tried to knee him in the groin, bit his wrist.

He released his hold on her hair and grabbed each of her wrists, holding her arms out at right angles to her body as he brought his left leg up to ward off her kicks.

"You could get a bad sunburn running around like you are in the altogether," he told her, grinning in spite of what had just happened to him.

The woman continued to kick at him, continued to try to break his grip on her wrists, saying not a word, her black eyes blazing, her mouth set in a thin tight line.

"Never would have taken you for a horse thief," he told her. "*Ow!*" he yelled as her foot slammed hard against his right knee. He threw her to the ground and then threw himself down upon her, pinioning her body beneath his, again gripping both of her wrists in his two hands. He stared down at her as she turned her head from side to side as if trying to avoid looking directly at him.

"Now what's this all about, honey?" he asked. "Just take your time. I'll just hold you here till you decide to tell me your story."

As her body struggled beneath his, Cimarron thought of the last time he had been in a similar, though different, situation. He thought of Emma Dorset.

The woman struggling under him was not white. She had the oval face of an Indian. Her skin was, Cimarron noted, as bronzed as his own, but unlike his, hers was smooth; he felt the sudden urge to touch it, but refrained from doing so. Her eyes were crow black, as was her long straight hair. Her lips were full but not thick, and above them was a narrow, almost aquiline nose. Comely, he thought to himself. A most comely young lady, he thought as he felt himself growing hard.

The woman beneath him suddenly went limp. She sighed, the soft sound of surrender.

Cimarron, staring down at her, saw her blink and then look up into his eyes. Then, turning her head, she closed her eyes and moaned.

"I'll let you up now," he told her. "But you just sit nice and still. You run, I'll down you. You try to hit me, I'll—well, you'd best not."

He released her wrists and stood up.

The woman sat up, wrapping her arms around her body, trying to hide her breasts. She crossed her legs and stared down at her thighs. "You're not going to . . .?"

At first, Cimarron didn't understand what she had intended to say. Then, he realized that she thought he had been intending to rape her.

"Honey, you got me all wrong. All I want you to do is tell me why you were trying to run off with my horse."

She looked up at him and then her eyes traveled slowly down his body to stop below his gun belt.

Cimarron looked down at the bulge in his pants. "Couldn't help myself, honey. Just a natural reaction as a result of our little set-to. Now about my horse—"

She looked up at him. "There were two men. He brought them to the house. They paid him and he—he turned me over to them." She shuddered.

"Who were they?"

"He said he'd met them while he was in Tahlequah and he arranged to bring them to me."

"Who is he—the one who brought the two men?"

"My husband."

Cimarron pushed his hat back on his head and stroked his stubbled chin. "Your husband," he repeated. "I've heard some strange stories in my time, but this is about the strangest and that's a true fact."

"He's not really my husband," the woman said. "I mean he is, but . . . he made me marry him."

Cimarron judged the woman to be no more than seventeen, possibly even younger. He hunkered down in front of her. And then immediately stood up. "I apologize for my manners, ma'am. But you being the way you are—it distracts a man! You just wait right here." He went to his horse, untied his bedroll, and brought her his blanket. As she wrapped it around herself, he asked, "How does a man go about *making* a woman marry him?"

"He gave me a choice. Either I married him or he'd shoot me to death."

Cimarron whistled through his teeth.

"It was all perfectly legal. We were married by a Methodist minister in Tahlequah."

"You're Cherokee?"

"Yes, my name is Sarah Lassiter. I mean, that was my maiden name, but now, legally, it's Mrs. Alfred Quince."

"Why couldn't Quince court you in the ordinary way?"

"He wanted our land. My land. It was my father's. He died. I was attending the female seminary just outside of Tahlequah. I came home for the funeral and afterward this man rode in one day—he didn't even have a permit to be in Cherokee Nation—and he made me marry him so he could gain legal title to my land. And then—and then—there were those two men. I got away from them after the first one had—had finished with me. I ran and hid in the woods. They rode out after me. I ran again. Oh, I ran so far and so fast, and then I came here and I tried to take your horse so I could get away and I—" She dropped her head in her hands and began to weep.

Made uneasy by her tears, Cimarron reached out to touch her, trying to think of something to say that might soothe her. As his hand came to rest on her shoulder, she drew back sharply, recoiling from his touch, her eyes afire again, obviously ready to fight him off.

"Hold on now," he said quickly. "I'd nothing more in mind than just trying to gentle you down some."

"Please," she said plaintively, huddling in the blanket, seeming to shrink into herself as Cimarron watched her. "Don't touch me." She grimaced. "I'll never let another man touch me again. *Never!*"

"Now, that's your right and there's no disputing it, ma'am," Cimarron said. "But never's an awful long time."

"If you try to touch me again, I'll—"

Cimarron hunkered down, facing her. He held up both hands, palms turned toward her. "I've no intention of doing you any kind of harm."

"I wish he was dead," Sarah declared vehemently. "I wish all three of them were dead!"

"You could see to it that they wind up dead."

She looked at him, frowning. "What do you mean? I had no weapon back there. I have none now."

Cimarron lowered his head and began to trace a pattern

in the dust with his index finger. "You see this spot?" He looked at her, and when she nodded, he said, "This here is where we are right now. This"—he drew a winding line—"is the Arkansas River. It meanders along southeast and pretty soon it hits Fort Smith." He made an X in the dust and looked at her again. "You could go to Fort Smith—"

"Like this?" she exclaimed, interrupting him.

He held up both hands again. "Not so fast. Let's take things in order. Now, like I said, you could go to Fort Smith and tell your tale to Marshal Fagan there and he'd issue warrants for the arrest of your husband and his two friends faster'n a hound can tree a coon. Like as not, Fagan's deputies would run those three to ground and bring them back to Fort Smith for trial. You could testify against them."

"But, in the meantime, if they found me—I mean, if my husband did, he'd kill me now for sure. He's got my land. There's no reason to keep me alive any longer."

"Isn't there?"

Sarah met Cimarron's steady gaze, and when the meaning of his question sank in, she shuddered again.

Cimarron said, "This wasn't the first time Quince brought you paying customers, was it?"

Sarah dropped her eyes and shook her head.

"You live far from here?" he asked her.

"Just northwest of Tahlequah," she answered. "About three miles from here."

"I'll take you home. You'll put on some clothes. You have a horse there?"

"Yes."

"Once you're dressed, you'll get on your horse and head for Fort Smith."

"What if they're there?"

"Well, I guess we'll have to meet that problem when it pops up, won't we?"

"I'm afraid."

"No doubt you are. But it appears to me that you don't have a whole lot of choice in the matter."

"No, I guess I really don't. Now that I'm free of Quince— But to go back there and find him there—"

"I'll be riding right beside you."

Sarah met Cimarron's gaze. "I'll do it," she said. And then, frowning again, she asked, "Can I really trust you?"

"You can try trusting me. You might be lucky and find I'm trustable."

Sarah started to rise. As she did so, the blanket slipped down over one shoulder and Cimarron's eyes dropped to her suddenly bared breast, the nipple of which was a darker brown than the rest of her skin.

Hastily Sarah adjusted the blanket and Cimarron turned and went to get his horse. Before he reached it, he heard the sound of riders and, his mind racing, he halted. More than one rider, he thought. Could be anybody. But not a posse. They were coming in from the north. Could be Quince and his friends.

He turned and raced back to Sarah. He ripped the blanket from her body and threw her to the ground.

She screamed as she went down.

Good, Cimarron thought, as he quickly removed his gun belt, dropped it, and threw himself down upon the startled Sarah.

"Don't," she screamed as he cupped her breasts in his hands and pressed his mouth on hers, holding it there, pressing down hard so that she could neither speak nor move her head.

As she clawed at his back, he released her breast and shoved his hand down to fumble with the buttons on his pants.

She hit him on the side of his head with her small fist and he let out a yelp.

"There she is," he heard a man shout, and then three riders were coming through the trees toward them.

Feigning surprise, Cimarron stumbled to his feet, fingers still fumbling with the buttons on his pants.

"Grab the bitch, Ross," one of the three riders shouted, and one of the men leaped from his saddle and came running toward Cimarron and Sarah, who was getting to her feet, her eyes darting in every direction, seemingly too frightened to flee.

The man named Ross grabbed her by the arm. "Got her, Quince," he bellowed happily.

Quince got down from his horse and strode over to where Cimarron was buttoning his pants. "You," he barked. "What you doing with my wife?"

"I didn't know she was your wife, mister," Cimarron said.

"You can see what he was *trying* to do just as plain as

day," the man who was still mounted declared, and guffawed. "But he never so much as got it out and into action!"

"She costs five dollars, mister," Quince told Cimarron.

"I just didn't know the lady was a workingwoman," Cimarron declared.

"Well, you know it now," Quince snapped. "Ross, you and Jansen get her up on one of your horses. We're going back."

"To finish what we started?" Ross asked Quince.

"You started and you finished. Unless you got five more dollars and the inclination, it's Jansen's go-round."

"I've got five dollars," Cimarron lied, and pretended not to see the anguished look Sarah, still gripped tightly by Ross, gave him.

Quince studied Cimarron through narrowed eyes. "For you the price just went up. To ten dollars. On account of you were trying to get it for free."

Cimarron shrugged. "I figure she might be worth ten dollars. But I'd be much obliged if one of you would hold her arms and the other her legs while she and me have at it. She like to have clawed me raw a while ago."

"Come on," Ross said, and went to his horse.

When Cimarron had retrieved his blanket and strapped on his gun belt, he rode out beside Quince.

Ahead of him rode Ross, Sarah mounted behind him. Next to Ross rode Jansen, his eyes on Sarah.

"If she tries to run again," Quince yelled to the pair, "shoot her in the leg! That ought to slow her down some." He turned to Cimarron. "Don't really know why she took it into her head to run. These squaws dote on it. They're glad to do it night or day." He scratched his head. "Maybe she was mad because I didn't split the fees with her."

Cimarron rode on in silence, his eyes on the gentle curve of Sarah's bare spine and the voluptuous spread of her buttocks.

8

As they rode northwest and deeper into Cherokee Nation, they passed an occasional farmhouse, and if the Cherokees working in their fields were surprised to see a naked Indian woman riding with four white men, they gave no sign.

In less than an hour, they halted in front of a one-story log house that had a pole roof covered with sod. In places, multicolored wild flowers sprouted from the sod. There was a privy some distance from the house on a raised piece of ground and to the left of the house was a small corral that contained two horses. Cattle grazed in a distant meadow and knee-high corn sprouted in a tilled field to the right of the house. Between the house and the meadow was a windmill that screeched noisily, its gears and bearings crying out their need for grease. Bunches of tansy hung in the door and windows of the house to repel flies and ants.

"Ross," Quince called out as he dismounted, "you take the bitch inside. Jansen, you turn our horses into the corral."

As Jansen gathered the horses, Ross led Sarah, who was vainly struggling to free herself from him, into the house, a grin on his face and a lusty light in his eyes.

Cimarron turned his horse over to Jansen and followed Quince inside the house. He found himself in a dim parlor which had a woven straw rug on the floor and was filled with heavy chairs and a sofa, all of them decorated with immaculate antimacassars. Beyond the parlor was the dining room, which contained a table and six chairs, all of them claw-footed.

"Take her into the bedroom," Quince ordered Ross. "You know where it is."

When Ross, dragging Sarah behind him, had gone through the dining room and disappeared, Cimarron said, "Seems like ten dollars ought to put me first in line."

"It don't," Quince muttered. "Jansen's first, then Ross, if he comes up with another five dollars. *Then* you."

"I wouldn't mind watching while I wait," Cimarron said almost laconically. "That is, if you don't charge extra to see the show and Jansen's not a modest man."

"Come on," Quince said gruffly, and Cimarron followed him through the dining room and into the bedroom, where he found Sarah lying in the middle of a brass bed with Ross, who was still grinning standing over her.

"Tie her ankles to the foot of the bed," Quince said to Ross, and Ross left the room, returning a few minutes later with a grass lariat that he used to lash Sarah's ankles to the foot of the bed.

"Her wrists," Quince said, and Ross cut a length of the lariat and used it to bind Sarah's hands to the brass uprights at the head of the bed.

She lay there, eyes closed, biting her lower lip.

Jansen came into the room.

"She's all ready to mount," Quince told him.

Jansen unbuckled his gun belt and tossed it into a chair. Less than a minute later, his trousers and grimy longjohns were around his ankles and he was climbing onto the bed.

Cimarron backed up until Quince was standing just ahead of him and to the right. Ross, who was still standing at the side of the bed, stripped off his gun belt. After draping it over the head of the bed, he began to unbutton his trousers.

"Don't move," Cimarron barked drawing his Colt. "I don't want to use this gun, but I will if any of you so much as twitch."

"What the hell . . ." bellowed Ross, staring at Cimarron.

"You're clearing out of here, all of you," Cimarron said.

"This is my house, goddammit," Quince yelled, his eyes on the gun in Cimarron's hand.

"You too, Quince," Cimarron said.

Jansen climbed off the bed, to stand beside Ross.

"Let's all of us move out now," Cimarron said steadily. "March on out, one by one. I'll be right behind you. You first, Ross."

Ross took a step toward the door and then dived for his gunbelt which was draped over the bed's headboard. He came up with his six-gun in his hand and Cimarron shot him, the bullet striking him in the chest, its impact backing Ross up until he hit the wall behind him.

Quince whirled, his hand on the butt of his gun.

"Don't draw," Cimarron told him, leveling his gun at the man's midsection.

But Quince did.

Cimarron's first bullet took him in his right arm. Cimarron's second shot shattered his skull, just above his left ear.

As Ross slid down the wall and hit the floor, Jansen grabbed for his gun. Cimarron let him unholster it, and then, as Jansen fired at him, Cimarron dodged to the side and squeezed off a shot that tore into Jansen's right arm.

Jansen's finger convulsed on the trigger of his revolver and it went off, the bullet slamming into the plank floor. The gun fell to the floor.

Cimarron stood his ground, his finger tight on the trigger of his .45. But he did not fire again. There was no need to do so. Jansen, blood seeping from his right arm, which he was clutching with his left hand, shuffled backward away from Cimarron.

Cimarron stepped cautiously forward and turned Quince over with the toe of his boot. The man, he saw, was dead. Ross was dying.

Ross tried to speak as he sat on the floor, his back against the wall, his legs twisted under him. Blood frothed from between his lips. He raised a trembling hand toward Cimarron.

"You're lung-shot," Cimarron told him coldly. "You got a few more minutes maybe. Maybe not."

Ross looked down at his chest and then up at Cimarron before listing to one side and crumpling to the floor.

Cimarron, holding his gun on Jansen, used his free left hand to untie Sarah's ankles. When he had freed them, he untied her wrists.

"You killed them," she whispered, a shocked expression on her face.

"Two out of three."

"I wanted them dead—all of them," she said, still whispering. "But now I—"

"Now you're not so sure, is that it?"

Sarah looked down at the two bodies littering the floor of the bedroom.

Jansen, still clutching his bleeding arm, said, "Listen, mister, I'll go. I'll go and never come back. Don't shoot me no more."

"Get up, Sarah," Cimarron said. "Tie his hands to the foot of the bed. Then tie his ankles together. Tight!"

Wordlessly Sarah did as she had been told, using the lengths of lariat with which she had been bound to the bed.

"I got to get to a doctor," Jansen protested. "I'm losing a lot of blood. At least let me pull up my pants!"

Cimarron remained silent, his gun aimed at Jansen as Sarah bound the man's wrists and ankles. When Jansen's hands were tied tightly to the foot of the bed, Cimarron holstered his gun and said to Sarah, "Quince and his friends won't be causing you any more trouble. Now it's time you were getting dressed. You've got some riding to do."

"I do?"

Cimarron nodded. "You're going to ride into Tahlequah. Get one of the Cherokee Light Horse to ride out here with you. Show him what happened. Tell him why it happened."

"But the Light Horse have no jurisdiction over white men," Sarah protested.

Cimarron held up a hand. "Hear me out. Get the Light Horseman to ride to Fort Smith. Have him get Marshal Fagan to swear out a warrant for Jansen's arrest on a charge of attempted rape. Have him send a deputy marshal out here to pick up Jansen.

"You'll have to ride into Fort Smith to testify at his trial. They'll put you up there. And one more thing."

When Cimarron hesitated, Sarah asked, "What else do I have to do?"

"Did you know any of the other men Quince brought around here—where any of them might be found?"

Sarah lowered her eyes. She pulled the coverlet from the bed and wrapped it around her. Softly she said, "There was one I knew—he's a Cherokee. He's a lawyer in Tahlequah."

"Tell the Light Horseman to have Marshal Fagan swear out a warrant for him, too. For rape."

"Who shall I say killed Ross and my husband and wounded Jansen?"

"Say you don't know the man who did it. That's true. You don't know me. Just tell the marshal how we met and then about what I did and why I did it."

"Mister," Jansen said to Cimarron, blinking up at him, "you just can't leave me here tied up like this and maybe on my way to bleeding to death. It could take her days to do all you told her to do."

"Most likely," Cimarron agreed. "But you'll keep. You don't, it's not that much of a matter." He turned to Sarah. "I'll be on my way now."

She nodded, and then, as she stepped over Quince's body, she lost her footing and stumbled against Cimarron. The blanket fell away from her body.

He caught her and was about to release her again when, to his surprise, she put her arms around him and placed her cheek against his chest. He let his hands remain where they were.

"When you seized me," Sarah said, "I thought you had been lying to me all along about wanting to help me."

"You thought I was one more of their ilk," Cimarron said.

"Yes, I did."

"I wasn't. I'm not. But I wanted them to think I was until the time was right to do for them."

"I know now you're not at all like them." Sarah looked up at him. "But you have to understand my position. I was a virgin before Quince forced me to marry him. With him, it was terrible. Not just the first time, although that was awful because he didn't care how much he hurt me. Every time with him—it was like being attacked by an animal. And then, when he started bringing men to me—none of them cared about me or my feelings or my desires. They just used me as if I were a—a *thing!*"

"You've had yourself a bad time, no doubt about it. But you're young, not to mention pretty. You've got time."

"Time?"

"Time to find out that all men aren't like Quince and

the others he brought here. Some men, they can be gentle with a woman. They can care. Be tender."

"Are you one of those men?"

He kissed her gently, and although she instinctively started to pull away from him, as his lips remained on hers she drew closer to him and opened her mouth.

His tongue slid between her teeth, and as it did, her arms tightened on his body. He moved his tongue about, running his hands lightly up and down her back, along her buttocks, wishing he had no calluses, hoping she would understand that his rough touch was due only to the hard work that had hardened his hands.

She began to suck on his tongue and he felt himself beginning to stiffen. Then she suddenly released him and stepped back.

"I guess I shouldn't have done that," he said softly. "Not after all you've been through."

"It's true," she said, and raised one hand and placed her palm against his scarred cheek. "You are a gentle man."

"When gentleness is called for," he amended, looking down at the two corpses at their feet.

"I'd like to know if it can be nice," she said.

"It can be," he assured her. "It can be a whole lot more than just nice. But maybe you'd better wait a spell. It's so soon after . . ." He gestured, and she looked down at the two dead men.

"I may never meet another man like you," she said, and withdrew her hand from his face.

"Odds are you will. Just take your time. Pick and choose. You're free to do that now."

She looked up at him. "I am. And I choose you."

Cimarron hesitated, a fiery longing rising within him. This woman—this little more than a young girl—he didn't want to hurt her. He had to leave. He would never see her again.

He told her his thoughts.

"I know all that," she said when he had finished. "But you could leave me a legacy of sorts."

"Beg pardon?"

"The knowledge that what you say is true—about men, I mean. That they can be gentle. That is, can be—what was it you said? 'A whole lot more than nice.' I know I'm shameless."

"You're not. You're still scared is what you are. You

think I might be lying just so I can use you and then ride on out."

"You want me," she said, her hand coming to rest on his hardness.

Cimarron took off his hat and tossed it on the bed. He untied his bandanna and pocketed it, his eyes on Sarah's face, not sure what he was looking for, not sure if he was, by his steady gaze, trying to hold her where she was, to keep her from fleeing from him now that his desire for her was almost overwhelming him.

"Not here," she said, taking his hand. "There's another bedroom next to this one."

He picked up his hat and let her lead him into the adjoining bedroom, where she lay down on the bed and stared up at the ceiling, arms rigid at her sides, lips pressed tightly together.

There was a single window in the room. Cimarron went over to it and shuttered it, dimming the room, turning it shadowy.

He did not speak, nor did Sarah, as he sat down on the edge of the bed and pulled off his boots. He removed his gun belt and then his clothes. He eased himself down beside her, and as he did so, Sarah flinched and closed her eyes.

"I'm not your husband," he whispered to her. "I'm not Jansen or Ross." He cupped her chin in his hand and turned her face toward him. Gently he kissed her lips and then propped himself up on one elbow and looked down at her. Her eyes remained closed. He bent and kissed her breasts, let his tongue lightly touch their nipples. He felt them begin to harden, and when his own hardness accidentally brushed against her, she opened her eyes wide. He kissed her lips, barely brushing them.

She reached up and tentatively pulled his face down toward hers. When their lips met, hers were open and Cimarron slid his tongue into her mouth, moving closer to her, feeling the warmth of her body, running his right hand down between her breasts, along the curve of her navel, and then letting it come to rest between her legs.

Her hands clasped the back of his neck and she eased her body toward him, but he did not move. But his hand did, coming to rest between her legs. He massaged her lightly, feeling the heat of her. Then, as he continued manipulating her, she moaned and spread her legs.

Cimarron eased himself over upon her but he did not enter her. Their lips parted. Their eyes met.

"You're a fine woman," he whispered to her. "Knew it the minute I laid eyes on you." He kissed her cheeks, nibbled her earlobes, feeling himself throbbing hotly between her thighs as he did so.

" 'Oh, young Lochinvar is come out of the west,' " Sarah whispered, tightening her hold on Cimarron. " 'So faithful in love, and so dauntless in war, There never was knight like young Lochinvar.' "

"A poem?"

"It's called 'Lochinvar.' Sir Walter Scott wrote it. We studied his poetry in the seminary. Being here with you, like this, it just came to my mind."

Cimarron murmured, " 'Thy two breasts are like two young roes that are twins, which feed among the lilies.' "

"That's from the bible, isn't it?"

"Song of Solomon."

"Isn't it wrong to quote the bible at a time like this?"

Before Cimarron could answer, Sarah sighed deeply and said, "I think I'm ready. I know I'm ready."

And as Cimarron gently eased into her, he knew she was right. The moistness of her made his entry easy, but he nevertheless was careful not to rush the matter. He continued to ease into her until she suddenly and unexpectedly clasped his buttocks in both of her hands and brought his body down upon her own.

When he felt her thrust upward beneath him, he plunged downward, withdrew partially, and then plunged again.

"Oh," she cried, her fingernails biting into his buttocks. She wrapped her legs around his thighs and he assumed an easy rhythm, holding himself back, mindful of her, wanting to wipe every memory of Quince and the others from her mind.

Suddenly her body was seized by a violent paroxysm and she thrust her loins upward to meet his steady plunging.

Cimarron, responding to her, thrust down as deeply as he could, his arms embracing her body.

She cried out, her head thrown back and her neck arched.

He kissed her neck, her lips, and then, his body seized

by the violence of his passion, which he had until now restrained for her sake, he thrust rapidly several times in quick and eager succession until the world around him exploded and he groaned with relief.

"Never before," she whispered in his ear, her hands caressing his back, her legs still wrapped around his thighs. "I never felt it before. I didn't know I could feel it. It was glorious."

"Depends a lot on the man, honey," he told her. "He has to keep his woman's needs in mind and not just his own."

"I feel like I should thank you," she said, placing her hands on the sides of his face and looking up at him.

"We both have a lot to be thankful for. Each other."

"But not for long."

Cimarron, breathing shallowly and still lying on top of her, felt a wave of sadness wash over him. " 'How fair is thy love, my sister, my spouse; thou hast ravished my heart with one of thine eyes, with one chain of thy neck.' "

"Must you go?"

Cimarron nodded and withdrew from her, to lay back on the bed beside her, his arms clasped behind his head.

She turned on her side and moved close to him, her left arm lying across his chest. "I'll remember you."

"You do that when you next set out to choose. Just be a bit careful about who you pick and you'll be fine."

"Who are you?" she asked.

Cimarron considered the question. Who was he? Her question led to another, far more difficult question: How could a man be defined, identified? Through his work? His ancestry? His abilities? He knew who he was and what he was, but as he tried to form an answer to Sarah's question, he realized that he could not do so. He was a man. That was all. But it was everything—and enough. He was sure that such an answer would not satisfy Sarah.

He said, "I'm called Cimarron."

"Cimarron," she repeated, and glanced at the wound on his thigh. "You've been hurt."

"Not bad, though."

"What happened?"

"Grazed by a bullet."

"And this?" She ran her fingers lightly over the scar on the left side of his face. "How did you get it?"

When he didn't answer her, Sarah said, "I want to know

you, Cimarron. I need to know you. Tell me how you got that scar. Tell me all about yourself."

"I was a boy at the time. We ran some cattle down on the home place. Once, when we were branding our cattle, I didn't tie down one of the calves firm enough and the critter up and started to run. My pa, he was just about to brand the animal, and when it up and run off on me, Pa's red-hot branding iron caught it across the eyes. Blinded the beast, my pa did, all accidental on account of me. Got mad, Pa did. He had him a terrible temper. Well, he swung at me with the branding iron for what I'd done—for what I'd not done right—and the iron, it raked my face." The fingers of his right hand rose and dislodged Sarah's. He ran them along the raised welt on his face.

"Where was your home place?"

"Texas."

"Were you happy there?"

"I made do," Cimarron answered, feeling the pain of the burning brand as it again, in vivid memory, seared the flesh of his face. "My ma was a good woman. Read the bible seemed like night and day to me. Taught me verses."

Impishly: "From the Song of Solomon?"

Cimarron grinned at Sarah. "Nope. She never did mention anything about that particular part. But I happened upon it once, and well, I guess you could say it appealed to me."

Sarah smiled down at him, bent, and kissed his lips. "I think I know why it did."

"Reckon you do at that."

"Do you have any sisters or brothers?"

"Had a sister. Cholera took her when she was but nine. A brother, older than me, he may still be working the home place."

"Your parents—are they living?"

"Nope."

"Then you're as alone as I am."

"That's a fact."

Sarah lay back on the bed. "My father was a good man. He worked hard. He loved me very much. When he died, I thought the world had ended. When Quince came, I knew it had. But then you came."

Cimarron began to feel uneasy. He sat up and swung his legs over the side of the bed. He began to dress.

"Why do you have to go, Cimarron?"

"I'm trailing someone."

"A woman?"

He nodded.

"I was sure of it." After a brief pause, Sarah asked, "Are you in love with her?"

Cimarron laughed. "Nope."

"But you're trailing her."

"Her and her man."

"Why?"

"It's a long story. Let's just say I intend running them both down. I've got a score to settle with them."

"Do they know you're after them?"

"Not likely."

"What if they try to—hurt you, assuming you do find them?"

"*They* might get hurt." Cimarron pulled on his boots and stood up. "I've got to go."

"Wait. Let me dress. I'll put up some food for you to take with you."

"That's real kind of you. Appreciate it."

While Sarah dressed, Cimarron went outside and stood staring out over the land on which cows grazed and corn grew. It was hard to believe, he thought, that here in this apparently peaceful land, lawlessness was rampant. But he knew it was. He knew that death lurked behind every deadfall and hid in the shadows of every hill. He found the thought oddly exhilarating. Knowing that fact kept him alert and, in the process, fully alive. Ready to take risks. Ready to match wits with the world and the dangers that inhabited it.

When Sarah called his name, he turned, to find her standing in the doorway of the house. She beckoned to him, and when he approached her, she said appreciatively, "You cut a mighty fine figure in that outfit of yours."

She was wearing a brown velvet dress trimmed with yellow velvet ribbons. It was full-skirted and high-necked. She had bound her hair into a coil on top of her head and it glistened in the afternoon sunlight. On her feet were buttoned-up patent-leather shoes.

Once inside the house, Sarah led Cimarron to the kitchen, and as he sat at the table watching her, she began to prepare a meal.

She cracked hickory nuts and separated the meats from the shells, after which she placed them in a pot of boiling water on the stove. While the nutmeats boiled, she mashed beans and added diced onions to them, sprinkling the mixture with sage and pepper. Then, after straining the nutmeats through a piece of cheesecloth, she added rice she had boiled and hominy she had cooked, and mashed them.

Then, after adding cornmeal to the bean mixture, she formed patties from it and fried them.

When she placed the food she had prepared before Cimarron and had seated herself across the table from him, he said, "This is the first real home cooking I've tasted in far too long, I can tell you." He forked food into his mouth, chewed, and said, "Just as fine as can be."

Sarah beamed and, pointing to the nutmeat mixture said, "We call this Connuche and this"—she indicated the bean patties—"is Tu Ya."

"Would I be out of line were I to ask for seconds?"

Still beaming, Sarah heaped food on his plate. "You are not out of line, Cimarron. Don't you know that cooking is one area of her life in which a woman hopes to receive compliments such as the ones you've just given me?"

"You do yourself proud in at least one other area of a woman's life I've gotten acquainted with," he said, and winked at her.

"But that area is usually not discussed publicly."

"A shame, I sometimes think." He gave her another wink.

Later, when they had finished their meal and Sarah had cleaned up, she wrapped some boiled beef and some bread in butcher paper, tied it with twine, and gave it to Cimarron. "For the trail," she said.

"You're not taking anything along for yourself?"

"I want to keep my figure, so I eat rather sparingly."

As they left the house, Jansen bellowed from the bedroom. "Let me loose, dammit!"

Cimarron ignored him. "Where's your saddle and gear?" he asked Sarah.

"There's a little shed behind the house. Everything's stored there."

Cimarron left her and, when he had gathered up her gear, went to the corral and saddled one of the two horses, a gelding, which had been in the corral when he arrived at the house.

Sarah watched him from outside the corral, and when he beckoned to her, she entered the corral and led the gelding from it. When Cimarron had joined her and closed the corral gate, she got into the saddle, adjusting her skirt after doing so.

As Cimarron stepped into the saddle, Sarah said, "*Au revoir*, Cimarron."

"I just about manage to get by in English," he told her, "but when it comes to foreign languages, I'm at a loss."

"It's French," she said. "It means 'till we meet again.' "

"*Au revoir*, Sarah."

She moved out on the gelding and Cimarron watched her head south. He was about to turn his horse when she looked back over her shoulder and waved to him. He returned her wave.

"Hey," Jansen yelled from inside the house. "Don't you all leave me here like this!"

Cimarron turned his horse and rode west. By midafternoon he had forded the Grand River and less than an hour later, he had also forded the Verdigris River. He continued riding west, two women on his mind. Sarah Lassiter. And Emma Dorset.

Au revoir.

Would he meet Sarah Lassiter again? he wondered. Emma Dorset?

He hoped he would meet both women again, but for entirely different reasons.

Not long after fording the shallow Arkansas River, he reached the point where the Chisholm Trail cutoff followed the river northward. Muncy's herd would be almost to Dodge City by now, he thought. And here I am crossing my own backtrail. He forded the river and rode on through a region of weathered outcrops and low hills. The sky above him was streaked by the setting sun with red and gold patches of clouds, those in the east puffy, those in the west spread out in long thin lines by a westerly wind. Gradually the gold faded. The red turned pale, and then it too faded as dusk descended.

He rode into a narrow valley that lay between two of the rolling hills and was surprised to find a small mesquite thicket growing there. Most of the trees were young, but one towered, Cimarron estimated, a good thirty feet into the air. Its trunk was thick, at least two feet in diameter, and it reached, he guessed, a good seven or eight feet before forking.

The majestic tree was in bloom and Cimarron could

smell the sweet scent of its yellow flowers brightly visible among its greenish-white petals. Its twigs were covered with sharp thorns. Its pods had not yet begun to form.

Looking at the tree, Cimarron was reminded of his father.

"When the mesquite buds, it's time to put out the tomato plants," he had said year after year.

Cimarron dismounted and led the quarter horse under the tree, where he stripped his gear from it and shook out his saddle blanket, draping it over a low branch of one of the young mesquites to air. The horse was lathered and he pulled up some grass to wipe it down. Then, as the animal got down on the ground and rolled in the low-growing bunch grass, Cimarron took from his saddlebag the package Sarah had given him. He sat down with his back against the tall mesquite and untied it, placing it on the ground beside him. As he ate some of the bread and boiled beef it contained, he surveyed the land around him. The mesquite grew close to the hill rising behind it. That was good, he told himself. Anyone up there on top of that hill behind him would be unlikely to spot him where he was because of the thick branches spreading out above him.

From across the narrow valley where the other hill rose he would also be difficult to spot if he and his horse sheltered for the night between the mesquite and the hill behind it.

He was glad Sarah had given him the food because it meant that he didn't have to light a fire to cook anything he might have been able to bring down on his way.

When he finished eating, he rewrapped and retied the package of food and replaced it in his saddlebag, which lay near the rest of his gear at the foot of the tree. Then he took a long drink from his canteen, which he had filled earlier.

Above him, the stars were appearing in the sky, but the moon was not yet visible. Cimarron stared up at the dark top of the hill opposite him, able to define its sloping crest by the wavering line of stars just above it.

He rose and carried his gear around behind the tree and then went to where his horse was standing grazing. He gripped its mane lightly, spoke to it, and led it around behind the mesquite. He hobbled it close to the base of the hill beyond the tree and then went back and lay down under the tree, his hat and unholstered Colt beside him, his saddle serving him as a pillow. Stretched out on his back, he stared up through the branches of the tree at the stars that winked on and off as the branches stirred in a faint breeze that whispered through them.

You're a long way from your native land, he silently told the towering tree. Like me. Some old southwestern cow must have eaten your seed pod a long time ago and then run off the Chisholm and dropped it down here.

The tree, Cimarron thought, had found a home. A place to grow and flourish. He envied it. It had more than he had had for too long a time.

He closed his eyes, shutting out the stars, aware of the sweetness drifting in the cool night air from the mesquite's bright flowers. Soon he slept.

His horse's nickering woke him. He remained on his back, not moving, listening. The sky was beginning to lighten above him. No star was now visible in it.

Something snarled.

There was a tearing sound.

Cimarron seized his Colt, sat up, and looked around.

He leaped to his feet when he spotted the cougar off to his left. It crouched not more than a dozen yards from where he stood, its forefeet clawing at his saddlebag, which it was dragging away from the mesquite.

The food, Cimarron thought. It's trying to get at the beef and bread.

His thumb eased back the hammer of his Colt.

The cougar, at the sound of the metallic click, laid back its ears and looked up at him. It snarled.

Cimarron eased to the left, intending to get behind the mesquite, putting it between him and the hungry cougar. His movement was a mistake, he realized as the cougar came out of its crouch and sprang at him.

9

Cimarron fired.

His bullet caught the cougar in the shoulder, leaving a bloody trail where it grazed the animal's tawny hide.

He tried to get out of the way of the cougar but the animal was too fast for him. The mesquite might as well have been a world away from him. The speed with which the cougar sprang gave him no time to dodge. The cat came down on him with the full force of its heavy body, knocking him to the ground and sending his Colt flying from his hand.

As he struck the ground with stunning force, the body of the cougar on top of him, he fought desperately to keep the animal's fangs away from his throat. The claws of its front feet raked his chest, tearing his shirt and drawing blood.

Cimarron tried to roll over but could not. He seized the cougar by the throat and squeezed with both hands. A harsh guttural sound came from the cat's throat. Its eyes remained on Cimarron's face as its tail thrashed in the air and its claws continued to mercilessly rake Cimarron's chest.

Cimarron, as the animal tore itself free from his grip, brought up both knees, unbalancing the cougar. He thrust hard again with his knees, and the cat, still savagely clawing, went over his head. He leaped to his feet and was about to retrieve his gun when the animal came at him again. He was able to sidestep it this time and the momentum of its spring carried it beyond Cimarron, who raced to the nearest young mesquite and leaped up. He caught a low-hanging branch and was swinging himself up onto it when it suddenly snapped and he fell to the ground.

Between him and his Colt was the cougar, ears erect now, lips drawn back over gleaming white teeth, eyes blazing as it bellied along the ground toward him, blood oozing from the gash the bullet had left in its flesh.

Cimarron seized the broken branch and, getting quickly to his feet, advanced on the cougar, the branch held high above his head. He brought it down hard on the animal's skull. The cougar howled and slithered backward along the ground, its glowing eyes fastened on Cimarron.

Near the hill beyond the tall mesquite, Cimarron's horse, terrified, snorted loudly and, in a frantic attempt to escape from the instinctively alarming scent of the cougar, fell because of the hobbles on its legs. It screamed.

Cimarron swung the branch a second time, but this time it glanced off the cougar's shoulder as it cringed away from the blow it had seen coming.

Then it leaped into the air, its feet splayed out in front of it. Cimarron leaped to the side. But the cat's claws slashed his right shoulder, tearing his flesh. He made a run for his gun, but the cougar, as if knowing his intention, cut him off from it.

For an instant he held his ground, staring at the cougar, which was crouching not far from where he stood, staring as steadily at him.

The crash of his horse falling for a second time barely registered in Cimarron's consciousness as he wished now that he had built a fire the night before. A burning brand, even a smoldering one, might be enough to drive the cougar away.

He waited, expecting the cat to spring.

It waited as if it were watching for his next move. And then it leaped into the air.

Cimarron, prepared for the move, dodged, and the cat went flying harmlessly past him. Instantly he turned and flung himself on top of the animal. As it thrashed beneath him, he managed to pinion its head by pressing both knees tightly against the animal's neck. Behind him, the animals hindquarters surged as the animal attempted to free itself from the headlock.

Cimarron seized the cougar's skull and, using most of his fingers, quickly gouged out both of the animal's eyes.

One fell to the ground. The other hung from its socket by a thread.

The cougar roared its agony and thrashed even more violently, managing to free itself from Cimarron as it did so.

Cimarron fell backward, but he was on his feet almost immediately and ran, his eyes on his Colt. Behind him the cougar screamed and leaped aimlessly, falling to the ground, then rising and careening blindly into a mesquite tree.

Cimarron scooped up his Colt, skidded to a halt, turned, and was about to fire when a new sound joined that of the cougar's agonized screaming.

The sharp clear *crack* of a rifle shot.

The cougar leaped high into the air and then fell heavily to the ground, where it lay thrashing about in the bunch grass. It took several minutes for the animal to die, during which Cimarron scanned the hill from which he believed the rifle shot had come. He saw no one.

When he was sure the cougar was dead, he ran to the tall mesquite, strapped on his gun belt, holstered his Colt, and carried his gear, which lay beneath the tree, over to his stumbling horse.

It took him a while to quiet the animal and remove the hobbles, time he regretted losing.

There was no way of knowing who had fired the shot that had killed the cougar. But Cimarron was not interested in finding out who had done it. Not here. Not in the middle of Cherokee Nation, where a man might have a motive for such an act that was not a benign one. Working as rapidly as he could without alarming his horse, Cimarron got his saddle and bridle in place. Not taking time to tie his bedroll in place or even to fold his blanket, he stepped into the saddle, the bedroll and blanket under his left arm. He turned the horse, intending to head out of the valley.

Directly in front of him was a rider. The man was coming toward him at an easy canter, leading a laden packhorse, a revolver in his left hand, with which he also gripped his reins.

Cimarron halted his horse, his shirt in shreds, his chest and shoulder bleeding.

He looked at the gun held apparently casually in the rider's hand and recognized it as an Adams 1869 double-action center-fire .45. "You won't be needing that," he said. "You dropped the cat with your first shot. It was you who did it, wasn't it?"

The rider nodded and shoved his revolver into the holster he wore on the right side of his gun belt, butt forward. "It's not the first painter I've shot and it probably won't be the last. You took a chance trying to gouge out its eyes like you did."

"Didn't try. Did it."

The rider was a short and slender man. As he sat his horse and stared at Cimarron with his dark-brown eyes, his head barely cleared that of his horse. His oval face was dark and impassive. There were wrinkles at the corners of his eyes and across his forehead. His straight hair was as black as Cimarron's but a little longer, reaching almost to his narrow shoulders.

On his head he wore a round-crowned stetson with a turkey feather stuck in its band. Over his gray flannel shirt he wore a canvas vest and his black trousers were almost as dusty as his equally black boots.

"You did me a real good turn," Cimarron told the man.

"Well, you'd about finished that painter," the rider responded offhandedly. "Once you blinded him like you did, he wasn't much good for anything."

"He just might have got me, though—accidental like."

"I'd have shot sooner, only you two were too cozied up together for me to take the chance. I might have hit you instead." The man drew a cloth pouch from his vest pocket and proceeded to build a cigarette. "Smoke?" he asked a moment later, holding out his pouch and papers to Cimarron, the cigarette dangling from his lips.

Cimarron shook his head.

The rider pocketed the makings, dismounted, and lit his cigarette. "Saw you ride into the valley last night," he said, blowing smoke through his thin lips.

"Thought I had myself pretty well hid," Cimarron said somewhat ruefully as he too dismounted.

"I like to nest on high ground. A man can see a lot from high up."

"And out here that's important."

The rider nodded his agreement. "My name's Abner Hawk. Actually it's Abner Big Hawk, but some of us Cherokee folk like to pretend we're fully assimilated into the white culture, so I generally drop the 'Big' from my name. I'm a Light Horseman."

"The law, are you? You hunting somebody out here?"

"I have been now for the past four days and nights. A Negro—a former Cherokee slave. His name's Small June. He robbed and killed a merchant in Tahlequah. Have you seen his sign by any chance?"

Cimarron shook his head, thinking that if Big Hawk was four days out of Tahlequah, he was not likely to have heard about him having broken out of jail back in Fort Smith. He looked down at the long gashes on his chest and those on his shoulder.

"Big Hawk—it's all right if I call you that?"

"Sure, it's fine with me. Now what would you have me call you?"

Cimarron hesitated a moment before answering, "Cimarron'll do."

"What were you about to ask me, Cimarron?" Big Hawk sucked on his cigarette and blew smoke into the air.

"I'm wondering, would you happen to have an ax in that pack on your horse?"

"I have one."

"Something I might boil up some water in?"

"That too. A small iron pot. What do you have in mind to do with them?"

"Well, I thought I'd best be about seeing to these wounds of mine. If you'll loan me your ax and pot, why, I'll be obliged to you."

Big Hawk snubbed out his cigarette using his thumb and index finger. Later when he had taken the long-handled ax and pot from his pack and given them to Cimarron, Cimarron, despite the sharp pains in his chest and shoulder, proceeded to chop lengths from one of the tall mesquite's roots that ran along the surface of the ground for a short distance. Then, after starting a fire, he filled the small pot with water from his canteen and set it on the stones he had placed in the fire. While he waited for the water to boil, he used Big Hawk's ax to chop the pieces of mesquite root into small sections. Then he sliced the bark from them.

Once the water was boiling, he dropped the root bark into the water and then took off his buckskin jacket and ripped the remnants of his shirt from his body.

Big Hawk, hunkered down on the opposite side of the fire, solemnly watched him. "You plan to eat that?" he asked finally, pointing to the brew Cimarron was stirring with a branch he had broken from one of the mesquite trees.

"Nope. Although some there are who claim it can be consumed. But I got more important things in mind for that bark."

When the bark had softened and become pulpy pieces, Cimarron fished them out of the pot and dropped them on the grass. Then he tossed the remains of his shirt into the still-boiling water and stirred them with the branch.

"Got to let the bark cool some," he told Big Hawk, "before I can plaster it on myself, else I'm liable to fry my hide instead of curing it."

A few minutes later, he used the branch to remove the strips of cloth from the boiling water. These too he placed on the grass. Once they had cooled, he wrung them out and then picked up pieces of the root bark and gently applied them to his flesh where it had been ripped open by the cougar. He bound the bark in place using strips of his shirt, and then put his jacket back on.

"I'll soon be as good as new, or almost," he said when he had finished tying the dressings in place.

"Where'd you learn to do that?" Big Hawk asked him.

"From an Indian who was a friend of mine down in Texas." He glanced at the dead cougar. "A man might make a meal off of that animal."

Without a word, Big Hawk rose and went over to the cougar. Cimarron watched him unsheath a knife and proceed to skin and butcher the animal. When Big Hawk returned, carrying several bloody pieces of meat, he handed two of them to Cimarron. Then, after breaking off a mesquite branch, he speared the large piece he had kept for himself, and after removing the pot from the stones, he began to roast the meat.

Cimarron followed his example, and as the sun eased up into the morning sky, the two men ate in silence.

"You been the law long?" Cimarron asked when both men had finished their breakfast.

"A number of years," Big Hawk answered.

"You like what you do?"

Cimarron thought he caught a glint in Big Hawk's eyes as the man replied, "Sure do. It beats being a shopkeeper or a farmer. Now, I've got nothing against farmers or shopkeepers, you understand. But I'm a man who likes to be on the move. More than that, I like life when it has an edge to it like a good blade."

"Know what you mean."

"Thought you might. You don't strike me as a man who'd stand still long enough to grow a cash crop or empty out his store's inventory."

Cimarron sensed that Big Hawk was prodding him in an indirect manner. Perhaps it was the man's way, he speculated. Lawmen, he reminded himself, tended to be questioners, a little on the suspicious side. They tended to think that every man was guilty of something until they had proved him innocent; the trick, for them, was to find out just exactly what it was that each man they met was guilty *of*.

"You strike me," Big Hawk said, "as a man who'd make a good soldier or an even better outlaw."

Cimarron wiped his lips with the back of his hand and shifted his position slightly so that he was once again sitting in the shade of a mesquite. "Soldier? Outlaw? Me?"

"Soldiers fight," Big Hawk said, "and never mind the odds. They have discipline. Good ones don't run from a fight, no matter what the odds. And a cougar against a lone man's mighty hard odds. Now, an outlaw, on the other hand, he's out to get what he wants and he's determined to stay alive in the getting. You're headed somewhere. Along comes a cougar. You don't let him stop you from going wherever it is you're going. An outlaw's a lot like a soldier in some ways, when you come to think about it."

"I was never a soldier," Cimarron said, deliberately taunting Big Hawk by making no reference to outlaws.

Big Hawk didn't rise to the bait. He did say, "I might have turned into an outlaw instead of a Light Horseman."

Cimarron recognized the bait and obligingly took it. "That so?" he prompted.

"You know anything about my people?"

"Know they came from the East."

Big Hawk's eyes flashed fire. "They didn't come. They were driven! Soldiers came in 1838 and drove most of my people off their farms and out of their homes in Georgia and Tennessee at gunpoint. They were allowed to take with them only what belongings they could catch up after they'd been given a few minutes' notice to move out. Before some of them had gone out of sight of their homes, whites came and looted them of everything worth anything that they could lay their dirty hands on."

"Heard tell of that," Cimarron said soberly. "It was General Winfield Scott who ran that show, wasn't it?"

"Him and his regulars plus some militia men he rounded up. Families were separated from members who weren't home when Scott and his men came down on them. They just herded everybody—I mean men, women, and children—into stockades and then later they marched them west under military guard.

"Most went on foot," Big Hawk continued bitterly. "A few rode horses. Some—not many—in wagons. Hundreds died on that march. *Hundreds!* It took my people six months to get out here, and most of the marching was done in the winter. When they arrived here, there were only about fourteen thousand of them left alive. They'd died on the trail from the bitter cold because they didn't have enough clothes or blankets. They died from dysentery and whooping cough—and the rigors of the trail."

"The Trail of Tears," Cimarron said, his voice somber.

Big Hawk's eyes narrowed. "You know more about the removal than you let on to me."

"It just don't do, seems to me, to tell all a man knows. Might make him seem to think himself a superior specimen of humanity. Or a fool."

"Some never came out here," Big Hawk said. "You know about them?"

Cimarron nodded. "They fought back and then they ran off and hid in North Carolina. They're still there."

"If I'd been there then," Big Hawk said, his hands tightening into fists, "I'd have fought the goddamn soldiers!"

"That's what you meant about you might have turned into an outlaw?"

"That's exactly what I meant."

"Well, a man never does know just what he might do. Not until he finds himself face to face with a situation, he doesn't. But you must have been not much more than a baby when your people were forced out of their homes back East."

"I hadn't even been born yet. But my mother and father used to tell me about the removal. My mother talked of the courage of our people. Even the old ones—old women carrying bundles and marching until they dropped dead.

Others, knowing they were dying, climbed out of wagons, to die beside the trail so that someone else, someone less sick, could take their places—and have a chance to live.

"My father—he was hard-living and, at the end, a harder-dying man—he told me all about the fighters. He admired them and he wanted to be one of them at the time; and he almost was, but my mother stopped him. Oh, not by any words. She doesn't talk a whole lot, my mother. What she did, that day, she grabbed his hand while the soldiers were yelling at her and my father to move out or they'd shoot them down where they stood, and she placed it on her belly and my father always said there was nothing else he could do after she did that. So he let himself be taken to the stockade and then he marched with the Nation. At times, my mother told me, he carried her. Her and me in her."

"The way I see it," Cimarron said, "you figure you can do more for your people by being a Light Horseman than an outlaw."

"I never put it to myself that way," Big Hawk said, frowning.

"It's there in your words. Or just behind them."

"It is, I guess," Big Hawk said, still frowning. Then, giving Cimarron an almost ingenuous smile, he said, "The outlaws are still back there in North Carolina, only they aren't outlaws anymore. They're law-abiding United States citizens now."

"A man can't expect to go through life without changing some along the way." Cimarron picked up the long-handled ax and went over to the big mesquite, where he proceeded to chop free a small section of one of the tree's roots. After removing the root's bark, he placed it on a stone, and then, using another stone, he began to pulverize the bark.

Big Hawk, some distance away, poured water from the iron pot to douse the fire and then headed for his pack-horse with the pot in his hand. "You through with the ax?" he called out to Cimarron.

"I am," Cimarron called back. "Just wanted to pulverize some bark to put on my hide once I start to heal up." He pocketed the bark he had pulverized and then picked up the ax, intending to take it to Big Hawk. He had taken only four steps when a rifle shot rang out in the stillness, causing sparrows that had settled in the mesquite thicket to fly up and away.

Cimarron saw the dirt shoot up at Big Hawk's feet. As Big Hawk dropped down behind his packhorse, Cimarron looked up at the hill on the far side of the little valley and saw the figure of a man skylined on its crest.

He ran back to his horse, pulled his rifle from the scabbard, and then ran as fast as he could along the flank of the hill behind the mesquite thicket, keeping the upper branches of the trees between him and the rifleman on the opposite hill.

He loped down the slope of the hill beyond where the mesquite thicket ended and then raced across the narrow valley and up the side of the other hill. When he reached its crest, he started down its opposite side. Halfway down the hill, he turned to the left and ran along the side of the hill, his eyes on the outlined figure in the distance ahead of and above him.

But before he reached the point below the man that he had been heading for, another shot rang out and the man started down the hill. In seconds, he was out of sight.

Cimarron ran on and then turned left again and made for the hill's crest. Just before he reached it, he bellied down on the ground and began to crawl toward it. Taking off his hat when he was near the top of the hill, he eased himself up and looked down into the valley.

Big Hawk's packhorse was there. Big Hawk still crouched behind the animal. And, firing as he went, the man who had tried to kill Big Hawk was zigzagging down the hillside toward his prey.

Big Hawk's head appeared above his horse, his rifle in his hands. He fired. The man on the hill dropped to one knee behind an outcrop and returned the fire. Big Hawk's head disappeared behind his packhorse.

Cimarron raised his gun—and hesitated. *He doesn't know I've got him in my sight,* he thought. He was certain he could drop the man with a single shot. Either kill or wound him. But backshooting—the situation bothered him.

"Drop it," he yelled to the man at the top of his voice. "We got you in a crossfire!"

The man didn't drop his rifle. Instead, he eased around behind the outcrop and sent a shot in Cimarron's direction.

Big Hawk fired again.

Then . . . silence.

It was finally broken by Cimarron's next shot, which sent splinters flying from the rocky outcrop.

The man left its shelter and bolted down the hill, running fast, heading for the mesquite thicket. When he reached it, he took up a position behind the tall mesquite. Big Hawk turned his packhorse to maintain the only shelter available to him.

Cimarron leaped to his feet and ran back the way he had come. Once across the valley, he raced up and then down the other hill and along it until he reached the point where he had earlier crested it. He climbed the hill and cautiously peered over its crest. Below him, the rifleman was on his right, Big Hawk on his left.

He raised his gun, but before he could fire, the rifleman did. Big Hawk's packhorse fell dead at the Light Horseman's feet. Big Hawk dropped flat on the ground behind the body of his horse.

The rifleman darted forward from tree to tree, shortening the distance between himself and his quarry.

Big Hawk fired at the man. His bullet embedded itself in one of the young mesquites behind which the man had taken temporary cover.

Cimarron again found himself aiming at the man's back. He backtrailed along the hill and then went over it and down into the mesquite thicket, moving cautiously forward, avoiding fallen branches as he went in order to make no sound.

The rifleman ahead of him fired at Big Hawk again.

Big Hawk's rifle flew from his hands as he toppled backward.

The rifleman ran forward and stood over the fallen Light Horseman, who was clutching his left arm where his attacker's bullet had grazed him.

"Throw your sidearm over here," the rifleman ordered, and Big Hawk did.

"I knew they'd send a lawman after me," the man said to Big Hawk. "Too bad, because you are about to be one real dead Indian." He raised his rifle, sighting down its barrel at Big Hawk.

"You fire and you're dead too," Cimarron yelled, stepping out from behind the tree where he had taken cover and slowly advancing on the man he now could see was a black man.

"Don't shoot," the man yelled, and dropped his rifle.

Cimarron continued to advance and then he circled around so that he was facing the black man.

"That's Small June," Big Hawk told Cimarron as he got to his feet, still clutching his bleeding arm. "The man I was trailing."

"Well, this is the beginning of the end of June's trail," Cimarron said.

"Maybe so," June said, grinning. "You gentlemen oughtn't've fired before. Men on the run like me, we hear shooting, we come investigating. And look what we find! A little Indian policeman and a great big white man in cahoots together."

"You got any rope you can tie him up with?" Cimarron asked Big Hawk.

Wordlessly Big Hawk bent and began to untie the pack his dead horse had been carrying.

"Turn around," Cimarron told the black man. "Put your hands behind you."

The black man turned and placed his hands behind his back, crossing his wrists, just above his buttocks.

As Big Hawk approached him, a coil of rope in his hands, the man suddenly turned, gave Big Hawk a shove, and sent the Indian, arms flailing, flying backward, to fall against Cimarron.

Cimarron's .45 was knocked from his hands as Big Hawk's body struck him. He immediately retrieved his gun, but June had seized Big Hawk in both hands, and before Cimarron could fire, he sent the Indian hurtling into Cimarron again. Cimarron lost his .45.

June bent to pick up his own rifle, but before he could straighten up again, Cimarron bent down and seized the long-handled ax that was lying on the ground much closer to him than his .45.

He straightened and, gripping the ax handle tightly in both hands, swung it high above his head and then brought it swiftly down, to split June's skull, which was coming up as if intending to meet the deadly implement in Cimarron's hands.

With blood and brains spewing from his shattered skull, June dropped facedown on the ground at Cimarron's feet.

Cimarron released his hold on the ax handle, leaving it embedded in June's head.

"Goddamn," exclaimed Big Hawk from where he lay still sprawled on the ground. "If you aren't the fastest-moving man I have ever met in my entire life!"

Cimarron, staring down at June, said, "There're times when it pays a man to move fast."

"And this, my good friend, Cimarron, was most certainly one of them," Big Hawk said, getting to his feet. He walked over to Cimarron and held out his hand. "You sure do manage to even things up, don't you?"

As Cimarron shook Big Hawk's hand, he said, "You made sure that cougar didn't get a taste of me. And I was lucky enough to make sure that June's bullets didn't get a taste of either one of us."

"Hell-fire and damnation," Big Hawk bellowed. "Lucky, my ass! It wasn't any luck. It was just coolheadedness on your part that kept the two of us alive."

"Have it your way." Cimarron looked away from June's corpse and into Big Hawk's eyes. "Now let's get that little iron pot of yours and that ax—June won't mind if we take it out of him—and let's boil up a little more bark and put a poultice on your arm. The bullet still in it?"

"It went through. It took a little bit of me with it when it did."

After boiling some mesquite root bark and applying it as a dressing to Big Hawk's wounded arm, Cimarron said, "It's time I was riding out."

"And I'll be moseying on back to Tahlequah," Big Hawk said. "Me and Small June. I'll have to lay him over the rump of my horse. Guess I'll have to leave my pack here. Maybe one day I'll get to come back for it. We Light Horsemen travel around more than a mite."

Cimarron grinned.

"You need a shirt," Big Hawk said to him. "Small June's got no more need of the one he's got. It might fit you, Cimarron, though June's a bit bigger than you around the middle."

"Rob the dead?" Cimarron asked.

Big Hawk shook his head in mock dismay. "Will you listen to the man? Will you, now? He doesn't hesitate to halve a man's skull, but he scruples when it comes to divesting that same man of his shirt."

Cimarron grinned again and bent to strip the brown

shirt from June's corpse. He put it on under his buckskin jacket, buttoned it, and said, "Not a bad fit."

Big Hawk held out his hand.

The two men shook hands and then Cimarron went to get his horse. He remade his bedroll and tied it behind his saddle, reloaded June's Winchester, then stepped into the saddle. He rode back to where Big Hawk was lifting June and tossing him over his horse's rump.

"*Adiós,*" he said to the Light Horseman.

"I'll remember you, Cimarron," Big Hawk said. "That's something easily done. You're the sort of man who, once met, is hard to forget."

Cimarron smiled and rode out, glancing down as he passed the ax lying on the ground that was stained with June's blood and brains; then he looked up again and spurred his horse, thinking of Emma Dorset . . . and the bogus Reverend Philip Griffin.

10

Cimarron rode out of the narrow valley and headed west. He scanned the high plains country through which he rode, but he saw no sign of any other riders.

By midafternoon he had reached the Arkansas River and he rode west along its southern bank, the wide expanse of the Santa Fe Trail paralleling his course on the opposite side of the river.

The sun sent down hammers of heat and sweat glistened on his face. The stubble growing on his cheeks and chin itched, and he idly scratched it as he rode along beneath the cloudless sky. Sweat covered his body, and as it oozed beneath the bark dressings he had applied to his chest and shoulder, he experienced the sharp sting of salt in his wounds.

He crossed a short expanse of gypsum flat, which was matched by an identical one on the far side of the river. In places, selenite crystals lay like a gray carpet beneath his horse's hooves. No grass grew on the barren flat; it had probably been formed, Cimarron speculated, by wind and rain that had eroded the gypsum deposits in the Glass Mountains to the north which had been carried south by the same elements over the years. Here and there on the flat grew scrawny tufts of gypsum surge, which were struggling to survive in the bleak and wind-shifted ground covering.

The quarter horse beneath Cimarron had slowed its pace as it moved across the unstable flat and he let the animal set its own pace as a warm breeze rippled the gypsum and the sun made wavering shadows along its newly formed low ridges, giving it the look of a gently surging dry sea.

Beyond the flat, tall stipa grass grew, bowing in the breeze and gleaming with the sunlight reflecting from the many tiny silver hairs topping each seed-bearing stem.

As Cimarron continued his journey westward, only the fitfully stirring breeze roamed the plain with him. The trail across the river was empty. As was the treeless plain. He saw no game. No birds flew in the sky above him. The monotonous landscape, combined with the heat and the faintly whispering wind, made him drowsy. It was not until he awoke that he realized he had been asleep in the saddle.

The sun, he saw, was now not far above the western horizon. He glanced over his shoulder. There was no one on his backtrail and no one on the Santa Fe Trail.

As he turned around, his eye caught a reddish mound in the distance near the north bank of the river. He kept his eyes on it as he came closer to it.

A horse. Dead.

A roan horse.

Emma Dorset, he remembered, had been riding a roan when he'd met her!

He turned his horse to the right and the animal splashed through the river, and when it came out on the far bank, Cimarron dismounted and went over to the horse. It had been stripped of all its gear. He examined it. The animal bore no wounds. Its body was intact. Ridden to death, he thought.

Emma's mount? He couldn't be certain. He hadn't paid much attention to the horse she had been riding when they met, except to note its color. And there were, he thought, countless roan horses in the West.

He sat on his heels, staring at the horse. If it had been Emma Dorset's horse, he thought, its death meant that she was now on foot. He rose and looked up the trail.

He saw no one on it.

He got back into the saddle and rode west along the trail, spurring his horse into a gallop, hoping that the dead horse had been Emma's and wondering if she would survive on foot long enough to reach Bent's Fort and achieve what he believed to be her planned rendezvous with Griffin.

He frowned, thinking about the fact that the horse's saddle and other gear had been taken from it. Not by Emma, he reasoned. He doubted that she would have been able to carry such a heavy load—at least not far—and he had not found it abandoned along the trail—at least not yet.

He slowed his horse when he spotted the wagon in the distance. It wasn't moving. The two oxen that had been pulling it lay on the ground to the left of the wagon.

Cimarron reined in his horse and sat his saddle, staring at the wagon. And then, after scanning the country again on both sides of the river, he moved forward, his right hand resting on the butt of his .45.

When he reached the wagon, he saw that the team that had been pulling it had been shot to death. One of the oxen had been butchered.

In front of the wagon was a naked man whom Cimarron had not been able to see from his backtrail because the man had been hidden from sight by the bulky wagon.

Cimarron quickly dismounted and hurried over to the man, whose feet and hands had been tied with strips of rawhide to wooden pins that had been pounded into the ground. The man's body, supported by his hands and feet, was sharply arched over a small fire that was burning beneath his back.

Cimarron saw that he was still alive, although barely, and his body was quivering in his efforts to keep himself from falling down upon the flames that were flickering below his painfully arched body.

Cimarron rammed a boot under the man and kicked the fire away. Then, walking around the man, he stamped it out.

With a barely audible groan, the man's body slumped to the ground and then shuddered spasmodically as his burned flesh made contact with it.

Cimarron kicked the four pins to which the man was bound out of the ground and knelt down beside him. He avoided looking at the man's bloody groin, from which the organs had been severed and thrown on the ground beside him.

The man's eyelids flickered, his eyes opened, and he stared dully up at Cimarron. "They've done me in," he said in such a low tone that Cimarron had to bend down toward him to catch his words.

"Who?"

"Kiowa," the man murmured.

Cimarron got his canteen and held it to the man's lips.

After the man had drunk, he tried to turn on his side but couldn't manage the maneuver. Cimarron helped him to do so. When the man was lying on his stomach, he whispered, ". . . took her."

"You had a woman with you?"

"She—walking. Horse died."

Cimarron's body stiffened as excitement coursed through him. "Her name—did she tell you her name?"

"Dor—Dorset."

"Which way did the Indians go when they left here?"

The man's lips moved but he could not speak.

"West?" Cimarron asked. "South?"

The man moved his head slowly from side to side. His lips opened again. "Up the trail," he managed to murmur, before his eyes closed.

Cimarron knelt helplessly beside the man who was obviously dying. It's not the burns, he thought. That's not what's killing him. It's the mutilation—all the blood he's lost.

He thought of Emma Dorset. Since the Indians hadn't killed her, he knew they must have other plans for her and he thought he knew what those plans were.

"How long ago were the Indians here?" he asked.

"Don't know." The man's eyes suddenly opened wide. "Made me watch while they—they—all of them—had her."

"How many were there?" Cimarron asked tonelessly.

"Four," the man whispered. And died.

Cimarron closed the man's lifeless eyes and then went around to the back of the wagon to see if it contained a shovel. It did. It also contained a saddle, bridle, saddlebags, and bedroll. Cimarron recognized them as having belonged to Emma Dorset.

After burying the victim of the Kiowa, he got back in the saddle and cantered up the trail, scanning the grassless ground ahead of him that had been heavily rutted by wagon wheels. He found an occasional hoof print made by an unshod pony, but most of the ground was too hard packed to register the imprint of a horse's hooves. His own horse, he noted, left almost no sign behind him of his passage along the trail.

When he spotted horse droppings, he got down from his horse and examined them. Even though they had lain, he estimated, for some time in the sun, which was now touching the western horizon, they were not completely dried out. Then the Kiowas weren't, he thought with grim pleasure, very far ahead of him.

Ahead of him too was Bent's Fort—just north of the trail. Bent's Fort . . . and, perhaps, Philip Griffin. Or whatever the man's real name might be.

Kiowa, he thought as the sun began to slide beneath the horizon and the last of its orange light glinted on the surface of the river to his left. What, he wondered, were Kiowa doing this far north? Most of them were, if not exactly pacified, he knew, at least confined in the south on the Fort Sill reservation. And last year, even Quanah Parker had finally brought the last of his free Kwahadi Comanche into Fort Sill after the cavalry had gone after them and the Kiowa in force.

A buffalo hunt? Cimarron doubted it. It was, of course, possible that only four men might set out to hunt buffalo. With or without permission from the Fort Sill agent. But four was too small a number, he believed, to head out after buffalo.

And the man back on the trail. What had been done to him told Cimarron several things about the four Kiowa who were somewhere ahead of him with Emma Dorset as their captive. It told him they were mad. It told him they were probably renegades. Reservation jumpers.

But why had they left the reservation? Or was it possible that these four had never been on it? Had they eluded Colonel MacKenzie's troopers during the cavalry raid on their Palo Duro Canyon village last fall?

Cimarron rode on until at last he spotted the Kiowas and Emma Dorset, her yellow hair unbound and hanging about her shoulders, riding ahead of him in the distance. Beyond them, on their right, the ruins of Bent's Fort were visible. There was a spring wagon standing on the eastern side of the ruins, its bed covered with a canvas tarpaulin. Tied to it, Cimarron saw with growing excitement, was his horse.

The dun meant that Griffin was probably there—somewhere. It meant that he had been right, Cimarron thought: Griffin had stolen his dun the night they had camped in the eastern woodland.

Griffin, Cimarron was now convinced, had murdered Marshal Brent. He was equally convinced that Griffin had persuaded Emma to testify against him.

He turned his horse, left the trail, and rode into the tall stipa grass, which, when he dismounted, reached almost to his chest. Crouching in it, he watched the Kiowas and saw them halt and dismount when they reached the ruins of the fort.

Bent over, Cimarron began to run to the north, leading his horse, knowing that he and his mount would be less visible in the grass. But he also knew that sharp eyes could pick him out. If not him, his horse. He increased his pace, running northward as fast as he could go.

He wondered, as he ran, if the Kiowas intended to make camp in the ruins. Or was there some other reason why they had stopped at the fort? A rest? A meal? Were they planning to use Emma Dorset again, as they had back on the trail, before riding on?

When Cimarron decided that he was far enough north of the fort, he turned left and ran on at right angles to his previous path. Once he was directly above the fort and as dusk began to deepen into darkness, he hobbled his horse and left it behind him, moving swiftly—bent over—through the grass toward the ruins in the south.

It didn't take him long to reach them, and as he did, he heard the sound of weeping. A woman's weeping. He climbed up and over the jumbled mass of adobe that covered more than half an acre of ground. Portions of the thick walls still stood, forming ragged battlements that loomed whitely above the dark ground as they pointed at the equally dark sky. He climbed over fallen walls and skirted a circular mass that once had been part of a tower. As he did so, his foot dislodged some loose rubble and he threw himself down upon it before it could rattle down to the ground and betray his presence by the noise it would make. He lay still, listening, the sharp edges of the adobe bricks pressing painfully against his chest wounds. He gritted his teeth and remained where he was, listening to Emma Dorset, who was still weeping.

Then, carefully, he crawled forward little by little to where he could see shadows flickering on a section of wall that remained standing. Someone, he realized, had built a fire. But his view of it was blocked by a mound of rubble. He eased around it and moved, his body bent low, to the left and into what seemed to have been a small room of some sort, placing the narrow portion of the low wall that still stood between him and the fire. He crouched down behind it and pressed his body against it.

A field mouse scurried over his leg and disappeared in the darkness.

"I told you red bastards that she's my woman!"

Cimarron recognized Griffin's voice. The man was obviously angry.

"We did not know that when we found her on the trail," a man with a clipped way of speaking said.

"Two Feathers," Griffin said, evidently addressing the man who had just spoken, "you know it now. And as I have so patiently explained to all four of you, she is staying with me."

Cimarron eased himself to the right and peered around the ragged edge of the crumbling wall.

Emma was sitting on the ground in front of the fire, her head resting on Griffin's shoulder. He sat cross-legged by the fire facing the four Kiowas, who formed a semicircle beyond it. They stared impassively at the unarmed Griffin, paying no attention to the man hunkered down on Griffin's right, a thickly built and bald man wearing a full red beard, a Peacemaker held casually in his right hand. The four Indian ponies stood stolidly behind their owners, their eyes glistening in the light of the fire.

Six to one, Cimarron thought. Seven, if you count Emma Dorset. He pressed his lips together and tightened his grip on the rifle he held in his right hand. I've no business to do with those Indians, he told himself. Or that man next to Griffin. But they might, if they lay eyes on me, decide to do business with me.

Two Feathers. The name meant nothing to Cimarron. But, he thought, Griffin apparently knew the Kiowa.

"Philip," Emma said, no longer weeping, "let's leave. Why can't we leave right now?" She cast a glance across the fire at the four Indians and moved closer to Griffin.

"I told you," Griffin practically shouted at her. "We'll leave when we've finished our business. Not before."

"I don't care about the money," Emma said, gripping Griffin's shoulders. "I told you what they did to me. I'm—"

He tore her hands from his shoulders. "Shut up!"

Then, turning back to the Indians, he asked, "How many of you are there, Two Feathers?"

The Kiowa who answered wore a headband, a white cotton shirt that covered his hips, leggings, and knee-high buckskin moccasins. "Forty now. More later."

"That's not such a helluva lot of men to go up against the cavalry," the man seated next to Griffin commented.

Two Feathers' expression did not change. "One Kiowa worth two, maybe three pony soldiers."

One of the Indians rose and left the fire. Cimarron watched him until he had disappeared around the eastern edge of the ruins, and then, after putting down his rifle, he began to crawl, swiftly but cautiously, in the direction the Indian had taken. When he reached the eastern side of the fort, he looked down, and because his eyes were accustomed to the darkness, he spotted the Indian at once. The Kiowa was relieving himself as he stood beneath the starless sky in which no moon had appeared.

Cimarron leaped from the rocky ledge on which he was perched and knocked the Indian to the ground. He straddled the Indian, who lay on his back, and pulled the knife from the red sash the Kiowa wore around his waist. Holding him down with his left hand pressing the Indian's throat, Cimarron raised the knife.

The Indian's hand shot up and grasped his wrist.

Cimarron struggled to bring the knife down, but the Indian's grip prevented him from doing so.

In response, he rose slightly and then brought both knees down on the man's chest.

The Kiowa's breath shot from between his lips and his grip on Cimarron's knife hand loosened. Cimarron slapped the Kiowa's arm away and brought the knife down. Instantly he pulled it free of the man's chest and plunged it deep into the Indian's throat.

The man made no sound.

He lay beneath Cimarron, not moving, not breathing.

Cimarron hastily wiped the blade of the knife on the Indian's shirt and then climbed back up into the ruins and made his way back to the spot he had just left.

"Quanah Parker's braves paid me well," Griffin was saying to Two Feathers. "They're jumping the reservation again in droves. I don't know where they're getting the money, but they are getting it and that's all I care about."

"You give us fifty guns?" Two Feathers asked.

Griffin laughed and slapped his thigh. "Give you? *Give* you?" His laughter came again, louder this time.

"We pay," Two Feathers said. "How much?"

"I've got good Winchester repeaters in that wagon out there. All new. Shells—all you can use. Thirty dollars each for the rifles. I'll throw in the ammunition at no extra charge." He paused and grinned at Two Feathers. "Kicking Bird would turn over in his grave if he knew about this little adventure you boys are planning."

Two Feathers spat into the fire. "Kicking Bird was weak chief of Kiowas. Kicking Bird was bloodless old woman. Took orders from Great Warrior Sherman. From Indian Agent Haworth."

"When they catch us in Palo Duro Canyon," said one of the other two Kiowas angrily, "they take us to Fort Sill. They put us in corral. Burn our property. Drive our mules and horses out on prairie and shoot them all."

Two Feathers said, "Me—others—they suspect us of leading Kiowa off reservation last year. They put us in cells. Some in icehouse with no roof. They throw us raw meat to eat as Kiowas feed dogs.

"Kicking Bird!" Two Feathers grimaced and spat again into the fire. "Last year Great Warrior Sherman order Kicking Bird to pick up twenty-six Kiowa to punish for leaving reservation. Kicking Bird pick. Lone Wolf he pick. Woman's Heart and White Horse. Mamanti the Sky Walker. Other braves. Some of our Mexican slaves.

"But Kicking Bird dead now. Good thing. We give you twenty dollars for each rifle."

"Twenty dollars," Griffin bellowed. "Sedge and I—my woman too—hauled these rifles all the way down here from Kansas. We took chances with our lives for your sake, Two Feathers. And we had trouble, let me tell you. A deputy marshal caught us after shooting my horse out from under me. He arrested us for gun running. But later I got the drop on him and shot him so he couldn't take us into Fort Smith to stand trial before the Hanging Judge. You've heard, perhaps, of Judge Parker?"

Without waiting for an answer, Griffin said, "I had to kill that lawman to keep him from taking us in. Besides, I needed his horse. But then two others started trailing us after Sedge and I split up. He headed here and my woman and I rode south, but we couldn't get those goddamn marshals off our trail. It wasn't until we spotted some dumb cowboy on the trail south of us that I was able to figure out how to shake those lawmen.

"I knew that they knew I was traveling with a woman. They'd spotted us right after I sent Sedge out here. So my woman and I planned to set it up so that the cowboy would be accused of killing the marshal. We did set it up, but it was a risky business.

"And now you offer me *twenty* dollars a rifle? Go back to the reservation, Two Feathers. Send somebody out here who knows the worth of what I've got to sell."

As Griffin and Two Feathers continued to haggle over the price of the rifles, Cimarron made his way back to where he had killed the Kiowa. He untied one of the ropes holding the canvas tarpaulin in place on the wagon and rummaged around in the wagon bed until he found what he had been searching for.

He took the boxes of shells and, using the knife he had taken from the dead Indian, began to work on their casings.

It took him some time, but he finally managed to build a conical pile of gunpowder on the wagon bed. He crept over to where the dead Kiowa lay and removed the man's sash. Back at the wagon, he twisted the sash, placing one end under the pile of gunpowder and letting the other dangle over the side of the wagon to serve as a makeshift fuse.

He struck a match and held it under the free end of the dangling sash. When it caught fire, he raced around to the rear of the wagon, freed his dun, and led it around behind the ruins.

A shot rang out.

Emma screamed.

Cimarron vaulted onto the ruins and made his way back to the spot where he had left his rifle.

Emma screamed again and another shot sounded.

"We take rifles and your woman," one of the Kiowas shouted.

"Over my dead body," Griffin roared.

"Look out," a voice warned, and Cimarron guessed it had been Sedge who had shouted.

He peered around the broken wall. Someone had downed Griffin, whose rifle lay on the ground. As Cimarron watched, Two Feathers drew his knife and hauled

Griffin to his feet, holding the man in front of him as a shield.

The red-bearded Sedge, his Peacemaker pointing at Griffin, blinked and stepped back.

"Don't shoot," Griffin roared at him.

"Put down gun," Two Feathers ordered Sedge.

As Sedge gingerly placed his gun on the ground, one of the Kiowas picked it up and aimed it at Sedge.

Emma, both hands covering her mouth, was backing toward the broken wall behind which Cimarron was crouching.

The gunpowder in the wagon exploded.

The Indian ponies bolted as burning boards flew through the air. One of them fell not far from where Cimarron remained hidden. Another struck Sedge and he let out a yell that was a mixture of surprise and pain.

The Kiowa holding Sedge's Peacemaker fired, whether from shock or intent, Cimarron wasn't sure. The bullet took Sedge below his cartridge belt and the man bent over, clutching his body, blood oozing between his clenched fingers. He staggered forward, his knees buckled, and he fell, still clutching the site where the bullet had invaded his body.

At the same instant, Griffin broke Two Feathers' grip, and as the Kiowa holding Sedge's gun turned toward him, he kicked the gun from the Indian's hand, dived for it, and came up shooting.

The gunless Kiowa dropped, his arms flung out, a low moan issuing from his parted lips.

Griffin fired again, but he missed the other Kiowa, who threw his knife at Griffin; he managed to dodge. He got off another shot and this one blew part of the Indian's face away on its journey into the man's brain.

Cimarron reached around the wall. He seized Emma's arm and pulled her toward him. He flung her to the ground behind him, and as she cried out, he said, "Quiet! You'll be out of harm's way here."

Looking up at him in the red light that flickered among the ruins from what remained of the burning wagon, she gasped, "It's you!"

"It's me."

Cimarron straightened and propped his gun hand, which held his .45, on the top of the uneven wall. He downed Two Feathers with his first shot.

The Indian whirled as if suddenly seized by an odd desire to dance. His hands wavered at the end of his arms, which were reaching out at right angles to his body. His head bobbed backward and then forward before he fell to his knees and then to the ground.

Griffin spun, Sedge's Peacemaker in his hand, toward the wall. His eyes widened as he made out Cimarron's features in the light of the campfire and he swore as he fired.

But Cimarron had dropped down behind the wall and Griffin's bullet went harmlessly over it.

Seizing Emma by the hand, Cimarron dragged her behind him as he made his way deeper into the ruins. He found a hollow down in the ruins and he shoved her into it. "Stay there. You pop up you might get your head blown off. There's going to be a gunfight or I miss my guess."

Emma stared up at him. "How did you—"

"Long story," he said, pushing her down deeper into the rubble-strewn hollow.

Then, he was up and looking away from the light of the fire, scanning the eerie landscape of the ruins where dark shadows scurried as the campfire and the burning wagon cast their dancing light.

The only sound was the crackling of the wagon's wood as the fire ate away at it. The campfire itself was invisible to Cimarron from where he crouched low, hugging the adobe rubble as he searched for Griffin.

A third fire lighted the darkness. This one had come from the Peacemaker in Griffin's hand, which had flared from that part of the ruins that were just in front of where the campfire burned.

Cimarron didn't return Griffin's fire. Instead, now that he knew Griffin's approximate position, he began to crawl toward it, his chest burning as it scraped against the shattered adobe bricks. He kept his eyes on the spot where the flame had flared briefly when Griffin fired at him, circling toward it, climbing up, dropping down, wriggling onward as soundlessly as he could.

When his boot dislodged a broken brick and it went tumbling noisily downward, Griffin fired again.

Cimarron swore softly. The man had changed his position. Now he was farther away. And circling away from Cimarron.

Cimarron remained motionless, waiting to see what

Griffin's next move would be. His body hugged the ruins, his .45 was half-cocked, his finger was on its trigger.

A dark figure darted between two crumbling spires in the ruins. Cimarron fired at it, aiming for its legs.

No cry of pain. So he had missed. Again, he swore. And began moving toward the spot where he had last seen Griffin, keeping low and sweating in the cool night.

There was a crumbling wall not far from the two adobe spires. He made for it and, when he reached it, went around behind it and then slowly raised his head to peer over it.

The burning wagon was now just a dull glow off to the east. The campfire was directly in front of Cimarron now and he avoided looking directly at it to preserve his night vision.

"Philip?"

Cimarron's eyes narrowed. Was Emma up and moving about in the ruins searching for Griffin? He didn't want to risk shooting her. But neither did he want to risk being shot by Griffin. He damned her silently.

Sweat slid down his body and oozed into his eyes. He blinked it away.

And then—there was Griffin, a shadow surrounded by shadows, a mound of a man amid the toppled mounds of adobe.

Cimarron's thumb pulled back the hammer of his .45 to full cock and he fired.

"Damn your hide, you son of a bitch," Griffin bellowed.

Must have got him, Cimarron thought, and there was no pleasure in the thought because he wanted the man alive. He cocked his Colt again.

"No way for a preacher man to talk," Cimarron called out to Griffin, deliberately trying to draw Griffin's fire, hoping that, if he'd hit him, the man hadn't been hurt seriously.

No shot sounded.

Cimarron edged between the two spires, moving toward the spot where he had last seen Griffin. Was he still there? Was he waiting, his gun cocked and aimed? He moved slowly on.

A sound made him turn to the right.

Griffin was standing now.

Before he could fire, Cimarron picked up an adobe brick and flung it. The brick struck Griffin's right arm and the gun fell from his hand.

Cimarron raced toward Griffin. When he reached him, he stood over him as Griffin fumbled frantically about in the ruins, searching for Sedge's gun.

"Move out into the open," Cimarron told him. "Forget that gun. You won't need it now."

Griffin looked up at him and then smiled. He shrugged. He moved out, stumbling through the ruins, Cimarron not far behind him.

When they came out into the open, Cimarron marched Griffin around the ruins to the campfire, around which the corpses lay as if they were pretending to be sleeping men.

"Emma said they were going to hang you," Griffin remarked almost pleasantly, as if he were talking to an old friend about better days. He touched his right hand with his left, which Cimarron's bullet had bloodied.

"They were. But me, I had other ideas."

"You saved my life when you shot Two Feathers," Griffin commented idly. "A sporting thing to do."

"We're riding out of here tonight for Fort Smith, the three of us," Cimarron told him. "I've got your horse hobbled out in the grass. Let's you and me go get him."

Griffin asked, "Which way?"

Cimarron gestured, and Griffin turned and started around the ruins.

"I'll kill you if you move, Cimarron," Emma said from the shadows behind Cimarron.

He stiffened. Did she have a gun? Had she found Sedge's gun, which Griffin had dropped? Or was she bluffing in order to give Griffin a chance to get away?

"Turn around," Emma said to him, and he did so to find himself facing her and his own rifle, which she was aiming at his heart.

11

Emma smiled at Cimarron and said, "When you first pulled me into the ruins and threw me down—quite roughly, I must say—I fell on your rifle. While you were trying to capture Philip, I went and got it and now— Well, you're not going to take him, or me, to Fort Smith."

Cimarron stared at her in silence, noting the merriment dancing in her blue eyes.

"Good girl," Griffin cried to her, and then, to Cimarron he said, "Just toss your gun over here, cowboy."

Cimarron threw his .45 toward Griffin, who picked it up and walked over to stand beside Emma, a broad smile on his face.

Cimarron dropped his eyes to the black barrels of the Winchester and the Colt. My own guns, he thought. He cursed himself for a fool. He never should have left his rifle in the ruins when he went after Griffin. But he had never thought that Emma would . . . But she had. He braced himself, waiting for one or both of the guns to fire, waiting for their bullets to tear into his body and rip the life from him.

Griffin stuck Cimarron's .45 in his waistband and held out a hand to Emma. "Give me that. If you were to fire it, its recoil would probably break your shoulder."

Emma handed him the Winchester. "Shoot him, Philip. Get it over with."

"Might as well," Griffin said, and raised the rifle to his shoulder, sighting along its barrel at Cimarron, one eye closed.

"You ever shoot an unarmed man before?" Cimarron asked him.

"Once or twice, as I recall," Griffin answered. "Shooting unarmed men is a lot safer than trying to get those that are armed. The odds of getting them are much better in the former case and I'm a man who likes the odds in my favor."

"Philip," Emma exclaimed. "Don't stand there carrying on a conversation with him as if you two were discussing crops or the weather. Do it, Philip!"

Griffin lowered the rifle slightly and glanced at Emma, the smile fading from his face. "I guess you did your best," he said to her. "But it does look as if your best was simply not good enough. This cowboy has more lives than most cats, or so it would appear."

Emma sighed. She folded her arms and impatiently tapped her foot on the ground.

Griffin turned his attention to Cimarron. "You know who killed that marshal, don't you?"

"Heard you talking a while back—to Two Feathers. Yes, I know you killed him."

"Emma knows too," Griffin said stonily, his voice low, his eyes still on Cimarron. "But you two are the only ones who do know."

Cimarron's eyes narrowed. What was Griffin getting at? There was something ominous, not only in his tone of voice, but also in what his words hinted at.

"Philip, will you please—"

"Stand over there beside him," Griffin barked at Emma.

"Philip, whatever are you—"

"You heard me, Emma. Stand over there beside the cowboy!"

Emma began to back toward the ruins.

Without taking his eyes from Cimarron, Griffin reached out. He seized her by the shoulder and sent her hurtling toward Cimarron, who caught her as she collided against him. She tore herself free and turned to stare, her eyes wide and disbelieving, at Griffin, whose smile had returned to his face.

"One day, Emma, you might develop a bad case of conscience," Griffin said. "I admit it's not likely, but it is entirely possible. You might decide to talk to the law at Fort Smith. You might decide to tell them the truth. I couldn't chance that.

"And I never intended to chance it. That's why I waited for you to get here. But then, before I could carry out my plans for you—well, things got a bit busy. They aren't any longer."

"You're—you're going to shoot me?" Emma asked, her voice weak, barely more than a faint whisper.

"I am, Emma. I must."

"An unarmed man," Cimarron said. "Now that strikes me as bad enough. But a woman, Griffin? Are you sure you have the stomach for that?"

Griffin nodded and raised the rifle.

He quickly turned immediately after hitting the ground Emma, knocking her to the ground. At the same instant, he hit the ground, and as the Winchester roared and the bullet whined over his head, he quickly scrambled forward on his belly and seized both of Griffin's ankles in his hand before the man could fire a second time. He jerked on them, pulling Griffin toward him. Griffin fired as he began to fall. The bullet went harmlessly into the dirt to Cimarron's right.

Cimarron gave Griffin's ankles another hard tug, and as Griffin completely lost his balance, he let go of the rifle and, his arms waving in a vain attempt to stay on his feet, fell backward.

He turned quickly after hitting the ground and reached for the rifle he had dropped.

But Cimarron put out a booted foot and kicked it out of Griffin's reach. He turned Griffin on his back and, straddling him, hit him with a hard right cross. He followed that up with a left uppercut.

Griffin's head snapped to the left and then backward as Cimarron's blows landed on his right cheek and on his jaw.

Then as Cimarron hauled Griffin to his feet, gripping the man's shirt with clenched fists, he muttered, "I've met some mean men in my time, Griffin. But you qualify without any question as the meanest."

He released Griffin, and as the man swung a clumsy left, he bent backward and then came in fast and sent his right fist slamming into Griffin's gut. The blow doubled Griffin over. Cimarron's next blow, a left uppercut, sent him flying backward.

As Griffin fell, Cimarron reached down and picked up his rifle. He walked over to Griffin, who lay sprawled on his back on the ground and pulled his .45 from the man's waistband.

"Cimarron," Emma cried, getting to her feet and running toward him.

When she threw her arms around him, he shoved her away, and she fell again. He stood his ground, his .45 in his right hand, his Winchester in his left and pointing at the ground. He stared down at Griffin and Emma and could not prevent his lips from curling in distaste.

"I wanted to thank you," Emma said to him. "For saving me from him."

"I saved you from him, all right," Cimarron said. "Because I wanted you alive just as I wanted Griffin alive. I'm taking both of you back to Fort Smith. Griffin, you're going to meet George Maledon, who's going to wrap a real tight noose around your neck."

Griffin merely stared up at Cimarron, his face expressionless.

"What about me?" Emma asked hesitantly.

Cimarron looked down at her as she sat in the dirt, a strand of her now dusty yellow hair hanging down over her face.

"You? You're going to do time for perjury. At the very least. Maybe as an accessory to murder."

"Cimarron," she said, managing the smallest of smiles. "Don't, Cimarron. I'll go with you. Anywhere you want. I'll be—nice to you, Cimarron, I will. You'll see. You can't have forgotten what it was like that night—what we were like together. We'll be that way again—anytime and anyway you want us to be. Cimarron?"

"I'd sooner eat swill with pigs than have you again."

Emma's head drooped forlornly and she raised one hand to cover her eyes.

"On your feet, both of you."

When Griffin and Emma were standing some distance away from him, Cimarron gestured with his .45. "Head north. Your horse is hobbled out there, Griffin."

Griffin turned and headed north, Emma following just behind him, her arms at her sides, moving stiffly, as if she were in pain and movement aggravated that pain.

Cimarron followed behind them, his .45 on full cock.

The clouds that had darkened the night sky began to break up as they walked, and by the time they reached the quarter horse a few stars glittered brightly above them.

"Take off the hobbles," Cimarron ordered Griffin, who bent down to obey the command.

When the horse had been freed, Cimarron, leading the quarter horse, marched Griffin and Emma back to the north side of the ruins where his dun was grazing.

Griffin said, "You'll never be able to prove I killed Marshal Brent, cowboy. The grand jury probably won't even indict me. Insufficient evidence. I'll bet on it."

Cimarron knew Griffin might be right. What proof did he have of Griffin's guilt? None.

"I'll testify against you," Emma screamed at him, her voice an anguished shriek in the night. "I will!"

"You will?" Griffin countered. "What the *hell* do you think a jury will say—if I should ever come to trial, which I'm betting I won't—when they hear that you testified against this big cowboy here, claiming he was the killer, and then you come along and say, no, you made a mistake. *I* was the one who killed the marshal. I'll tell you what they'll say, Emma. Either way, that strumpet is a liar—got to be—is what they'll say. She either lied about the cowboy or she's lying about poor Mr. Griffin."

Emma flew at Griffin and began pummeling him with her fists.

He laughed as he easily pushed her away, and when she came at him again, he kicked her shin.

She cried out in pain and Cimarron said, "Enough! Stand apart, you two!"

Emma began to sob, overwhelmed by the impotent rage that was twisting her features and making her look aged.

Suddenly she stopped sobbing. She raised her head, her eyes widening as she stared at Griffin. A smile, more of a sneer, parted her lips. "I'd forgotten," she said, and a look of wild triumph suddenly glowed on her face. "But now I remember!"

She spun around to face Cimarron while she pointed at Griffin's no-longer-bleeding hand. "That ring he's wearing," she shouted to Cimarron. "It's the one he stole from the marshal! That's proof that he killed the man!"

"Give me that ring," Cimarron said to Griffin.

Griffin was already sliding it from the finger of his right hand. He threw it away from him.

Emma ran in the direction in which Griffin had thrown the ring and dropped to her hands and knees, searching about in the grass for it.

"Damn you," she shouted. "Damn you, Philip Griffin!"

And then she rose and slowly turned, holding out her hand to Cimarron. On her palm rested the gold ring Griffin had been wearing. She walked slowly toward Cimarron, her eyes on the ring in her hand.

He reached out, took it from her, and pocketed it.

"That will prove he did it, won't it?" Emma asked Cimarron, the hopefulness in her voice an oddly ugly sound.

"It'll help some," Cimarron replied. "Climb up on your horse, Griffin."

When Griffin was in the saddle, Cimarron beckoned to Emma, and when she came toward him, he helped her climb up behind Griffin.

He stepped into the saddle of his dun, holstered his .45, and pointed east with the Winchester he had shifted to his right hand. "Let's go," he said. "And if you should take a notion to try to make a run for it, Griffin, I'll shoot you right through the lady's back. One bullet'll do for both of you."

They moved out.

When they reached the ferry on the western bank of the Arkansas River, Cimarron said, "Griffin, pay our fares."

Griffin, still on his horse with Emma behind him, paid their fares, and as he was about to step down onto the deck of the ferry, Cimarron said, "Stay up there on that horse where I can keep an eye on you."

He got out of his saddle and leaned back against the railing, his rifle aimed at Griffin, conscious of the afternoon's hot sun on his body.

One of the ferrymen, who was gripping one of the stern lines, looked nervously at Cimarron. "You ain't planning on shooting up this here old boat, now are you, mister?"

"Nope, I do any shooting it'll be at him and all over before you can say Fort Smith."

The man nervously threw off the stern line he was gripping, and moments later the ferry moved out into the river.

Cimarron kept his eyes on Griffin, who was staring across the river at the busy waterfront of Fort Smith. In the saddle behind Griffin, Emma rested her left cheek against his back, her arms hanging limply at her sides, her eyes vacant.

When the ferry slid into one of the slips on the Arkansas' eastern bank, Cimarron got back into the saddle.

Griffin kneed his quarter horse and the animal walked off the ferry, Cimarron riding close behind it.

"Cut across the railyards down there," Cimarron called out to Griffin, "and head down Garrison Avenue."

Griffin did, and a few minutes later Cimarron ordered him to turn right at an intersection, which he did. When they reached Rogers Avenue, Cimarron told Griffin to make another right onto it.

People in front of the shops and houses stared at the passing procession, at Cimarron's rifle, at him, and at the pair on the quarter horse in front of him.

Suddenly a woman cried out, a sound of alarm. "That's the man they were going to hang," she shouted. "The one who broke jail!"

Out of the corner of his eye, Cimarron saw the woman pointing at him. He turned toward her and waved. She hastily drew back as if he had spat at her.

A man ran up the dusty street past Griffin and Emma and disappeared through the gate of the compound a block away.

Cimarron knew why the man had run to the compound. But the reception committee that met them just inside the gate of the compound was smaller than he had expected. It consisted merely of two deputy marshals with drawn six-guns, both of which were aimed, not at Griffin or Emma, but at him.

"Nice day, gentlemen," he said to the marshals. "We could use some rain, though. Things are drying out."

"Get down," one of the marshals said in a strained voice.

"Be happy to," Cimarron said, and swung out of the saddle. "Brought you these two prisoners. You can toss the gent in that basement sty you call a jail, but I confess I don't know what you're going to do with the lady."

"Women prisoners are housed over there in the courthouse yard," one of the marshals said, pointing to a small brick shack.

"Shut the hell up, Moore," the other marshal barked. "Don't you know who that man is?"

"He's the one who got away a while back, Clinton."

Cimarron laughed. "I plead guilty to that, but I've got a question. What do you plan to do with these two?"

"It's what we're planning to do with you that matters," Moore declared, brandishing his six-gun.

Cimarron sighed. "You're a good shot, are you, Mr. Moore?" Without waiting for the man's reply, he added, "You'd best be, and that's a fact. On account of I'm good. And real fast."

Moore and Clinton, indecision etched on both their faces, stared uneasily at Cimarron.

"Now I'm not going to try to escape again," he told them. "I just want to have a little talk with Marshal Fagan. I mean to tell him some things he ought to know. Will you boys take me to him?"

Both marshals looked at each other.

"It can't hurt, Moore," Clinton suggested.

"I guess it can't hurt, you talking to Fagan," Moore said. "But remember. We'll shoot to kill if you run."

"Do I look like I'm ready to run, Marshal?" Cimarron asked. "Why, I just rode right in here as brazen as you please. Right into the open arms and gun barrels of the law. Would I do that if I were planning to run?"

Moore stroked his chin with his left hand and then gestured with his right, which held his six-gun. "Fagan's office is in the courthouse."

"Who—what . . .?" Fagan blustered as Cimarron threw open the door of the marshal's office and herded Emma and Griffin inside it. He lined them up against the wall as the two deputies entered the office behind him, their guns drawn, puzzled looks on both their faces.

"Moore, Clinton," Fagan said. "What's going on here?"

"Well, Marshal," Clinton said sheepishly, "neither one of us knows for certain."

Fagan looked from them to Griffin and Emma and then at Cimarron. His eyes widened. "You! I know you!"

"Reckon you do, Marshal." Cimarron gave the man a smile. "Now, that jasper over there and his lady friend, you'll want to make their acquaintance too. Man claims his name's Philip Griffin. Maybe it is and maybe it isn't. Point is, he murdered your Marshal Brent. I didn't."

"The lady," Fagan said, rising from behind his desk and peering at Emma. "She looks familiar."

"Ought to," Cimarron said. "She was the chief witness against me at my trial."

Fagan banged a fist down on the desk. "Of course!"

"She lied," Cimarron said bluntly. "You can try her for perjury."

Fagan leaned over his desk and glared at Cimarron. "You have any proof of your accusations?"

Cimarron pulled the gold ring from his pocket and dropped it on the desk. "The lady—her name's Emma Dorset—says Griffin took this ring from the marshal before he killed him."

"It's true," Emma cried. "He did. I was there and I saw him do it."

Fagan sat back down in his chair and stared hard at Emma. "You were also sure recently that this man here"—his finger jabbed in Cimarron's direction—"killed Brent."

Emma lowered her head. "I lied at his trial."

"Young woman," Fagan said, "do you realize you're confessing to having perjured yourself?"

Emma nodded, her eyes on the floor.

"Do you realize," Fagan continued, "that you'll draw a jail term if you stick to your confession?"

Emma nodded a second time and looked up at Cimarron. "That man who calls himself Cimarron is innocent." For a brief moment, her former sauciness appeared on her face as she added, "At least he's innocent of the killing of Marshal Brent. I know he's not innocent where certain other matters are concerned."

Fagan picked up the ring and turned it over in his fingers. Then he looked up at Cimarron and asked, "Can you prove that this ring belonged to Brent?"

"I can't," Cimarron said. "But the lady can. Seems to me you ought to ask some of Brent's friends if they can identify it as his. I'm no lawyer and I hope this isn't some kind of trial you're conducting here on the spur of the moment."

Fagan harrumphed. "You'll testify at their trials?"

"Glad to." Cimarron shot a glance at Emma, but she did not meet his eyes.

"Remand these two to the men's and women's jails, Moore," Fagan said.

As he spoke, Judge Parker strode into the room, and when he saw Cimarron, he said, "Fagan, you've done good work. I take it Clinton and Moore brought him in?"

"Not exactly, Isaac," Fagan said hesitantly.

"Who captured him?" Parker asked. "And why haven't you disarmed him?"

"Nobody captured him, Isaac," Fagan answered. "You see—"

"I do not see," Parker said, an edge of anger in his tone. "I'd be most grateful if you'd enlighten me. This man escaped from jail. Now I see him standing here before me with a gun in his hand. Well, Fagan?"

"I brought myself in, Judge," Cimarron said quietly.

Parker nodded. "A wise thing to do. The arm of the law is long and justice will be served. You realized the grievous error of your ways, I take it?"

"Isaac," Fagan said, and when Parker turned his attention to him, he continued, "this man claims those two killed Brent." He pointed at Griffin and Emma. "Cimarron brought them in to me."

Parker's gaze impaled the pair.

"He's a liar," Griffin yelped.

"He's not," Emma said quietly. "It's true, your Honor. Cimarron didn't kill the marshal. This man did," she concluded, indicating Griffin.

"She's another liar," Griffin yelled.

"*Silence*," Parker thundered, and the room's walls seemed to quiver.

"You," he said to Cimarron, "will tell me why you have done what you have."

Cimarron explained what had happened since he escaped from the Fort Smith jail, concluding with the remark, "I wanted to clear my name and this seemed the only sure way of doing that."

Parker's eyes narrowed as he carefully studied Cimarron. "That ring—you could have removed it from Marshal Brent's finger after you killed him."

"Reckon I could have, Judge," Cimarron said. "Only I didn't. Never laid eyes on your marshal. And Emma Dorset saw Griffin rob that ring from Brent before he shot him."

Parker said, "You claim she perjured herself at your trial. Perhaps she is not telling the truth now about Griffin."

"She wouldn't confess to perjury for me or any other man, Marshal. Not her. She's got a motive for telling the truth now about Griffin. Tell the judge what happened out at Bent's Fort, Emma."

"Your Honor, Philip was going to kill me because I knew he had killed the marshal. He was going to kill Cimarron for the same reason. He didn't want to leave anyone alive who knew what he had done—anyone who might someday testify against him as I intend to do now."

"She says she lied once," Griffin said. "You can't possibly believe her now!"

Ignoring Griffin's outburst, Parker said thoughtfully, "Marshal Fagan, wasn't Deputy Tracy a good friend of Brent's?"

"He was, Isaac. In fact, they were next-door neighbors here in Fort Smith. The two families used to go on outings down on the Poteau River together."

"Is he in town now?"

"I believe he is, yes."

"Send someone to see if they can locate him, please."

Fagan sent Moore, and when Moore returned, Tracy was with him.

"Tracy," Parker said, "will you please take a look at this ring?" Parker handed him the ring. "Have you ever seen it before?"

"Lots of times," Tracy said. "It belonged to Marshal Brent."

"When you remanded Cimarron to jail, you made him hand over his personal possessions, did you not?"

"It's the custom," Tracy said.

"Did he give you that ring?"

Tracy shook his head.

"Was he wearing this ring at the time?"

"No, your Honor. I would have noticed it if he'd been wearing it because we always confiscate personal jewelry—stickpins, rings, that sort of thing."

"Thank you, Tracy," Parker said, and waved his hand in dismissal. When Tracy left the office, he said to Fagan, "Your deputies here will take Miss Dorset and Mr. Griffin into custody immediately."

Fagan gestured and Moore and Clinton quickly marched Griffin and Emma from the room.

When they had gone, Parker sat down in a chair that faced Fagan's desk. He waved Cimarron into a chair near his own.

"Cimarron," he said, "we will require your testimony before the grand jury and at the trials of Miss Dorset and Mr. Griffin. Will you give it?"

"With real pleasure, Judge."

"Good. Without it, I am doubtful that a grand jury will indict." Parker placed the tips of his fingers together and stared solemnly at Cimarron. "Tell me about yourself."

"Not much to tell. And anyway, all you really need to know about me is that I didn't kill Brent."

"You brought to justice the man who did," Parker said, placing the tips of his fingers against his goateed chin. "Cimarron, I have a proposition to make to you."

"You have, Judge?"

"This court is always in dire need of reliable men to serve it as deputy marshals. Would you consider taking such a job?"

Cimarron stroked his stubbled chin, trying hard not to show the surprise he felt. "I never thought I'd have the chance to consider turning myself into a lawman," he temporized. Was Parker serious? he wondered. Do I want to ride for the law? he asked himself.

"I regret to say," Parker continued, "that the pay is not munificent—far from it. If you are sent out to subpoena witnesses, you will receive six cents for each mile you travel—one way only, however—and you will have to pay your expenses and transportation costs out of the mileage fees you receive. You will also receive fifty cents for the first witness contacted and thirty-five cents for each additional witness. For each prisoner you bring in, you will be paid two dollars, but I must hasten to add, you must forfeit that fee if you kill your prisoner.

"All in all, you can expect to earn perhaps five hundred dollars annually. But, in addition, you may collect any rewards offered by local or state authorities, and in some cases these rewards may be greater than your annual salary. Unfortunately you are not eligible for rewards offered by the federal government for such crimes as mail robbery or the murder of a federal employee because, Congress in its wisdom contends, you are already paid fees by the federal government as an officer of this court."

Cimarron was thinking fast. Questions exploded in his mind as he considered Parker's offer. Should he accept the job? What were his alternatives if he turned it down? Not much, he decided. He was going nowhere. He had been just drifting, turning his hand to whatever presented itself. Now a job had presented itself. But a risky job. One in which he might get himself killed.

He thought of his years as an outlaw. And that thought

brought rushing back to him the memory of that fatal day in Texas—the bank, his father. Again, in his mind, he saw himself fire, saw his father's body lurch, saw his father fall and die. Again he felt the gut-wrenching pain that he had felt then, the pain that was not physical but that racked both his mind and his body in a way worse than any knife or bullet might have done. The sense of guilt that he had felt at that moment, and that he had never stopped feeling since, swept over him again.

He closed his eyes and put one hand over them as he lowered his head.

"Cimarron?"

He heard his name spoken from a great distance as the racking sense of guilt flooded him worse than it had at any other time and the old familiar pain rode through him.

"Are you all right?"

He uncovered his eyes and raised his head, to find Parker rising from his chair, a look of grave concern on his stern face.

"Are you all right?" Parker repeated.

Cimarron drew a deep breath and nodded. "I'm fine," he lied. "Just fine."

Parker resumed his seat. "And so, as I was saying, the work is hard and dangerous and the pay cannot be counted a princely sum by any means. I continue to issue pleas to Congress to authorize higher fees for the court's deputies, and Congress continues to turn a willfully deaf ear to each and every one of them. But, Cimarron, a man could do much worse than live his life as a United States deputy marshal in Indian Territory. Many have."

"I know that, Judge."

"You're young," Parker observed. "You're strong. You have an innate sense of justice, which you've displayed by returning here after risking your life in the pursuit of a murderer to clear your name. You would do well as a marshal, I am convinced. Your performance as a lawman would be, I believe, superb."

Cimarron looked down at his hands and was surprised to find them clenched on the arms of the chair in which he was sitting. Sweat was beading his forehead. He felt as if he were being tortured, not by whips or branding irons but by an awful memory, that one terrible memory of that deadly day in Texas.

"Will you consider the offer?" Parker asked him, leaning forward in his chair toward Cimarron.

"No."

Parker sighed and leaned back in his chair. "I'm sorry. I truly am. I'd hoped that you would—"

"I'll take the job, Judge," Cimarron said. "When I said 'no' I meant that I wouldn't *consider* the offer. I meant that I'd already made up my mind to take the job. My father—he was a sheriff once down in Texas and I . . ." His voice trailed off.

"Ah, I see," Parker exclaimed happily. "The son will follow in the father's footsteps!"

"In a manner of speaking," Cimarron murmured. Was he being offered a chance to atone, he asked himself, to make up for what he had unwittingly done—a chance to expiate the deed that had caused him so much suffering all these years? The answer came to him through his body. He felt himself beginning to truly relax for the first time since that day in the Texas bank. He felt light-headed. His hands loosened and he released the chair he had been gripping. His mind seemed to soar, finally free of the burden it had borne for so long.

There was a knock on the door.

"Come in," Fagan called out.

The door opened and Sarah Lassiter stepped into the room, halting just beyond the threshold. "I'm sorry," she said. "I didn't know you had someone here, Marshal. I can come back."

As she turned, Cimarron got to his feet and crossed the room. "Sarah," he said.

She turned to him and her words came rushing from between her lips. "They said—everyone in town is talking about you. They told me a marshal had brought you in. They said you had broken jail and that you'd been caught—that you'd hang. They said you were here. Oh, Cimarron!"

Cimarron took her in his arms and held her tightly.

"People have a way of mixing things up, Sarah. I'm not going to hang, although I did break out of the jail here before I met up with you. I'll tell you all about it later."

"Miss Lassiter," Parker said. "I take it you know this man?"

"Yes, sir, I do," Sarah said as Cimarron released her and they both faced Parker.

"Miss Lassiter was a witness at a trial that concluded earlier this afternoon," Parker told Cimarron. "Two men—one of them her husband—were murdered at her home and she testified against a man named Jansen and a Tahlequah lawyer who had—uh—molested her. They were found guilty of—uh—attempted rape."

Cimarron and Sarah exchanged glances.

Parker said, "I am vexed with you, Miss Lassiter, as you know." Glancing at Cimarron, he said, "Miss Lassiter refused to tell the court who rescued her and killed two of her attackers."

"Is that a fact?" Cimarron asked, his tone bland.

"How do you happen to know Cimarron, Miss Lassiter?" Parker abruptly asked.

"He visited me once," she replied. "I—I entertained him." Her eyes were on the floor.

"Was that before or after the—uh—incident that took place at your home?"

Sarah glanced at Cimarron, who remained silent. And then she said, "He did it to save me, your Honor. He had to kill my husband and that other man Ross or they would have killed him for trying to stop them from—from doing what they intended to do to me."

Parker turned his attention to Cimarron, his expression stern. "You will recall that I told you earlier that if, as a deputy marshal, you kill your prisoners you forfeit the two-dollar fee you would have received had you brought them in alive."

"Well, Judge, if I'd brought Jansen in I would have made two dollars, so it all wouldn't have been a total loss, now would it?"

"I just wanted to impress upon you the profitable aspect of the job you will be undertaking. Marshal Fagan, swear Cimarron."

"But, Judge," Fagan protested, "we don't know anything about his background and he admits to having shot Quince and Ross, and he—"

Parker held up a hand and Fagan fell silent. "Marshal," he said, "you know very well that our deputies are not saints, not a single one of them. You know that they are often foulmouthed and as frequently taciturn about their past lives. You also know that we are obliged to take such material for deputies as prove efficient in serving the process of this court. I should also point out that none of our deputies are cowards, and although a coward may be a highly moral man, he could not successfully serve as a marshal in Indian territory. Do I make myself clear?"

"You do, Isaac," Fagan said with a grin.

"Then swear Cimarron in as a deputy marshal of the District Court of the United States for the Western District of Arkansas."

Fagan promptly did.

And then he shook Cimarron's hand.

So did Parker.

Cimarron said, "I'd best be seeing to my horse. And I sure could use a meal, if one's to be found in this town."

"Report to Marshal Fagan first thing in the morning," Parker ordered Cimarron.

"Begging your pardon, Judge," Cimarron said, "but I'd just as soon have a day or two to rest up before I start working for your court." He glanced at Sarah.

She smiled and said to Parker, "You do want him to be fresh and fully rested when he begins work, don't you, your Honor?"

For the first time since entering the office, Parker smiled. "And you, I take it, Miss Lassiter, plan to see to it that Cimarron is looked after while you two renew your acquaintance."

"Well, I shall do my best," Sarah said demurely, "to see to it that he doesn't want for anything during the next day or two."

She put her arm around Cimarron's waist and he laid a light hand on her shoulder as they left the office together and made their way to Sarah's hotel.

SPECIAL PREVIEW

Here is the first chapter from

CIMARRON RIDES THE OUTLAW TRAIL

second in the new action-packed Cimarron series from Signet

1

Cimarron dragged the pine saplings he had felled out of the grove of trees. He began to haul them toward the southern edge of the encampment of United States deputy marshals that was sprawled on the western bank of the Arkansas River.

As he passed canvas army tents and crude lean-tos, he was only half-conscious of the sounds that the other deputies in the camp were making; he was thinking about Sarah Lassiter.

The clang of a horseshoe as it hit the iron spike that had been driven into the ground rang in the early June morning's still and humid air. A man shouted. Another swore. Another clang sounded and it was quickly followed by a loud argument between two men who were bending over the spot near the railroad spike where the thrown horseshoe had landed.

She's gone, Cimarron thought, as he slapped at a mosquito that had landed on his neck. He used three of the saplings to form a wide-based tripod after lashing them together at one end with rawhide. He wondered if he'd ever see Sarah Lassiter again. He hoped he would. And he might. She lived just northwest of Tahlequah, the capital of Cherokee nation, and Tahlequah, he knew, wasn't a very long ride from Fort Smith, the frontier town that squatted on the other side of the Arkansas.

A man shouted—a name. There was an answering shout. Then, booming laughter from several throats.

They had spent three days together, Cimarron and Sarah, in the small and none-too-clean hotel in Fort Smith. Yesterday she had returned to the female seminary she had been attending just northwest of Tahlequah.

But to Cimarron it seemed like it had been weeks since he had seen her—had gently touched and eagerly held her. Thinking of those arousing nights—and days—they had spent so happily together in the big brass hotel bed brought a smile to his face.

Someone in the camp behind him snickered as he leaned more poles against the top of the tripod and then began covering them with a tarpaulin.

He used wooden pegs he had whittled to fasten the tarpaulin to the ground and then he ducked down and went inside the tepee he had built and gripped the length of rawhide that dangled from the top of the tripod and that lay in a coil on the grassy ground.

He pounded another wooden peg into the ground directly beneath the apex of the tripod with one booted foot and then tied the rawhide tightly to the peg to keep the tepee stable in even the strongest wind.

"Ain't a tent good enough for you?" someone asked, and Cimarron glanced over his shoulder to find Deputy Marshal Pete Smithers peering into the dim interior of the shelter.

"Don't happen to have a tent, Smithers," Cimarron replied amiably. "Nor do I have the wherewithal to buy myself one."

He left the tepee, shouldering Smithers out of his way as he did so, and proceeded to insert the ends of two saplings in the small pockets he had made in the top of the tarpaulin in order to control the makeshift smoke flaps he had fashioned there.

Smithers, a wooden toothpick between his lips, said, "You wouldn't happen to be part Injun, now would you be, Cimarron?"

"Might be. My pa, he was a wandering man. There's just no telling what he might have gotten himself into in his traveling down in Texas." Cimarron gave Smithers a smile, unbothered by the lie he had just told—more of a joke on himself than a genuine lie—and then tested the two poles, opening and closing the smoke flaps.

"You mean *who* he might have gotten himself into, don't you?" Smithers asked with a sly grin.

Cimarron anchored the smoke-flap poles in place and then turned around. He studied Smithers for a moment—the man's mirthless grin, his feral eyes, his smooth, faintly pink complexion.

Smithers said, "That there thing you just put up, it looks a whole lot like an Injun house to me. That's why I asked if you were part Injun." He paused, his eyes on Cimarron, before adding, "That, and the fact that I heard you were living over in the hotel in town with a Cherokee squaw."

"What people hear," Cimarron said, "is more often than not best left unrepeated."

"You hold anything against your own kind?" Smithers asked. "I mean, against white women?"

"Smithers, don't you have enough business of your own to mind without mixing yourself up in mine?"

"How was she, Cimarron? I hear some of those squaws are awful eager to snuggle up tight against big and brawny white men like you. Was she good?"

Cimarron sighed. "Miss Lassiter is no concern of yours, Smithers. Nor am I."

Smithers slapped his thigh and hooted. "You hear him, fellas?" he called out to the other deputies in the camp. "Touchy sort, now ain't he just?"

"I'm going to ask you real polite, Smithers," Cimarron said in a low tone as several idly curious deputies wandered over to join the pair. "I'm asking you to let it lie, Smithers."

"You fellas heard about this here squaw man?" Smithers asked the deputies and, without waiting for a reply, continued, "This old Cimarron just barely manages to slip his neck out of Maledon's noose last month and before you can say shit he slipped his—"

Cimarron's right hand shot out and seized Smithers by the throat, cutting off the man's words. With his left hand, he unbuckled Smithers' gun belt and tossed it to the ground some distance away. Only then did he release Smithers and proceed to unbuckle his own gun belt, from which hung the holster that housed his single-action Frontier Colt .45, from which he had cut away the trigger guard. He tossed it to the ground.

"Now what exactly might you have in mind?" Smithers asked him as he rubbed his throat.

"Murder, for one thing," Cimarron answered. "Only I'm not a murdering man as a rule, though gents like you do sorely try the patience of a peaceful man like I usually am."

Smithers' eyes widened in mock surprise. "You want to murder me?"

Cimarron sighed again. "I'll ask you just one more time, Smithers. Let it lie."

"And if I don't?"

"You'll wish to hell and back that you had."

"You think you can take me?"

"I plan on trying my best to."

"Oh, you do, do you?" Smithers growled, discarding his hat and gnawed toothpick. "Don't see what you're so all fired up about. A Cherokee squaw ain't much better than a nigger gal, you come right on down to it."

Cimarron swung. His right uppercut caught Smithers on the jaw and sent him staggering backward.

Almost immediately, Smithers regained his balance. His fists clenched. He said, "I got twenty, maybe twenty-five pounds on you, Cimarron. I'm going to pound you so far into the ground it'll take a crew with shovels to find you."

"Time for talking's past. Let's have at it."

Smithers lunged, his right fist drawn back. Although Cimarron was much lighter than his opponent, he made up for his lack of bulk with a litheness that was more characteristic of a cougar than of most men. He leaned to the right and Smithers' blow glanced off his left shoulder.

He turned and brought the heel of his right fist down hard on the side of Smithers' head. Then, as the man turned toward him, Cimarron followed up with a fast left jab, driving his fist into Smithers' fleshy gut.

Smithers doubled over, gasping for air, and then, both of his fists flying wildly, he hurled himself at Cimarron.

Cimarron took a right and a left to the ribs, losing his hat in the process. He reached out and grabbed Smithers' shoulders with both of his hands. He pulled the man toward him, turned him, thrust his right leg behind Smithers' knees, and threw him to the ground.

Smithers, propping himself up on both elbows, blinked up at Cimarron. Then, struggling to his feet as Cimarron stepped warily backward, he aimed a vicious kick at Cimarron's shin.

Cimarron had seen the kick coming and he shunted Smithers' booted foot aside with his own right foot.

When Smithers tried a second time to kick him in the shin, Cimarron grabbed the man's raised ankle, twisted it hard, and again Smithers hit the ground. This time, when he came up, he began to circle Cimarron, his fists raised, his eyes fiery.

Cimarron, also circling, suddenly moved in and landed a savage succession of blows to Smithers' head and body.

"Don't dance, Smithers," one of the deputies yelled. "*Fight* the man!"

As if the words had been a sharp goad, Smithers moved in and Cimarron failed to step aside quickly enough. Smithers' fist smashed into his jaw and his head snapped backward. Recovering, he swiftly raised his left arm to ward off the next blow Smithers was throwing at him, and his knees slightly bent in order to maintain his center of gravity, he jabbed hard, avoiding Smithers' ribs and going again for the man's gut, where he knew he could do more damage.

...s blow connected and the winded Smithers sagged but did not fall.

Then he lunged at Cimarron again.

Cimarron sidestepped, and as Smithers went past him, he turned, grabbed the man from behind by the shoulders. At the same time, he slammed his right leg against the back of Smithers' knees and Smithers' body bent backward. Cimarron jerked hard on Smithers' shoulders, and Smithers, thrown off balance, fell on his back.

Cimarron waited beneath the hot sun, his face slick with sweat.

Smithers slowly rose, his hands swinging at his sides, his chest heaving. And then he made a grab for Cimarron.

Cimarron's left fist shot out. But Smithers slapped it aside and locked both hands behind Cimarron's neck. He brought his right knee up as he bent Cimarron's head down toward the ground. It smashed into Cimarron's nose, from which blood immediately began to flood.

Cimarron butted Smithers with his head, sending him hopping backward and breaking the grip on his neck.

He moved in fast then, and opening his fist, his fingers outstretched and held tightly together, he gave Smithers a chopping blow to the Adam's apple.

Smithers gagged and clutched his throat.

His nose still bleeding badly, Cimarron seized Smithers, spun him around, and shot two fast fists into the small of the man's back. Before Smithers could recover from the blows, which had been meant to hurt both his lower spine and kidneys, Cimarron spun him around and threw another punch that hammered against Smithers' chin.

Smithers retaliated with two swiftly thrown punches, and for more than a minute they slugged it out toe to toe.

Cimarron came in under Smithers' swing and his fists began to savage Smithers' face. They opened a cut on his left cheek and badly bruised his right eye.

Smithers staggered backward. His knees buckled

under him. But he stood his ground, swaying, blinking, blood from the cut on his cheek reddening his face.

Then he lunged again, clumsily, and Cimarron gave him two short but sharp punches—a ripping right that got Smithers just below the ribs and a stunning left uppercut that crashed against his lower jaw.

Smithers fell.

"He's about finished," one of the deputies remarked, pointing to the downed Smithers and sounding disappointed.

Smithers managed to get to his knees. He swayed drunkenly for a moment and then pitched backward into a sitting position.

Cimarron shook his head to clear it of the grogginess he was experiencing. With the back of his right hand, he wiped the blood from his upper lip. Then he untied the bandanna from around his neck and blew his nose in it, soaking it with blood in the process. His eyes still on Smithers, he gingerly felt his nose and winced in pain as he did so.

"Broken?" someone asked him.

Cimarron turned, to find a deputy he didn't know standing beside him. "Don't think so," he answered. "Hope not."

"You're some fistfighter," the deputy commented, his eyes appraising Cimarron. "One of the best I've seen so far."

"My brother and me, when we were but knee-high to a small horse, used to go at it from time to time more for fun than much of anything else. We each of us picked up a trick or two."

Two deputies were helping Smithers to his feet. As they led him away, the deputy beside Cimarron asked, "What started it all?"

"Deputy Smithers said some unkind words about a lady who happens to be a friend of mine."

"That'll do it every time," the deputy commented laconically. "By the way, my name's Cass Renquist."

"Cimarron."

"I know," Renquist said. "You're well-known over in Fort Smith. People talk about you. Point you out to each other."

Cimarron glared at him.

Catching the glint in Cimarron's eyes, Renquist held up his hands, palms toward Cimarron, and took a step backward. "Hold on, now. I'm not aiming to take you on. I figure you could do for me, even though you're bruised and beat up some right now."

Cimarron went over to where he had dropped his gun belt. He picked it up and strapped it on, adjusting it until it hung low and easy on his hips. Then he retrieved his hat, clapped it on his head, and strode down to the river, where he knelt and rinsed the blood from his bandanna. As he stood up, Renquist joined him.

"Cimarron, Jim Fagan sent me out to look for you."

"That a fact?"

"Jim wants to see you. He's got a case he wants to send you out on."

Cimarron nodded. "It'll be my first since I was sworn in as a deputy marshal. He tell you what kind of case it is?"

"Jim said something about a witness he wants brought into town. But I'd better let him spell it out for you himself. I might get it all garbled up."

Cimarron wrung the water out of his bandanna, and as he started toward his tepee, Renquist called out to him, "Jim wants to see you as soon as possible."

Cimarron waved a hand and ducked into his tepee. He spread his bandanna out on the grass inside it and then went and got his saddle, rifle, and other gear and placed them inside the tepee.

On his way to the ferry slips, he passed Smithers, who was sitting disconsolately and alone beside his brush-covered lean-to. Neither man spoke.

Cimarron walked on, and after boarding the ferry, he stood alone on its deck, his back braced against its railing.

Cimarron was a tall man. His body was lean but solid, with broad shoulders and almost nonexistent hips. His chest was thick and his arms were strongly muscled. Now, his body bruised and aching, he stood stiffly on the deck of the ferry as the stern lines were freed by deckhands and the boat began to move out into the river, but usually he assumed an easy, almost loose stance that nevertheless gave him an air of wariness, as if he were making himself ready for anything the unpredictable world around him might have to offer.

The skin of his face had been bronzed by the sun and there were wrinkles at the corners of his eyes, the result of his having squinted long and often as he stood or rode beneath that sun. His features were strong and distinct. A square jaw. Thin lips beneath a wide-nostriled nose. Slightly sunken cheeks beneath prominent cheekbones. A broad forehead that was deeply creased.

His was a face that showed clear signs of weathering and one that hinted of pain that had been endured because it could not be escaped.

His eyes were the color of emeralds and they were deeply set, alert, and some men had, at times, found them uncomfortably keen.

A livid scar on the left side of his face began just below his eye and curved down along his cheek to end just above the corner of his mouth.

His straight black hair buried both his ears and the nape of his neck.

He had never been able to bring himself to believe that he was handsome, although there had been women in his life who had claimed that he was. Just as there had been men he had known who had insisted that he looked like a man only recently escaped from hell.

He wore a gray flannel shirt above his jeans, which were tucked into dusty black boots that reached almost to his knees. Their toes were scuffed and their underslung heels were worn down on their outer edges. On his head he wore a battered and sweat-stained slouch hat. His gun belt was made of untooled leather as was the holster containing his .45.

Cimarron was the first passenger off the ferry when it docked in its slip on the eastern bank of the Arkansas. He hurried past the railyards, excitement surging within him as he thought about the case Fagan was about to assign to him. What was it that Renquist had said? Something about a witness that had to be brought in to testify at a trial in Judge Parker's court. Cimarron's excitement began to wane as he passed the waterfront saloons and turned left on Rogers Avenue. It didn't seem to him that bringing in a witness was much of a job for a federal lawman.

As he passed through the gate and entered the stone-walled compound of the old fort, he headed for the federal courthouse.

He took the steps leading up to it two at a time, as if he were trying to escape from the gallows that loomed so threateningly in the otherwise empty compound.

Later, as he knocked on the door of Marshal James Fagan's office, Cimarron felt his earlier excitement returning. Maybe the case would involve more than merely serving a summons on a witness. Maybe Marshal Fagan hadn't told Renquist everything about it.

"Come in!"

Cimarron opened the door and stepped inside Marshal Fagan's office. Fagan was seated behind his desk in a big brown leather chair and he looked up as Cimarron closed the door behind him.

"So Renquist found you," he said abruptly. "Well, don't just stand there, Cimarron. Come over here and sit down. I'll be with you in just a minute."

Cimarron crossed the room and sat down as Fagan leafed through some papers that were littering his desk; then he threw them aside in evident disgust and said, "Bill Clayton has fallen into the nasty habit of giving me more work to do than ten men might be able to handle in half a lifetime!"

"I guess the prosecutor himself's kept pretty busy," Cimarron observed, referring to Clayton.

Fagan leaned back in his chair and closed his eyes. "Seventy thousand square miles in the Indian territory," he said softly. "And every inch of it's infested with thieves, murderers, rapists, and every other base form of humanity that crawls across the face of this sad earth of ours. No wonder this court's always so busy. No wonder Judge Parker has to hold night sessions as well as day sessions. No wonder I sometimes feel so tired that I could drop in my tracks and let myself be trampled to death by defense lawyers without so much as whimpering."

"Renquist told me you had a case you were going to send me out on."

Fagan opened his eyes and stared dreamily at Cimarron. "What's that you said? A case?"

"Renquist said—"

"Oh, yes." Fagan shuffled among his papers, pushed them aside, pulled open a drawer of his desk, rummaged about in it for a moment, and then triumphantly sat up straight in his chair and waved a paper at Cimarron. "Here it is!"

Cimarron waited, his eyes on the paper in Fagan's hand.

"You're to take this summons and ride out of here, Cimarron. Somewhere out there in the Nations is a man named"—Fagan peered at the paper in his hand—"a man named Archie Kane. You're to find him and bring him back here. Kane was an eyewitness to a horse theft. We've got the thief—his name's Dade Munrow—locked up in the jail down in the basement. But without Kane's testimony against him, Bill Clayton is convinced he'll never get a conviction."

"This Archie Kane—he's not wanted for any crime?"

Fagan shook his head. "We desperately need him as a witness for the prosecution in the case against Munrow."

"Seems to me you could send the court bailiff out on an errand like that," Cimarron said, frowning. "Maybe even the court clerk or reporter."

"See here, Cimarron," Fagan said, leaning over his desk and brandishing the summons. "You decided you wanted to be a deputy marshal for the United States Court for the Western District of Arkansas, did you not?"

"You swore me in yourself, Marshal."

"Then you must have realized by now that you take your orders from me. And the order I'm giving you right now is quite simple and straightforward. Find Archie Kane and bring him in to Fort Smith." Fagan peered through narrowed eyes at Cimarron. "What the hell happened to your face?"

"Got in a fight."

"With whom?"

"Deputy Pete Smithers."

"You deputies are supposed to work together—to cooperate with each other. You're not supposed to try to kill or maim one another. Deputies are hard to find. At least, good ones are."

Cimarron said nothing.

"Bully boys," Fagan snapped angrily. "Brawlers, every one of you! If the outlaws I send my deputies out after don't kill them, they'll probably do each other in themselves."

"Maybe you could send somebody else out after Kane," Cimarron suggested hopefully. "I wouldn't mind one bit going out after a killer. Or even a thief. But a witness? Now that strikes me as too tame by far. I'd been hoping to find a little excitement in my new line of work."

Fagan groaned. "You'll find all the excitement you can—or maybe can't—handle out there in the territory. It'll pop up from behind every boulder and come roaring out at you from every deep draw. Believe me, I know what I'm talking about.

"I was once a deputy of this court myself and just as green as you are right now. I rode day after day and year after year through those hills and the long grass. I passed more lonely cabins and ranches than I can count. I've been in more frontier towns than I care to recollect.

"I've been shot at. Hit a time or two. Men have come at me with knives. Women have come at me with—Never mind. I've buried friends out there. I've still got enemies out there.

"Oh, you'll find excitement in the territory, all right. But until you've learned how to handle yourself in this job, you'll take the easy assignments for a while. Although, I hasten to add, no assignment in the Nations can truly be called an easy assignment. The territory is a first cousin to hell."

"I was out there in the Nations," Cimarron said, wondering if Fagan might have forgotten that fact. "So I guess you're right."

"You're damn right I'm right," Fagan exclaimed. "You ran into that jasper who was running rifles to the Kiowas—what was his name?"

"Philip Griffin."

"And his woman—that Dorset woman."

"Emma Dorset." Cimarron recalled the night he had shared a campsite with Emma and she had come to him in the middle of the night and they had . . .

"So you know what can happen to a man—lawman or not—out there, or at least you ought to know by now," Fagan said, and Cimarron's thoughts of Emma Dorset fled. "Hell, you were almost hanged because of what happened to you out in the Nations last month."

Cimarron's hand went to his throat and rested there as an image of the man they called the Prince of Hangmen—of the gaunt and stony-eyed George Maledon—crossed his mind.

"Maybe you don't really want to be a deputy marshal," Fagan prodded.

"Where can I find Archie Kane?"

Fagan leaned back in his chair again. "I can't tell you where to find him."

"Then I'm supposed to fiddle-foot my way around seventy thousand square miles of country looking for a man who might be anywhere, that it?"

With his eyes still closed, Fagan said, "Two weeks ago another of my deputies served Kane with a summons to appear here in court. Kane never came in and Judge Parker was forced to postpone Dade Munrow's trial. My deputy caught up with Kane that time in Catoosa. You know where that is?"

"It's north of Tulsey Town, isn't it? Catoosa borders on the Frisco railroad that comes down from Vinita through Cherokee nation, if I recollect correctly."

"You've got it," Fagan said, opening his eyes and beaming at Cimarron. "If I were you, I'd start hunting Kane in Catoosa. Ask around about him. You might stumble on him there or on somebody who can point out his trail to you."

"If I don't run Kane to ground—if I have to come back empty-handed—"

"Don't," Fagan said sternly, and his eyes glittered.

Cimarron nodded thoughtfully. "I'll find Kane. Bring him back."

"That's the spirit," Fagan declared enthusiastically, beaming at Cimarron again.

Cimarron got up and started for the door.

"*Dammit,* Cimarron!"

Cimarron turned around to face Fagan. "Marshal?"

Fagan held up his hand, which still clutched the paper he had taken from his desk drawer. "The summons, Deputy. You *will* be needing it."

Sheepishly Cimarron recrossed the room and took the paper from Fagan's hand. Thrusting it into the pocket of his jeans, he made for the door and went through it.

As he left the courthouse, he avoided looking at the gallows, and once out in the town, he walked briskly through it, conscious of the stares that were being sent his way by both women and men. Passing the hotel, he found himself once again musing on the time he had spent in it with Sarah Lassiter. He supposed that the people staring surreptitiously at him all knew about that rendezvous as well as the fact that he had been convicted by a jury in Judge Parker's court and sentenced by the judge to hang. He wondered idly which event—his conviction or his having briefly shared Sarah Lassiter's bed—was considered to be the more heinous crime by the law-abiding citizens of Fort Smith.

Once back on the western bank of the Arkansas, he made his way to the deputies' encampment and his tepee.

He picked up his Winchester '73 repeater, slung his saddle over his shoulder, and carrying the rest of his gear, made his way to the western flank of the encampment, where a picket rope had been set up.

He went to his dun and proceeded to saddle and bridle the animal. He examined each one of its shoes, and satisfied that they were in good condition, he freed the animal and swung into the saddle.

Turning the horse, he rode northwest, the Arkansas on his right, the lightly forested flood plain of the river affording him some relief from the blasting heat of the sun high in the sky above him.

As he rode, the creaking of his saddle leather beneath him was the only sound in the stillness that lay like a pall on the flood plain.

It was midafternoon when he spotted the small flock of grouse ahead of him. He reined in his dun and pulled his rifle from its saddle scabbard. He brought the rifle up and, a moment later, fired.

The grouse went winging away—all but one that lay dead on the ground.

Cimarron cantered up to it and dismounted. Pulling his bowie knife from his right boot, he lopped off the bird's head and legs and then gutted it, after which he proceeded to remove its feathers.

He built a small fire in a circle of stones and then spitted the bird, using a branch he had broken from a willow. He sat cross-legged on the ground as he held the bird over the flames, turning it slowly. When it was evenly browned, he began to devour it, holding the spit in both hands.

When nothing of the grouse remained but a white litter of bones that lay between him and the fire, he opened his canteen and took a long drink of water. Then, after kicking out the fire, he got back in the saddle and continued his journey.

Less than an hour later, as he was approaching the foothills of the Boston Mountains, he suddenly turned his horse, spurred it, and galloped toward a stand of nearby aspens.

He heard the rifle shot. The bullet passed harmlessly behind him.

The rifleman, he thought as he rode in among the aspens, was a fool. Whoever it was who had shot at him from the mountains had made the mistake of skylining himself. A moment after Cimarron had spotted his unknown assailant, he had seen the glint of sunlight on the man's rifle barrel and he had wasted no time, asked himself no questions. He had merely moved and moved fast. As a direct result, he was still alive.

He slid out of the saddle and positioned himself behind an aspen, from which point he scanned the mountains looming in the distance. He saw no one.

Fagan, he thought grimly, had been right. Indian territory was not a safe place to be. He knew that every outlaw west of the Mississippi had taken refuge in the territory at one time or another.

Who, he wondered, was the man who had just fired at him?

And then he asked himself an even more important question: *Why* had the man fired at him?

About the Author

LEO P. KELLEY was born and raised in Pennsylvania's Wyoming Valley and spent a good part of his boyhood exploring the surrounding mountains, hunting and fishing. He served in the Army Security Agency as a cryptographer, and then went "on the road," working as dishwasher, laborer, etc. He later joined the Merchant Marine and sailed on tankers calling at Texas, South American, and Italian ports. In New York City he attended the New School for Social Research, receiving a BA in Literature. He worked in advertising, promotion, and marketing before leaving the business world to write full time.

Mr. Kelly has published a dozen novels and has several others now in the works. He has also published many short stories in leading magazines.

JOIN THE CIMARRON READER'S PANEL

If you're a reader of CIMARRON, New American Library wants to bring you more of the type of books you enjoy. For this reason we're asking you to join the CIMARRON Reader's Panel, so we can learn more about your reading tastes.

Please fill out and mail this questionnaire today. Your comments are appreciated.

1. The title of the last paperback book I bought was:
   TITLE:____________________ PUBLISHER:____________________
2. How many paperback books have you bought for yourself in the last six months?
   ☐ 1 to 3 ☐ 4 to 6 ☐ 7 to 9 ☐ 10 to 20 ☐ 21 or more
3. What other paperback fiction have you read in the past six months?
   Please list titles: ____
   ____
   ____
   ____
4. My favorite is (one of the above or other): ____________________
5. My favorite author is: ____
6. I watch television, on average (check one):
   ☐ Over 4 hours a day ☐ 2 to 4 hours a day
   ☐ 0 to 2 hours a day
   I usually watch television (check one or more):
   ☐ 8 a.m. to 5 p.m. ☐ 5 p.m. to 11 p.m. ☐ 11 p.m. to 2 a.m.
7. I read the following numbers of different magazines regularly (check one):
   ☐ More than 6 ☐ 3 to 6 magazines ☐ 0 to 2 magazines
   My favorite magazines are: ______________________________
   ____

For our records, we need this information from all our Reader's Panel Members.

NAME:____

ADDRESS:____

CITY:____________________ STATE:________ ZIP CODE:________

8. (Check one) ☐ Male ☐ Female
9. Age (Check one): ☐ 17 and under ☐ 18 to 34 ☐ 35 to 49 ☐ 50 to 64 ☐ 65 and over
10. Education (check one):
    ☐ Now in high school ☐ Graduated high school
    ☐ Now in college ☐ Completed some college
    ☐ Graduated college
11. What is your occupation? (check one):
    ☐ Employed full-time ☐ Employed part-time ☐ Not employed
    Give your full job title:____

Thank you. Please mail this today to:

CIMARRON, New American Library
1633 Broadway, New York, New York 10019